THE PACIFIC
BILLIONAIRE BOSS

TONI KENYON

apeople
Publishing

Published by:

Apeople Publishing

Copyright © 2017 Toni Kenyon

All rights reserved.

ISBN: 978-0-9941488-0-3

The Pacific Billionaire Boss is a work of fiction. Names, characters, places, and incidents are the products of the author's imagination or are used fictitiously. Any resemblance to actual events, locales, or persons, living or dead, is entirely coincidental.

INTRODUCTION

Welcome to the world of my Pacific Billionaires*

If you want to know when my next billionaire is available join my book club by visiting my website at www.tonikenyon.com and you'll be the first to know.

*Stories set in New Zealand (and sometimes Australia & the Pacific Islands) that are filled to the brim with unapologetic instalove, angst, drama and dirty sex.

Author note: I live in New Zealand and I write in British english. Here in New Zealand we have **footpaths** not side-walks and **taps** not faucets. We talk about the flavour of ice cream and the colour of the sky. I apologise in advance if you find any of our idiosyncrasies confusing and I hope you enjoy your visit to my homeland. Feel free to email me if there's something you need me to explain—I'll do my best and be happy to oblige.

The Pacific Billionaire Boss

Hannah Scott's bucking the southern small town mindset. She's not going to settle down and marry a man who spends his days working in the local milk factory and then have a couple of children. She's come to the big city to stake her claim on freedom and independence.

Robert Redfern is the equivalent of Auckland royalty. He's been groomed to be the CEO of the family empire all of his life. But when he discovers that part of the requirement to maintain his position is that he take a wife, Robert's not too happy.

When the curvy and attractive, Hanna Scott crosses his path, Robert seizes the opportunity to strike a bargain with the attractive redhead that will bring them both what they want.

But, what neither of them anticipates is their magnetic attraction to one another. Can the boss and his executive assistant keep their dealings purely professional?

For Kevin - a great love

CHAPTER 1

*H*annah
I was way out of my comfort zone.

I walked the balance of the boardwalk by the harbour and realised that I'd experienced nothing like this before.

On one side of me, I could see the Hauraki Gulf reflected in the bright windows of the tall corporate towers that had been built on the edge of the harbour. On the other side of me, the eastern edge of the North Shore and its famous beach suburbs ran as far as the eye could see.

In the middle of the harbour sat the majestic peak of the dormant volcano, Rangitoto with its iconic lighthouse standing like a tall guardian at the edge of pohutukawa tree covered slopes.

The ocean looked like a washing machine as numerous boats and ferries zigzagged their way across the busy waterway.

This was so far removed from the windswept, empty beach that tucked itself up against the green fields of my hometown in the deep south. I felt like a girl from the boonies who'd arrived in the big city and I guess that's how I should have felt.

I checked out where I needed to be tomorrow. I'd received an urgent phone call from the temp agency this morning. I didn't think I was qualified for the job they wanted me to take on, but they'd insisted that I'd be fine.

When I asked who I'd be working for and what the job entailed, they'd been strange and vague in their details. I'd been corresponding with the agency for some months now. Ever since they'd come on a recruitment drive to Gore, my home town. The lure of the big city had been too much and here I found myself. What I hadn't expected and what the agency had omitted to inform me was the cost of living in a city like Auckland—and now I had some understanding of why they were recruiting out of the city. The phone call for this assignment couldn't have come at a better time.

My savings were vanishing at an astonishing rate.

I was happy to take anything that the agency offered.

When I took in the sight of the building where I'd be working, I couldn't imagine why anybody would want to leave this amazing city.

Maybe the people who lived in Auckland didn't like coming into their city centre to work. I couldn't understand why. I found the city to be alive and vibrant and full of colour. The polar opposite to the tiny, backward town I'd escaped.

When I arrived in the city, I'd located a tiny bedsit apartment not too far from where I was standing now. It didn't have a view of the water. In fact it looked at the side of an office building. But it was warm and dry and it had everything I needed.

The rent was nearly as much as a family of six paid for an entire house and a quarter acre to grow their own vegetables down south, but I would be paid a good salary and I'd saved up for this day.

I was bright and dependable. I'd managed to get a job in our local corner store and I'd saved hard. I hadn't spent my money on booze and going to the movies like my friends. I'd stayed at home and read up about the places I wanted to go, when I had the money.

This was the first step.

Auckland.

From here I planned to travel the length and breadth of the globe.

I could earn more here in a year than I would have earned back home in ten years. I knew no one in the city, so there would be little to spend my salary on. I was planning to stay in Auckland for as long as necessary before packing my bags and seeing the world.

Life became untenable for me at home after Dad died.

My older brother, Daniel had taken over running the dairy herd. Mum had wanted me to stay down south and find a nice boy to marry who had a secure future in the dairy factory. Her idea of a future was the life her and Dad enjoyed. Find a house, settle down and then provide her with a son-in-law and grandchildren.

I wasn't going there.

Mum always said that girls didn't need an education. That it didn't take much thinking to bring up a couple of kids.

Mum and Dad has scrimped and saved to help Daniel find his way to Palmerston North so he could get a degree in farming.

He'd worked hard and become a share milker and now he was working his way towards owning his own farm. All my parents ever thought I was good for was being a dairy work-er's wife.

When the recruitment agency came around town, I had other ideas.

I'd worked hard at school and kept my focus on business qualifications. My parents had agreed to me doing a business course, because they thought I could help my brother manage the farm, or it would put me in a good position with a potential husband.

I had ideas for my future, but none of them ever included marriage or babies.

Leaving home had been hard.

I looked at the tall buildings to my left and I knew Dad would have loved them. It still hurt to think about him. The heart attack had taken him real quick. Then when Daniel married Trudi and she moved in with us—well I decided it was time for me to be on my way.

Trudi and I didn't get on well. She was everything that my mum wanted me to be. Quiet, thoughtful and she worshipped the ground that Daniel walked on.

No. I was better off out of there and Trudi had been happy to help me pack my bags.

Mum cried when I got on the train. I promised her I'd come home for holidays, but both of us knew that wouldn't happen.

Sometimes, when I'm standing in a crowd of people in Auckland, I'll see someone who looks like her, with a shock of short red hair and I think it's mum, but it's not. I miss her, but not enough to remain living in what had become Trudi and Daniel's home.

I've found the building. Redfern Towers. It looks like two buildings in one, but somehow they're joined by an amazing looking atrium that hangs suspended between the imposing glass towers.

Everything on the waterfront looks new and clean as if it's only been here for a few years. Where I'm from all the buildings have a dirty, damaged look about them. Almost as if no-one cares. I wouldn't be surprised if there was someone who climbed these buildings at night and polished them, they shone so bright in the midday Auckland sun.

The yellow globe came out from behind a cloud and I was blinded for a second. The next thing, I found myself plastered up against a hard wall of muscle.

"I'm sorry," I muttered, appalled that I'd walked straight into someone. I must have looked like a country hick wandering around with my head in the air staring at the buildings.

"It's okay," said a deep voice that ran over me like treacle and made all my nerve endings dance, "I take my life in my hands every day when I run here."

I shaded my eyes and looked up into the face of a giant of a man. He pulled an ear bud from one of his ears and I realised that he'd been out jogging along the waterfront.

No doubt one of the workers who frequented this part of the city, or perhaps a close neighbour of mine. I took in the sight of his dark hair with its odd strand that glowed amber in the sunshine. The sheen of the moisture that coated the strong muscles of his body and his achingly beautiful face. I decided on the spot that I'd made the right decision to move to the city if this man was any kind of example of the male population domiciled here.

The stranger took a step around me and I couldn't help but turn around and watch him as he jogged away. Did he sense that I was watching him? For some reason, he turned, jogging on the spot while he looked back at me.

I felt a deep flush of a blush creep up my face. I shouldn't be staring at him, but there was something about him that meant I couldn't look away.

The stranger turned away from me and continued to run

along the waterfront. I had a ridiculous urge to run after him... And say what?

Introduce myself? Invite him back to my bedsit that overlooked the office building next door.

I watched him jog out of view and then, satisfied that at least I knew where I was supposed to be tomorrow, I turned and continued on my way back to my bedsit.

It was only a short ten minute walk. On my way I passed many bustling businessmen and women who were on there way somewhere at speed.

Everyone walked fast here in Auckland. It was as if there was a huge time clock ticking over their heads. I was surprised that I didn't bang into more strangers on the street, the number of people who seemed to walk while staring at a cell phone screen.

I admired the crisp lines of the expensive business suits worn by those who worked in the financial and banking district. In comparison, I couldn't help noticing the reflection of my fuller figure in the shop windows I walked by. I looked like one of the tourists that I'd watched step off the ferry at the waterfront terminal. My bright yellow sundress, with its circle skirt and my matching sun hat with the bright red rose looked somewhat out of place.

Since I'd been in town, I'd scoured the secondhand designer stores looking for corporate cast-offs. I'd put together a meagre office wardrobe. But looking at these women now in their tall, strappy shoes and their pencil-thin skirts, I'd begun to have doubts about whether or not I'd made the right decision to come here at all.

CHAPTER 2

Robert

I'd been in the office since before the sun rose this morning. Living within walking distance of the headquarters of the family business had its advantages. Some might say the time I spent in this office was unhealthy, but the business was my life.

It was all I cared about.

Today I couldn't make these figures work, no matter how hard I tried to wrestle them into submission. It didn't help that most of the due diligence material I needed was scattered far and wide.

The agency had promised me they would have a replacement executive assistant to me by now. I'd gotten hold of the principal of the firm and she'd advised me that they would have someone with me tomorrow.

How difficult could it be to get a decent EA in this city? I didn't think I was that difficult to work for, but apparently, every EA the agency had sent me lasted less than a week.

I was at my wits end.

All I wanted was someone competent to do the work.

They kept sending me women who looked the part, they dressed the part, but for some reason they didn't seem to be able to make a sensible decision for themselves, or keep a pile of paperwork in order.

I looked again at the five cardboard boxes of files that sat on the other side of the room and cursed the fact the company we were looking at still used paper filing systems.

Why we hadn't received an electronic copy of all of their records was beyond me. Every EA who had been through the door of my office seemed incapable of sorting the information into some kind of discernible order. How hard could it be to sort and scan documentation?

I wasn't going anywhere near that hell-hole they called a copying room ever again. If the agency couldn't get someone decent to me tomorrow, I was canceling the contract and going elsewhere.

I knew I needed to get out of this room. Exercise was in order. I grabbed my running gear and changed in the bathroom adjacent to my office. I should just be done with it and move a bed in here and I'd never need to go home to my apartment again.

By the time I'd pounded the hot concrete for half an hour, I began to feel better. Nothing like a few endorphins and the scent of the sea in the air to settle my thinking. I thought I might even do a workout at the gym before I went back to my office.

I looked down at my wrist to check my vitals and to see how far I'd come and the next second I was bouncing off a woman. She looked as if she'd just arrived in the city from who only knew where. She certainly wasn't the kind of woman who gravitated to this part of town.

I immediately apologised for my lack of concentration and then turned around to take another look at this woman. There was something about the way the sun caught her bright red hair, or the curve of her hips in her yellow sundress. Maybe it was the shy smile she'd given me.

I was almost tempted to jog back and give her my card, except I carried none in my running gear. Maybe I'd see her again. Who knew? Auckland was a large enough city for someone to lose themselves in if that was what they wanted to do.

If you were me and your family were one of the wealthiest in the country, it was pretty hard to keep a low profile.

I'm sure that was one of the reasons I couldn't get a decent EA. They were all coming to work for me for the wrong reasons. Recently it had felt as if I was starring in my own peculiar version of a dating show. Every woman who'd walked through my office door seemed more intent on trying to persuade me to take her on a date, than work with me on the projects I had to manage.

If this one tomorrow didn't work out, I wasn't sure what the hell I was going to do.

I checked my watch.

I didn't have time for the gym. Grandmother Mary was in town for her annual fundraiser.

My family had worked hard to ensure that the Redfern name was respected around town and I wasn't about to be the first to tarnish our reputation by not meeting my required deadlines.

All my life I'd been groomed for the position of heading our business interests and I had no intention of letting the family name fall into disrepute.

My younger brother, Edward had always coveted my position, but he simply couldn't have coped running the company.

Dropping the ball while Grandmother was in town was unthinkable for several reasons, not the least being she still had the power to persuade the Board to her line of thinking.

I may be the head of the Redfern Corporation, but for all intents and purposes Grandmother Mary remained the powerhouse behind the throne.

"*A*h Robert, it's nice you could make time to get to the office." Grandmother Mary sat on one of the couches with a cup of tea looking at me as if I'd just crawled out of bed.

"I've been here since 5am," I said as I swooped down and gave my beloved grandmother a kiss on the cheek.

"You know how much I like to tease," Mary said with the twinkle in her eye that she'd shared with me ever since I could remember.

I sat down opposite Mary, grateful she was here. A towering pile of files and paperwork sat between us. I picked some of it up and put it on the floor

"Don't you have someone to take care of that for you?" Mary asked as she put her cup and saucer down on the table in the space I'd just made.

"The agency are looking after it," I sighed, "but if they don't get it sorted for me soon, I may just lose the plot."

"Well, don't lose it before tomorrow night, now will you dear?"

"No, not a chance," I said with a beaming smile. All the family were expected to show at Grandmother's annual fundraiser.

"And you will be bringing someone with you now, won't you dear?"

"Of course," I said, shuffling in my seat.

"It's about time a man like yourself found a suitable wife. I'm sure there's plenty of eligible women in the city."

There weren't, but I wasn't going to share that information with my grandmother. She'd been on about me finding a wife since my 30th birthday and I still wasn't in any kind of hurry to share my home with any of the so-called *eligible women* who had been introduced to me.

Finding someone suitable to bring along to the annual fundraiser seemed to be as difficult a task as finding a decent EA.

Something else I needed to turn my mind to this afternoon as well, but the manilla folders on the floor held far more interest to me than locating a woman that would meet with grandmother's approval.

"I don't particularly want to add to the chaos, Robert but the other reason I'm here today is to discuss your future with the company."

My head snapped up. "What do you mean, my future with the company?"

My future had been assured from the day my mother had given birth to me. A Redfern man had headed the company for generations. We were somewhat like royalty. Born to assume the position.

"What I mean is that it's time for you to settle down and to find yourself a wife. I thought that when your parents passed, you'd have put your single life behind you," Grandmother said eyeing me over the rim of her tea cup. "But I can see now that it's going to take a little more than their loss to help you crystallise your position."

Grandmother always had a pinched and forlorn look about her when she discussed my father. Since the air accident that had taken my mother and father it had fallen to me to be the head of the Redfern family. It wasn't part of the natural order, for a mother to bury her son. Something about the way she looked out beyond my shoulders, to the ocean made me hold my tongue. Now wasn't the time to argue that finding a wife needed to be a part of the job specification.

It was as if Grandmother suddenly realised where she was sitting.

"There's been a Redfern man sitting behind that desk," she pointed a thin, gnarly finger in the direction of my cluttered desk, "for generations. Those men have had the good, steadying influence of a woman of character standing beside them."

How many times had I heard this lecture?

"Now, this evening there will be a number of women at the fundraiser that I believe will be a suitable match for you."

"What do you mean, a suitable match?" I didn't like the sound of where this conversation was going.

Grandmother handed me a thick manilla envelope. "It's all in here, Robert. If you don't find yourself a wife within the next six months, then the board have agreed that your appointment will be terminated in favour of Edward.

"Edward!" I couldn't hide my fury. "Ed's not cut out to run this company."

"Your brother is married and Nicki's baby is due in less than four months. He's the kind of family man that we need running the business and that's all there is to it."

"You can't be serious," I said. "You can't just fire me."

"I think you'll find if you read the company's constitution that we can."

"How come no-one's told me this before now?"

Grandmother Mary sighed as she stood up. "You'll recall, Robert that you and I have been discussing a suitable wife for you for years now." She made her way to the door, but stopped half way across the room. "I'm sorry it's come to this, really I am. There's a copy of the appropriate part of the constitution in that envelope, together with the required notice from the Board."

And with that last comment hanging in the air, Grandmother Mary left my office.

I closed my eyes, took a deep and calming breath and then opened the envelope. There in black and white, a letter confirming I'd been served notice of termination of my appointment due to my failure to meet Article VI of the constitution. What was this, some kind of archaic monarchy? I pinched the bridge of my nose and tried to think.

Clearly, I wasn't going to get out of this without either gaining a wife, or losing the position that meant more to me than life itself. I folded the pages and tucked them in the inside pocket of my jacket. There was no reason to believe that Grandmother Mary wouldn't have a bevy of suitable *brides* waiting for me at the fundraiser tonight.

Now, on top of finding myself an EA I had to find myself a suitable wife, or worry about being set up with one of the women deemed 'suitable' by Grandmother.

I shuddered.

I could imagine the kind of young women she thought were suitable. I looked around again at the shambles that my office had become. Somehow it seemed to reflect my personal life as well.

Damn it.

I didn't have time to be worrying about finding a wife, I had a company to run.

CHAPTER 3

*H*annah

I stood staring at the clothes rack. It couldn't be described as a wardrobe, it was a tiny alcove where a steel stand with plastic black wheels had been set up. It had a crude little wire basket sitting in the bottom where I'd housed my three pairs of shoes. My sneakers. A pair of black lace-up shoes with a comfortable heel that I planned to wear to the office and my sheepskin boots. I didn't wear my sheepskin boots anywhere except around the house to keep my feet snug and warm.

With the heat beating in today through the glass window of my apartment, I didn't know when I'd ever need to wear sheepskin boots again.

I knew I was missing the strappy sandal-type shoes I'd seen the women wearing in the streets of Auckland, but I couldn't worry about that today. Hopefully something nice would turn up at one of the secondhand shops I'd been frequenting—otherwise my feet were going to be a swollen mess by the time I got back here tonight.

I slipped into the skirt and blouse ensemble that I'd decided I would wear on the first day of my new job. I failed to quell the host of butterflies that were doing circuits in my tummy.

I was good with people I knew that. The agency wouldn't have phoned me and begged me to take this assignment if they didn't think I could cope with it, would they? A sudden moment of uncertainty tugged at me. I gave myself a good shake. I'd made it this far on my own and I knew I could cope with whatever was in front of me now. If I was going to make it in the biggest city in the country, then I had to get out there.

Dad would have clucked me under the chin with his fingers, given me his trademark smile and told me to get out there and go for it. He might not have believed that a girl's education was important, but he was a great believer in being a part of something bigger than yourself and that was just what I was about to do. I was heading out to be, what had the agency called it? Yeah, *an integral cog in the wheel of a great machine.*

I was up for that.

Who was I kidding? I'd taken the job because the bond and advance rent on this shoebox in the middle of the city had practically cleaned out my bank balance. I had enough money in the bank for two more weeks rent, but I had to make this job work, or I'd be back on the train home before I'd even gotten started.

I took at look at myself in the small mirror in the bathroom.

My makeup was tidy.

My red hair pulled back into a tight bun on the top of my head.

"You'll do," I said to myself as I buttoned the top button

on my blouse. I wanted to make sure that I looked the part of an executive assistant. I had little idea of what that title meant, but the agency had assured me that I had the qualifications to deal with the job. Who knew that a couple of courses completed by correspondence could get you so far in the city.

I picked up my bag. Inside I'd stored my sandwiches for lunch and a piece of fruit. At least I wouldn't starve during the day. I'd already scouted out the coffee places and food stalls around my new workplace. It didn't take me long to work out that I could make my own lunches for a week, with the money they were charging for one overpriced, open sandwich.

I took a deep breath and pulled the door closed behind me.

Now I had somewhere to go and a purpose for stepping out of the building's front door, it didn't seem so odd to be joining the tide of pedestrians all scurrying to their destinations. A strange sense of belonging stole over me that I'd not felt since I stepped foot in the city nearly a week ago.

With a smile on my face and a spring in my stride, I climbed the front steps leading to the imposing glass doors of the Redfern Corporation. The man on the front desk in the huge, marble reception area looked at me.

"Can I help you," he asked.

"Hannah Scott," I said, "it's my first day."

He looked at the page in front of him and replied, "Yes, you need to go up to the 26th floor." He handed me a small tag coated in plastic that had the word VISITOR written in blue on one side. "Take lift E and make sure that you give that card to the receptionist." He indicated to the long corridor behind him where a bank of 10 lifts fed people to various floors within the two buildings.

"Thank you," I said hurrying to ensure that I made it to

the correct lift in time. I gripped the small plastic card and realised that my palm was wet. The walk downtown, or maybe just the beginning of the nerves that I'd managed to squash until now, I couldn't be sure?

I stood amongst a number of other people, some who swiped cards hung on long colourful lanyards from their necks and others, like me, who waited for their allocated lift to allow them access to the building.

The ping of the lift's arrival gave me a fright and I jumped. I stepped inside and found myself alone as the doors closed on me.

A sudden clenching panic grabbed at me. What if this lift jammed, or the door didn't open, or I arrived at the wrong floor? Had I gotten in lift E? For the life of me, now that I was travelling up into the building proper I couldn't be sure if I'd stepped into the correct lift.

I took a deep breath.

In through my nose and let it out slowly through my mouth. "You can do this, Hannah Scott," I said to myself under my breath as I checked my reflection in the walls of the lift. I don't know how many times I'd checked myself this morning, but it seemed like at least a thousand. My makeup remained perfect and my skin still looked flawless. It surprised me every time I saw myself with my hair up in a tight bun. I was used to seeing it free and flowing down my back like a river of red. I might be a country bumpkin come to the big city, but I hoped I didn't look too much like one today.

"Get through the next ten minutes and you'll be fine." I closed my eyes and thought about my options. If I didn't pull this off, then it was back down south for me. I wasn't going to live in a tiny house in the middle of nowhere, at the beck and call of a man.

"No, Hannah Scott," I said to myself, "you were made for better things and this is just the beginning."

The lift shuddered to a stop and the doors opened. I took a deep breath and stepped out into my new future.

CHAPTER 4

*R*obert
My phone buzzed. A message from my receptionist. The new EA had arrived. Not a moment too soon, I thought as I put my phone back in my pocket.

The door opened and I looked into the face of someone strangely familiar.

I stood and then stepped around my desk offering my hand to the attractive and curvaceous woman who stood in the centre of my office.

"Hello, you must be Hannah."

"Yes," she said in a voice that immediately piqued my interest. "Hannah Scott, it's nice to meet you."

The way she shook my hand and the way that her easy smile travelled to her green eyes made me feel immediately at ease. That was strange in itself. Usually the women who arrived from the agency put me on edge, but I didn't feel that around Hannah.

"Could we have a couple of coffees please?" My receptionist looked at me as if I'd just asked her to jump off the Harbour Bridge.

"How do you take your coffee?" my receptionist asked Hannah.

"I don't drink coffee," Hannah said, "I drink tea."

"You live in Auckland and you don't drink coffee?" I said, "I find that hard to believe." I sat on the front of my large desk, enjoying the way that Hannah squirmed under my gaze.

"I've only just moved here," she said.

I leaned forward slightly, "Do you like chocolate, Hannah?"

She nodded, "Yes."

I looked over at my receptionist, "Bring Hannah a moccachino and I'll have my usual."

My receptionist nodded and closed the glass door behind her. From my desk, I could see the entire floor set out in front of me. All ready I knew I was going to enjoy the vision of Hannah sitting outside my door.

"You're sure we haven't met before?" I indicated for Hannah to take a seat on one of the red leather couches in the middle of my room. I took up residence on the one directly opposite. A chrome and glass low table sat between us that was littered with folders and files.

She screwed up her eyes as if she were trying to remember something.

"Do you run around the waterfront?"

"I knew it," I said, "you're the girl I bumped into yesterday. I never forget a face." How long had it taken Hannah to pin up her hair? "You looked like a tourist yesterday." I saw the blush rise up her perfect cheeks.

"I only moved here just over a week ago. I wanted to make sure that I wasn't late this morning."

Punctual and pretty. I liked that.

The door opened and my receptionist returned with a hot

black coffee for me and a frothing chocolate delight for Hannah.

"Let me move these," Hannah said, piling files with infinite care so there was some space to put out the coffee.

I scrubbed my hand through my short hair, "As you can see, I need some help getting things into shape around here. I've been without an efficient EA for too long."

"Well," Hannah said, bringing the mocha to her nose and sniffing it suspiciously, "you tell me what you want me to do and I'll get started." She looked at the chocolate froth with concern.

"It's delicious, I promise," I said, "and if you're going to work for me there's going to be long hours and you'll need the caffeine to keep you going."

Tentatively, she took a sip. "It's not bad," she said, "but I think I prefer my cup of tea."

She was different this woman. I could tell all ready she had spirit and spunk and she wasn't afraid to disagree with me. I hadn't had someone working with me like this for a long time.

In fact, I wondered if I might not just have another job that would suit her.

$\mathcal{H}$annah

I'd enjoyed a quick cup of coffee with Robert, stowed my bag and my lunch in the drawer in my desk and then been ushered by his receptionist, Cynthia into the clutches of the HR department.

Ms Prescott, head of Human Resources, reminded me that I was here on a trial and if I wasn't up to Mr Redfern's expectations that I'd be shipped back to the agency in a nano-second. From her tone of voice and the way she looked at me over her half spectacles, I assumed that plenty had been *shipped back to the agency* before me.

After I'd been issued with my security pass and Ms Prescott had shown me around those parts of the building that I'd been allowed access too, I was returned to my post outside Mr Redfern's office. Ms Prescott handed me a large staff manual with *Redfern* emblazoned on the front cover.

"Everything we have discussed is inside the folder," Ms Prescott said, "together with a copy of the contract we've signed with your agency. I suggest that you make yourself familiar with the contents if you think that there's any chance you'll be staying here for long."

I had the feeling that not many people stayed here for long as I watched Ms Prescott turn on her heel and leave.

"Ah good. You're back," Robert arrived at my side the second that Ms Prescott left. "Can you come into my office please?"

I left the folder on my desk and followed Robert back into his office.

I couldn't decide whether it was the shot of coffee and chocolate that was making me shake, or being in the same room as Robert.

The agency didn't explain that I'd be working with the most gorgeous man I'd ever set eyes on in my entire life.

If my libido didn't stop behaving like it hadn't seen a man before, there was little chance that I'd be able to keep my mind on the job at hand. I'd been here an hour and my mind was full of so much information I wasn't certain that I'd be able to process it all.

"I trust that you've been shown around and that you've got your bearings?"

"Yes and no," I said.

"Don't let it overwhelm you," Robert replied, "just come and talk to me if you get into trouble."

"Of course, Mr Redfern," I said thinking of the kind of trouble that I'd like to get into with this gorgeous man.

"Call me, Robert," he smiled and all of a sudden I felt as if I couldn't breathe.

"O-okay, Robert," I said. I liked the sound of his name when it came out of my mouth. In fact, I realised that there were far too many things about Robert that I really, really liked. If I had any chance of remaining in this job and, by implication, remaining in Auckland then I had to try to keep my dirty mind on the job and not keep wondering what Robert would look like out of his business suit.

CHAPTER 5

*H*annah
      I'd spent most of the morning acquainting myself with Robert's systems—or lack of them. The man was lucky. My adolescence had been spent keeping my father's small business accounts in order. Once I figured out the filing system that actually was in place—thanks to my company employment manual—I knew I'd have his office in order in a day or two.

"Hannah, can you come in here, please?"

Robert arrived at my side, his sudden appearance giving me a fright. I jumped and he put his hand on my shoulder to settle me.

"I'm sorry," he said, "I didn't mean to frighten you."

I didn't want him to think that I was a bag of nerves, which of course I was, but he didn't need to know that. But the touch of his hand on my shoulder should have been soothing and, in fact, it had the opposite effect of putting me more on edge.

"It's okay." I stood up, allowing his hand to fall naturally off my shoulder. I could still feel the heat of his touch as I followed him into his office.

"Take a seat," he said indicating to the chair that sat opposite his desk. The large expanse of glass and steel could easily have doubled as a boardroom table. I wondered why someone would need such a large desk. At the moment, it was covered with files and documents and I itched to be able to make some kind of order out of the chaos in front of me.

"This might seem a strange request," Robert said as he steepled his fingers and leaned back in his chair. He seemed so at ease in his environment. Here was I, perched on the edge of a chair almost as if I was waiting for the ground to move beneath me, ready any moment to leap up and make a run for it. I'd never felt so on edge under the scrutiny of a man before.

Under the intense examination of Robert's gaze I felt somehow naked. That thought should have terrified me— instead it excited me.

I needed to keep my mind on the job, or I'd be fired on the first day.

Robert continued, "But my grandmother is in town to host a charity event and I'd like you to attend the event with me." He leaned forward, waiting for my response.

I took a deep breath trying to clear my thoughts. The beauty of the man in front of me, with his chiseled jaw and jet black hair seemed to have the effect of scrambling my brain. The way Robert had carefully constructed his words it was clear to me that I could say no to this request. But there was something about the tone of his voice, the demanding edge to his words that compelled me to agree. But then I thought about my wardrobe. What the hell would I wear?

"Thank you for asking me," I said trying to convey how much the invitation did actually mean to me, "but I'm afraid I'll have to decline."

"Why?" He leaned back again waiting with infinite patience for my answer.

I could feel the heat of embarrassment creeping up my face.

"I don't have anything suitable to wear," I squeaked.

"Not a problem," Robert said as he pulled out his phone, scrolled through for a number and never took his eyes off me as he began to speak.

"Rob Redfern here. I'm sending my EA, Hannah down to see you. She needs a dress for tonight. Good. She's on her way." He put the phone back in his pocket and scribbled a name and address down on a piece of paper and handed it to me.

Our fingers touched as I took the paper from him and a strange sensation ran through my body.

"There's the address. Go and see Stacy she'll organise something for you and I'll see you when you get back."

Robert went from intently studying me to focussing on the documents in front of him in a millisecond. There was no need to dismiss me, his actions said far more than any words could say. Those actions spoke to me in ways I was all ready too terrified to acknowledge.

"*H*ello, You must be Hannah." A tall, platinum blonde woman dressed in black who didn't have a hair out of place addressed me. How could she have known I was Hannah?

"Yes," I said looking around the room to see if anyone else was in the boutique. Maybe not many people came here to shop, it seemed sparse and deserted.

"I'm Stacy and I've picked out some things that I think would be suitable for tonight, they're on the rack over by the chaise."

I took in my surroundings. *Olive's* was the kind of designer boutique that I would only have dreamed about entering.

The small, exclusive boutique sat in amongst a strip of high fashion and designer shops. The boutique was located in a part of the city that I'd purposely stayed away from. The people who frequented the narrow lane seemed to somehow be a cut above the rest of the city's population. Whether or not it had to do with the tenure of the tenants, or the location—so close to the financial district—I couldn't tell. But I was certainly intimidated by my surroundings.

Stacy directed me toward the chaise in the corner of the sparse, well lit space. I smiled to myself, the polished concrete floors and the steel frames that housed the designer garments reminded me of a milking shed. I didn't think that Stacy would like the comparison, so I kept my thoughts to myself.

"Hmm…" Stacy walked a small, tight circle around me, her finger to her vibrant red lips as if she were working out some mathematical equation in her head. She continued to mumble to herself as she flicked through the dresses lined up on the rack. "This. This is perfect and it's near enough to your size. I can make a few adjustments before the fundraiser if need be."

She held in front of me a bright red dress made of luxurious fabric that was delicately trimmed with what looked like tiny clusters of white beads. It had a deep cut up the front from floor to thigh.

"I'm not so sure about the colour," I said remembering my mother's insistence that with my red hair I couldn't wear red.

"Nonsense," Stacy said, "with your colouring you'll look stunning and believe me," she glared at me as if I should know better, "if you're going to enter a room on the arm of Robert Redfern, you want to make sure that you make an impression." She carried the garment as if it were a precious package, then she hung it on a large brass hook on the wall. "And of course, you'll remember to tell the photographers that your gown came from *Olive's*."

"Photographers?"

"Darling," she said as she began to pull a yellow curtain that I'd not even noticed around the dress, "you're going to the Redfern's gala fundraising event of the year. Anyone who is anyone will be there. That's why Robert sent you to me." She said the last sentence with pride in her voice. How many women had she supplied dresses to in the past for Robert? "Although, I have to say that I've never been asked to outfit one of his staff before."

She pulled another curtain from the other side of the dress. "Now, come on we need to get this dress on you and checked for fit if I'm to have it ready in time for you to wear tonight."

Before I knew what was happening, Stacy had me out of my blouse and skirt and into a gown that seemed to hug my curves like a second skin.

"Perfect," Stacy crooned as she circled me like an approving mother. "Try these shoes." She supplied a pair of silver, strappy sandals not unlike those I'd seen the women of the city wearing. I caught sight of the price tag, an astonishing $699. If that was the price of the shoes, I could only imagine the cost of the gown that Stacy was now busy pinning at the waist and at the hem.

"You'll wear this with a pashmina," Stacy said. "It's only needed if it gets cool later," and she artfully draped a light, but incredibly warm and soft shawl across my shoulders. Then she showed me how to tie it so that it accentuated my hourglass figure.

"Almost perfect," she said as she handed me a clutch purse

that matched the shoes and pashmina. "What are you doing about your hair and makeup?"

I stood looking at myself in the mirror. I couldn't believe the transformation.

"Hair and makeup?" I repeated the words, still stunned at the reflection peering back at me from the mirror.

"Right." Stacy picked up the phone.

"Robert. Yes, we've found the perfect outfit it will have to be altered." There was a short silence while Robert must have been saying something. Stacy indicated for me to walk up and down the room. I felt like a different woman than the one who had walked in the door. How could clothing and shoes make you feel so different? "She needs her hair and makeup doing. I can arrange for Tim to be at your apartment at 5pm."

Another silence.

"Done," Stacy said, "you won't regret it. I promise."

She put her phone back in her pocket and looked at me with the first wide smile that I'd seen on her face since I'd walked in the door.

"You won't know yourself once Tim has finished with you," Stacy beamed.

I already felt like Cinderella, on her way to the ball. Stacy was some kind of control-freak fairy godmother. This wasn't what I'd expected from my first day on the job and I couldn't imagine what tonight had in store for me.

*R*obert

Hannah had barely said a word since she'd returned from Stacy's boutique, but I was pleased to see that there was some order being restored to the chaos that was my office.

The alarm on my phone buzzed. It was time to leave. I had to get Stacy to my apartment for her meeting with Tim.

I closed my laptop and put it in my satchel. I knew I'd have a few moments to look over some figures while Tim was working his magic on Hannah—not that I thought Hannah needed much magic. There was something about the way she looked that intrigued me. Hannah piqued my interests in so many ways. I hadn't been intrigued by a woman for such a long time. The fact that she'd managed to restore some kind of order to the chaos that I'd surrounded myself with here made her even more adorable.

"Hey you," I called across the office to Hannah, she was on her knees on the floor shuffling her way through various pieces of paper.

"Yes, Robert." When she looked up at me, with those green eyes I had a sudden vision of her in that position between my legs and my cock twitched.

Maybe taking her to the fundraiser tonight might not have been such a great idea. Hannah was clearly a major asset in my office, even after the first day. How many ways could I fuck up a good thing, I wondered?

"It's time to get going," I said as I stepped toward my office door. "Tim's not the most punctual man, but even I don't like to keep him waiting. It's a short walk to my apartment, but we need to leave now."

I held the door open for Hannah and she gave me a slight smile as she walked through to her desk. I watched her shut down her computer and then collect her bag from the drawer below her desk.

It didn't even look as if she'd been in residence by the time we walked out past reception. My receptionist looked at me as if I'd wet my pants, I never left the office before she did. "You're leaving?" she asked.

"Yes, we've the annual gala tonight. We'll see you in the morning."

"You don't usually leave this early?" Hannah asked, obviously seeing the shocked expression on the middle-aged lady's face.

"No," I said as we waited for the lift. I liked the idea of leaving the office with Hannah. I liked the idea of doing a lot of things with Hannah.

My grandmother had been harassing me to find someone to settle down with for more years than I could remember. The idea didn't appeal. I could never imagine coming home to the same woman night after night. My attention span wasn't good—I was easily bored. That was why company acquisitions and disposals suited me so well. New projects were my specialty and that translated into my personal life as well.

The lift arrived and I stood back and allowed Hannah to enter ahead of me. It wasn't just so that I could watch the enticing sway of her backside.

I couldn't wait to see what Stacy had chosen for her to wear tonight.

As the lift doors closed behind us and we were alone in the enclosed space, I was suddenly hyper-aware of Hannah.

The floral scent of her perfume filled the space between us, drawing me like a magnetic force toward her body.

I leaned back against the cool mirror surface of the lift and tried to concentrate on the changing floor numbers as we descended from the top floor of the building. Instead, I found my eyes wandering to the reflection of Hannah in the mirror.

It had been easy to keep my eyes away from her while we were working, but here in this confined space, with nothing but the two of us, I struggled to find a distraction more attractive than the gorgeous woman stood by my side.

I needed to find some self-control. It had taken months to find someone who'd made it past lunchtime in my office. I didn't need to screw up a good thing by taking this woman into my bed.

No matter how much my body screamed to touch her, I was going to remain a gentleman and leave this woman alone.

CHAPTER 6

Hannah

We'd walked the short couple of blocks to Robert's apartment in near silence. I didn't need to say anything, anyway. I was terrified. It had dawned on me as soon as we got in the lift together what I'd agreed to do. How the hell was I going to pull off going to a gala event with this man?

When we got to the front door of his apartment, I had an idea that I was out of my depth, but by the time we were inside, I knew I was in way over my head.

We stood in an enormous room that looked up the width of the Auckland harbour. I could easily have been standing on the deck of a cruise ship.

We were across the other side of the harbour from where Redfern Towers stood and I could easily see the outline of the building from the deck of Robert's apartment.

"With a good pair of binoculars you could see your office from here," I joked, trying to break the awkward silence that had developed between us on the walk.

"I wonder some days why I even bother having an apartment," Robert said as he handed me a glass of sparkling water. "I spend so much time over there," he indicated with a tilt of his head toward the office towers, "and then when I do come back here I usually bring work with me."

He was a workaholic. It was pretty clear to me that was the position, even after only spending six or so hours in his office. Maybe that's what you have to be if you want to live like this.

"You can use the guest wing, I'll show you through," Robert said as he led me away from the balcony overlooking the harbour and back into the apartment. He appeared to have the entire floor of the building. His guest suite turned out to be large enough to house four of the tiny bedsit spaces that I'd been residing in for the last week.

"Your dress has arrived," Robert said, "the concierge has hung it in the wardrobe. Make yourself at home. There's plenty to eat in the kitchen if you're hungry, just help yourself. I'll leave you to shower and there's a robe in the wardrobe too. Tim shouldn't be long. He'll need your hair washed, so I'll leave you to it." And with that he was gone.

I checked the wardrobe and there it was, the beautiful dress and next to it, in a golden box with the name Olive's written across it in embossed green lettering, the silver strappy shoes with the matching clutch purse and pashmina.

My head had begun to spin.

I was certain that any minute I was going to wake up and this would all be some kind of crazy dream.

The guest suite was like a sumptuous five star hotel room. A huge bed sat in the middle of an opulent room.

A vision of Robert sprawled across the bed came to mind and my head really did begin to spin. He was my boss. I couldn't think about him like that.

Probably best at this point in time to get myself in the shower and turn the water on cold.

*T*im was ushered into the room while I was still towelling off my hair. A tall, skinny man wearing drainpipe jeans and a green and white striped shirt. His short, spiky black hair looked as if it contained more hair product than I had in my bathroom cabinet.

"Beautiful," he cooed as he ran his fingers through the long damp rat-tails of my hair. "We'll have you looking like the belle of the ball before you know it."

He sat me down in front of the dressing table and then rolled out an assortment of what looked like hair torture devices.

"Just relax, darling," he said. Tim's frivolous manner did nothing to hide the nature of his sexuality. There was nothing about me this man would find attractive. I didn't think I could say the same about the man who stalked the office that I'd just started working in.

I closed my eyes, allowing the sensations of the pull and tug of my hair to lull me into some sort of trance. Thoughts of Robert clouded my mind.

Him out jogging yesterday.

The way he looked sitting behind his desk today.

The long length of his body as he strode around his office.

The vision of him relaxing in his beautiful home.

It had been a tough day and eventually sitting down and having someone else take care of my needs made me sleepy.

The buzz of Tim's hairdryer and the soft breath of the heat around my head and the back of my neck was the undoing of me.

I must have fallen asleep.

When I awoke, I barely recognised the woman sitting in front of me.

"You like?" Tim asked. It was clear that any answer other than in the affirmative would be the wrong thing to say.

He flicked a mirror to the back of my head to show me how my hair sat in what looked like neat little bows.

"It's beautiful," I said and I wasn't lying. I'd never seen my hair shine the way it shone. I had no idea what Tim had done, but I thought it would be wonderful to have him around every time I went out.

He stood tall, hands perched dramatically on the top of his hips. A hair clip sitting on the pocket of his frayed jeans and another hanging from the short sleeve of his t-shirt.

"That's hair. Now for make-up," Tim said as he expertly rolled his hair equipment back into its small pouch and replaced it with a large, double height make-up tray.

When he pulled back the plastic top of the box and separated the layers, I thought I'd walked into the make-up department of one of the upmarket boutiques dotted around the city.

Tim stood in front of me, studying my face with a zeal that made me uncomfortable. He put his fingers under my chin, tipping my head from side to side as he surveyed my face. All the time muttering to himself like a craftsman surveying his work.

"Where's your gown?" Tim asked. The question, coupled with his sudden focus on me, made me jump.

"In the wardrobe," I said. "What's that got to do with anything?"

"Everything, darling," he said, waving a hand in the air as he walked towards the wardrobe. "It's all about making you shine."

As Tim slipped into the walk in wardrobe to take a look

at the gown, not for the first time today I wondered what I'd gotten myself into.

*R*obert

I'd shown Tim out of the door. In the wake of his gushing what a wonderful subject Hannah had been, I couldn't wait to see her walk into the room.

I'd donned my regulation tuxedo and for some reason I'd taken extra care tonight. I'd chosen a pair of cufflinks that Grandmother had gifted me from my Grandfather. As much as I professed to hate the family's annual charity bash, deep down I still wanted to please Grandmother.

While I checked through the drawer where I kept my cufflinks, a small cat-toy caught my eye. A tiny white mouse, with a pink eye. I swallowed hard. I didn't have time to think about this right now and I pushed the toy to the back of the drawer.

I turned my mind back to my grandmother. She had a hold over me that I couldn't explain—and it had nothing to do with the ultimatum she'd issued me with yesterday.

I'd always been her favourite and for some reason that made me want to please her the best I could. The fact I'd not yet settled down and spawned an heir for her was the one prickle of disappointment that sat between us.

"You don't think this is a little over the top do you?" Hannah asked as she stepped through the double doors from the guest wing and into the living room proper.

I turned to look at her and she took my breath away.

A vision in red, Hannah eclipsed everything in the room —and my home had been filled with beautiful things that I'd acquired over the years.

I swallowed and tried to remind myself that I'd eventually found someone who could take control of the writhing chaos of my office—I didn't want to mess it up by contemplating her taking a hold of my cock.

"You're perfect," I said and I wasn't making any kind of overstatement.

The bright red of the dress contrasted perfectly with the pale colour of Hannah's skin. Tim had been right. He'd done a fantastic job with her hair. It hung in glossy spirals around her kissable neck.

But my eyes fell to the rise and fall of her perfect chest. How I wanted to bury my face in the soft swell of her breasts.

Reluctantly, I dragged my eyes back to Hannah's face and put out my arm.

"Come, my driver's waiting with the car downstairs. We shouldn't keep my Grandmother waiting. It makes her grumpy."

I could imagine what Grandmother would have to say about me arriving with this endearing woman on my arm.

"You're sure it's not all a little over the top?" Hannah asked again as we made our way down in the lift to the street below.

"No," I assured her, "you're perfect."

"I don't think I've ever worn a dress like this before and Tim…" her stream of babbling ceased as she saw the limousine parked at the side of the street. I found her reactions to the baubles of my life both endearing and amusing.

"Tim's fantastic and so is Stacy. They're a team that I've used for years." A small voice in my head said I might not ever be sending anyone else but Hannah to them.

I buried it.

The thought of tying myself down to one woman terrified me. *Yet, the seed of a plan had begun to form in my head.*

The nervous tension in Hannah's body was evident as I slipped my hand into the small of her back, helping her into the rear of the limousine.

"Do you always travel like this?" Hannah asked, as she took in the interior of the vehicle, with its plush seating and mini bar.

"No. I prefer to walk or run, but I don't think I could arrive at the fundraiser in my sweats."

The competent woman who had been sifting her way through the papers in my office had gone. In her place sat a woman so clearly out of her depth that I almost felt sorry for her.

I'd arranged for a half bottle of champagne to be waiting for us in the car. "Would you like a drink before we get there?"

Hannah looked at me, her eyes wide, as if I'd asked her if she wanted to take her clothes off. I might be thinking about asking that question later. Keeping my hands off this exquisite creature would be more difficult than I'd originally anticipated.

I poured us both a glass of champagne and then settled down in the seat beside Hannah.

"Thank you for coming with me tonight," I said as I raised my glass. The ping of the two crystal flutes touching each other echoed through the tension filled space.

"Who's going to be there tonight?" Hannah asked.

"Anyone who's anyone in Auckland and the greater part of the country."

I felt the shudder run through Hannah's body.

"You've no need to be nervous," I said. "You wouldn't have made it past lunchtime today if I didn't think you could cope."

Hannah took another sip of her champagne and looked out of the window. The lights of the outer Auckland suburbs had given way to the dark of the countryside. We were heading to a private estate on the fringe of the suburbs.

Grandmother liked to ensure that the gala evening was shared out between her patrons.

There wasn't a person in Auckland who could fail to conform to her wishes—except maybe her favourite grandson. But that was about to change. I pulled out my phone and began to tap out a text message to Grandmother Mary.

CHAPTER 7

*H*annah

The tension in the vehicle was palpable. I hadn't expected to feel such an intense attraction to Robert. I kept reminding myself that he was my boss.

Bedding the boss wasn't a great idea.

I blamed him for putting me in this position. I should have been in my tiny bedsit, sitting in front of my computer watching some crap on the internet—not sitting here in a limousine drinking the best champagne and preparing to meet with half of the who's who of Auckland and beyond.

I was so relieved to pull up outside our destination that I didn't have a chance to take in the opulence of our surroundings before we were accosted by a bank of photographers.

Shit!

We were standing on a red carpet.

I couldn't stop the trembling that began in my body. No amount of champagne on the way here had calmed the nervousness that I was feeling now.

Some reporter called Robert's name from behind the velvet barriers that lined the red carpet.

"Robert, over here," called another.

"Are you okay?" Robert asked, concern etching his perfect brow.

"Yes," I lied. He put his hand in the small of my back and the touch went some way to calming the fluttering in my body. Robert directed me towards the photographer who had called his name first.

"Just smile nicely and don't say anything," he said.

We worked our way down the line of photographers. Some asked questions of Robert in a way that suggested they spent far too much time photographing him at events like this one.

"Who's the beautiful lady this evening, Rob?" one of the photographers asked.

"Ms Hannah Scott," Robert replied as he took a step away from me to allow the photographer to take a shot of me standing alone.

"Have you been going out with Rob long?" the photographer asked as he took another shot.

"Well, we're—"

Before I could utter another word, Robert's lips were on mine. A belt of heat shot through my body and before I had a chance to recover my composure, we were walking the rest of the red carpet to the house.

"I told you not to say anything," Robert hissed as we made to enter the grand home.

My head was still reeling from the kiss and more importantly, my body's reaction to his lips on mine.

"What were you thinking, kissing me in front of the press?"

"I told you not to say anything," Robert smiled as he handed me a glass of champagne. I feared if I drank any more of that tonight, I was no longer going to be responsible for my actions.

"Look," Robert said as he almost frog-marched me into the middle of the throng of people who had gathered in the ornate room. "No matter what I say tonight, or how things look I want you to take your lead from me."

I knew I shouldn't be here. This was really taking the job to the extreme. Shit. I'd only been employed for a day.

I had a bad feeling about this. "What exactly is going on?" I asked.

Before Robert had a chance to answer my question a rather elderly woman arrived at our side. She was dressed in an immaculate black evening gown, but my eyes were drawn to the multiple strings of stunning pearls that sat at her throat.

"Grandmother," Robert acknowledged the elegant woman in black, "I'd like you to meet, Ms Hannah Scott."

"Ah, Robert I'm so pleased to see that you've brought someone with you." Robert's grandmother looked me up and down and, despite the line of photographers that we'd just walked by, somehow standing in front of Robert's grandmother felt far more intimidating.

"Mary Redfern," she said holding out a hand to me, upon which wrist sat another amazing pearl bracelet.

I barely resisted the urge to curtsey and was surprised by the strength of Grandmother Mary's grip. "I'll look forward to speaking with you later in the evening," Mary said as she released my hand and turned to Robert.

"I do hope that you'll be making an announcement this evening, Robert. I think that after the auction would be perfect." Grandmother Mary turned back to me. "I'm so looking forward to getting to know you dear, now that you're going to be one of the family."

I watched her walk into the crowd and turned to Robert.

"What's she talking about and what exactly is going on?"

*R*obert

I could tell by the look of confusion on Hannah's face that this wasn't going to go well.

"Do I need to ask the question again, Robert?" The tone of her voice told me that this was going to become a wild ride.

I knew I hadn't handled this well, but the thought of the women that grandmother may have set up for me had driven me to desperate measures.

"It's another job that I need you to do for me," I said taking Hannah by the elbow and ushering her out through the ballroom to the privacy of the garden beyond.

"Come and walk with me," I said and I held out my arm. I picked up another glass of champagne on the way out the door. "Would you like another drink?"

"I think I need to keep a clear head around you," Hannah said, her tone almost menacing.

I was the one who probably needed to keep a clear head. But even though I'd barely thought this through, I knew my thrown together plan could work.

Formulating my thoughts as we walked through the manicured gardens, we came to a stop where the path turned to the left. In front of us lay a small square of grass, it too perfectly groomed like the topiary bushes and hedges we'd walked by all ready. The entire garden was illuminated by tiny little yellow lanterns that lit the many curving pathways through the estate.

When I was sure that we were out of the earshot of anyone else at the gathering, I began. "This may sound odd, but I want you to hear me out."

Hannah nodded in agreement.

In the soft light of the moon she looked even more stunning. The silver light cast an ethereal glow over her curvaceous body and the dress she wore hugged her in all the right places. I took a deep breath and said, "I want you to pretend to be my fiancée."

"What?" She looked at me, blinking several times in quick succession. Then she took the champagne from my hand and took a large sip before handing the fluted glass back to me.

"You heard me." I wasn't going to repeat myself.

"Why would I do that?"

"Because I'd pay you two hundred thousand dollars." I watched her eyes go wide with shock. "And I'll have my solicitor draw up the contract tomorrow so we can both sign it."

Hannah looked at the champagne flute again. I passed it across to her and she took another drink.

"Why would you need anyone to pretend to be getting married to you?"

"It's complicated." I pinched the bridge of my nose. "Look. Do you want the money or don't you?"

"Do I still get to keep my day job?"

"Of course. I need you in the office."

I could see the possibilities beginning to swim in her head. "And how long do I have to pretend to be engaged to you?"

"Just until we get married."

I offered Hannah the champagne flute before she reached for it. This time she shook her head and took a step back from me. "No way. If I'd wanted to get married, I'd have stayed down south. I came to Auckland to make something of my life."

"You'll make one million dollars on top of the two hundred thousand if you marry me."

There was a pause.

Silence.

I could hear the hum of chatter coming from the house

across the expanse of the gardens. I thought I heard a horse whinny in the distant night.

Still Hannah said nothing.

I stayed silent.

Waiting for her to make a decision. I needed her to take me up on this offer, but I'd be damned if I'd resort to begging.

Minutes ticked by and still nothing.

Maybe I would have to resort to meeting the women that Grandmother Mary had summoned to tonight's event.

I knew I wasn't going to give the business up to Edward. I'd worked too damn hard. I'd do what it took to make sure that I stayed in the job. Even if Hannah wouldn't go along with my outrageous plan.

Hannah reached for the champagne flute. I handed it to her and watched as she took another sip. "I'm dreaming right? You haven't just offered me 1.2 million dollars to marry you?"

The fish was firmly on the hook. Now I had to play this with care.

"No. I'll pay you two hundred thousand on our official engagement and one million when we get married."

"What else is involved besides an engagement and a marriage?" Good, she was interested. She hadn't told me to stick my offer.

"You'll come and live with me and we'll behave like a happily engaged couple and then we'll get married."

"Live with you?" Shock began to register on her beautiful face.

"Not as husband and wife." She visibly relaxed at those words. "You'll have your own guest wing in the apartment. Where you were tonight. You'll have a driver at your beck and call and you'll get to keep your day job." I needed to make this as sweet a deal as I could. Brokering deals was what I did all day, surely I could close this one right now. "All you have to do is pretend that we're getting married." I retrieved my champagne glass from Hannah and this time I took a drink. "Call it an extension of your day job."

She hadn't gone running for the hills. I watched as Hannah took in the information, assimilated it. I liked the way she wrinkled her nose while she thought about things.

"What's this about, Robert?"

"I need a wife."

"That's it."

"Pretty much."

"Can I think about it?"

"No. I need your answer now, or I'll withdraw my offer."

CHAPTER 8

*H*annah
    The prospect of 1.2 million dollars disappearing in an instant was all the motivation I needed, or maybe it was the champagne making the decision for me.

"Okay," I heard myself say, "I'll do it."

I'd been to his home and spent the early evening in his guest wing. I already knew I could fit my small apartment in the bedroom alone. In six months I'd be able to leave New Zealand and see the world. Robert was offering me instant access to my dream. I'd be a fool to turn down an offer like this one.

Without any kind of warning, Robert pulled me to him. "I think we should seal the deal with a kiss, don't you?"

My traitorous body responded to the call of his. From the moment I'd laid eyes on him this evening in his tuxedo, I'd been dancing around the spectre of my attraction to him. Now, as he leaned in over me, waiting for me to consent to the brush of his lips on mine, I wondered not for the first time since I'd met Robert, whether or not I was doing the right thing.

"One little kiss wouldn't hurt," I heard myself say.

The moment I felt the heat of his mouth on mine, I knew I was in way over my head.

I heard a dull thud as the champagne flute landed on the grass beside the path. Robert's hands were in my hair, his palms flat against the back of my neck.

Despite myself, my hands slid inside his jacket, caressing the hard muscle of his back through his silk shirt.

Robert exhaled at the touch, a warm breath of air caressing my lips. As if of its own accord, my body pressed itself against his. I felt the peak of my nipples through the soft fabric of the dress. Robert's tongue found the inside of my mouth and I opened for him.

My body melded into his. I felt the touch of his hand in the small of my back as it travelled lower. All the while I continued to kiss him with a fervour that I'd never experienced in my life.

There was no denying the hard mass of cock that wedged itself against my hip.

When his hand found the soft flesh of my buttock I groaned. It was as if the sound somehow broke the spell between the two of us.

Robert pulled back from my mouth, looking down into my face. He swiped his thumb across the top of my chin with infinite care.

"We should go back to the party," he said his voice didn't sound like it had the usual control that I'd become accustomed to hearing. "I think the deal's well and truly sealed."

Most of the evening passed in a blur of boring conversation with people that I'd only seen in the tabloids before now.

People who I'd worshiped from afar via the media were on first name terms with Robert. Most of them barely acknowledged my existence. I didn't care. I was too busy thinking about the kind of life I was going to be living once I'd gotten through this strange employment arrangement with Robert. I tried not to focus on the way my body had reacted to our kiss in the garden.

I smiled my way through a delicious array of finger-food that was delivered on large silver trays by women not much older than myself.

I made sure that I ate my fill and felt sorry for the other women in the room who seemed to say no to every offering.

Never mind. I'd make up for it.

"I'm pleased to see that you have an appetite for the finer things in life," Robert said as he watched me eat another slice of lobster tail with its smattering of tiny black caviar.

"These taste so good," I said. Grateful for the food. It was taking the edge off the strange feelings I'd had after drinking so much champagne and then kissing Robert in the garden.

"You need to try one of these," he said as he held what appeared to be a tiny, perfect chicken burger to my lips. No more than a single mouthful, I went to take it from him and he held my hand.

"Open," he said as he held the tantalising morsel under my nose.

I did as he asked. The intimacy of the gesture wasn't lost on me. He never took his eyes from mine as he popped the delicious treat in my mouth.

"I'm pleased to see that you two lovebirds are partaking of the refreshments." I jumped at the sudden arrival of Grand-mother Mary.

"We are," Robert said as he moved to my side and casually slipped an arm around me as if it were the most natural thing in the world for him to be doing.

"Robert, I've arranged with the auctioneer that you'll both take the stage prior to the commencement of the auction. You can make your announcement then."

"Perfect," Robert said as he squeezed my back.

"Yes," I said.

"We'll arrange a formal engagement shortly, but this will be a good way for the auction to begin." Grandmother Mary leaned in to me and whispered, "Good news and good champagne, the two things needed to help these people loosen their wallets for charity."

I didn't know what to say. "I'm glad we could help," was the best I could come up with on short notice.

Grandmother Mary checked her watch. "We'll begin in a few moments, I think you should both come with me. Get yourselves a glass of champagne each. This is a celebration, remember."

"You ready for this?" Robert asked as he hailed a passing waitress. When the young lady arrived, he passed me a glass of champagne and took another from the tray for himself.

"I think so," I said with complete honesty. It was when I went to take a sip of the champagne that I realised my hand was shaking.

*R*obert

I'd been used to taking the stage at these kinds of functions for many years, but I could see by the faltering way that Hannah stood by my side, that she wasn't comfortable. What was I expecting? Of course she wouldn't be comfortable. I'd basically railroaded her into a pretence engagement and marriage.

I looked across at her and took her hand in mine.

She was shaking. I could feel the trembling of her body. There were other ways that I wanted to make her body tremble and I found that thought discomforting.

I needed to keep a calm head around Hannah and if the

kiss we'd shared in the garden was any indication of how things might progress. I could be in trouble.

"Ready?" I asked her.

"Yes," she nodded.

"Your life's going to change in ways that you can't imagine after I make this announcement," I said wanting to make sure that Hannah was completely aware of what she was getting involved in.

"It has all ready," she whispered. Then she looked up at me. Long, sculptured eyelashes fluttered as she blinked. I didn't really want to throw her to the dogs that were waiting out there for the two of us. The press were a pack of bastards. This story would be out on the internet tonight before they'd even finished auctioning the first piece of artwork.

Something inside of me wanted to protect Hannah from all of that. But marrying me, whether a marriage of convenience or not, would put her at the mercy of the bottom-dwelling scum bags who sold their souls to the highest bidder.

There was nothing I could do about that, but I'd do my damnedest to make sure that she wasn't hurt or destroyed in the process.

I tapped the microphone and began with the usual platitudes.

"But the real reason I'm up here tonight," I said as I held my hand out toward Hannah. I still couldn't get over how beautiful she looked. She'd appealed to me since the first time I'd set eyes on her down by the waterfront and now, stood here in all her finery, she was stunning. Even if this was going to be an engagement of convenience, I couldn't have picked a better woman to share the journey.

"The reason that I've welcomed you all here on behalf of my family is because I'd like you to meet the woman who is going to become the newest member of the Redfern family. My fiancée, Miss Hannah Scott."

Hannah came forward and I slipped my arm around her again. I couldn't believe how well she fit beside me. There were flashes from the floor as some of the photographers took photographs.

"Rob," one of them called from the floor, "have you set a date for the wedding?"

"We'll announce one soon," I said tightening my grip on Hannah. The closer I held her to me, the less she trembled. For some strange reason, I liked that. "But it will certainly be within the next six months."

By the time we dealt with the extra photographs that the press and Grandmother Mary insisted we have taken and we'd done the round of well-wishers after the auction, I could see that Hannah wasn't going to be able to deal with much more.

"That's enough," I said taking in her pale complexion. "You look exhausted."

"It's been an eventful day," she replied.

"Come on. I'm taking you home."

We were barely out of the driveway and back on the road before the weight of Hannah's body fell against mine. There was something sweet and comforting about the way she leaned against me in sleep. I couldn't keep my eyes from the valley between her breasts. The way they rose and fell as she breathed.

I hadn't been this attracted to a woman in an age. The last thing I needed was to get involved and screw up the one thing that meant the world to me.

The business.

It was the likelihood of losing the business that had gotten me in this predicament. Now a growing attraction to Hannah threatened to put me in even more jeopardy.

CHAPTER 9

*H*annah
I hadn't even been aware that I'd fallen asleep. When Robert gently shook my shoulder and announced that we were home, I struggled to remember where we'd actually been.

It was as if I'd awoken from some strange dream.

Then I remembered.

The man who had his arm around me and was helping me from the car to the apartment was my new fiancé.

"You've had a long day," Robert said as we waited for the lift.

"An eventful day," I replied. "It's not often that you get a new job and then get engaged to the boss all in the same afternoon."

When we reached the apartment, it was as palatial as I recalled. I still couldn't believe that I was going to be living here, with Robert. I began to understand how Alice must have felt when she fell down the rabbit hole.

"I guess I should show you around, since you're going to be living here now."

"Can it wait until the morning?" I couldn't stifle my yawn.

"Right," Robert said a slight smile curling the side of his mouth, "I'm so interesting I can't keep you awake."

"It's not that," I countered, searching for the appropriate words. But exhaustion had taken its toll. Then it dawned on me. "I've got no clothes here." Panic clawed at me. "In fact, I've got nothing here except the clothes I arrived in this afternoon.

"I've arranged to have them washed and pressed, they'll be here in the morning again in time for you to go to work with me and anything else you need you'll find in the guest wing."

"Goodnight," I said and I turned and went to move towards the guest wing, but Robert stopped me. A strong hand on my shoulder turned me back around towards him.

The blazing fire in his eyes told me more than I wanted to know.

"You haven't kissed your husband to be goodnight," he purred. The promise hidden in the sound of his voice sent ripples of desire through my body.

I knew I shouldn't be feeling this way. What the hell was Robert doing? This was supposed to be a purely commercial arrangement.

"You wouldn't ask me to kiss you goodnight if I was leaving the office at the end of the day," I said.

I knew I was playing hard to get. But I was enjoying watching this powerful man's emotions play out across his handsome features.

"You're right," he said as he pulled me closer to him. Close enough that now I could feel the heat radiating from his body. "But we're not in the office. We're in our home."

He stressed the word, 'our' and my stomach did a little flip.

If this was a business arrangement and I'd never see

Robert again after I'd pocketed my money, the racy side of my brain said, why not enjoy myself now? If I lived a hundred lifetimes, how many times would a girl like me have a man like Robert to herself?

I'd had far too many glasses of champagne and I was too tired to fight the attraction any longer.

"I guess another little kiss isn't going to hurt," I whispered. Well aware now of where another little kiss could likely take me.

This time, when Robert's lips touched mine something inside of me exploded. A hunger that I didn't even know I possessed took over.

I wanted him and I wanted him bad.

"Do you have any idea how beautiful you are?" Robert growled as he slipped the shoulder straps of my gown down, exposing my breasts and pinning my arms to my side.

His lips were on my nipples before I had a chance to answer him, my moans of pleasure echoing around the large living space.

Robert guided me backward and lay me down with care on a large sofa. The cool of the leather on my back made me gasp.

My arms were still pinned to my side by the straps of the dress, so no matter that I wanted to touch Robert, now I couldn't.

"I want to touch you," I moaned as his hand found its way up the inside of my thigh.

"No, let me do this for you," Robert said as his teeth raked the hard tip of my nipple.

I surrendered to the pleasure and relaxed, allowing Robert free reign as he pinned my body to the soft leather of the sofa.

As his fingers found their way to my wet heat I moaned and arched into him.

His mouth covered mine and his tongue and fingers plundered my body.

I didn't want to close my eyes but the pleasurable sensations and the tight dress rendered me helpless in the hands of my new boss and fiancé.

Robert slipped out of his jacket and relieved me of my panties. The next thing I knew I could feel the heat of his breath on my inner thighs. My entire body shuddered in anticipation of the pleasure that I knew was forthcoming.

A tiny voice in the back of my head screamed that I should make him stop.

I told it to fuck off.

Robert worked me to a frenzy with his mouth and his fingers. Playing me. Taking me to the edge of a screaming orgasm and then expertly letting me down.

When I didn't think I could stand it anymore, I began to beg.

"Please, let me come."

"I like the way you say please," Robert said and he pushed me to the edge of the cliff again and again.

"Soon," he growled.

The promise in his voice was almost enough to push me over.

"Robert…" I moaned, desperate now for some relief from the excruciating pleasure of his fingers and mouth.

He sucked my clit.

My body exploded.

I fell, long and hard from the heady heights where he'd driven me.

Robert picked up my limp body and said, "I think that's enough for one day."

He carried me through to the room that would be mine while we played out this charade of an engagement.

He lay me on the bed, slipped the designer gown from my body and dropped it on the floor as if it were a rag.

He pulled the sheets up over me and then stood looking at me for a moment. His hair was ruffled, his tie undone and his lips swollen and red.

"Sleep well," he said. "We've a big day in the office tomorrow."

Then he left me and closed the door.

I wasn't sure anymore what the rules were. Why had Robert put me in this room and gone to his own to sleep?

It was too late now to try to get back to my own apartment. I should have gotten in the shower, washed off the makeup and taken down my hair.

Instead, I let the exhaustion wash over me and squash the raging fears running through my head.

I was in way too deep.

What had I done?

CHAPTER 10

*H*annah
        I'd had a fitful night's sleep.

When I woke I had a strange feeling of disorientation and a dreadful headache. The disorientation I could put down to being in a strange home. But the headache? I couldn't decide whether the headache was to do with the amount of champagne I'd consumed the night before, or the terror of realisation that filtered into my head as I open my eyes.

Robert had awoken so many things in me last night.

I'd had experiences that I could only ever have dreamed about when I was living down south.

I stepped over the beautiful gown I wore last night and went to make my way to the bathroom. Something inside of me simply couldn't leave the expensive dress lying in an abandoned heap on the floor.

I stared at the bright red fabric bundle, with its tiny marble-like beads that looked as if each and every one of them had been hand sewn on with infinite patience. I wondered how anyone ever came to the position of being able to cast something aside as valuable as this dress without a second thought.

Then I remembered the money that Robert had promised me if I went through with his outlandish plan.

Is that what great wealth afforded someone? The ability to throw something as beautiful as this gown aside as if it were worth nothing.

My southern upbringing wouldn't allow me to leave the exquisitely crafted garment on the floor. I picked it up. Smoothed out the creases and went and found a hanger in the wardrobe.

The walk-in wardrobe was nearly as large as my bedsit.

If I was going to spend the next six months living here with Robert, then I would at least need to get the few clothes that I owned from my bedsit.

Should I keep paying the rental?

I pondered that thought as I inspected myself in the bathroom mirror and began to unpin the hard nest of my hair. By the time I'd teased out the toffee-textured strands, the vanity was full of long, thin hair clips.

As much as I wanted to get in the shower to soften my hair, I didn't want to wash away the scent of Robert from my skin. Surely last night was some kind of insanity.

As I stood under the heat of the water, I wondered whether or not he'd come to his senses this morning and realise that the offer he'd made me was untenable.

I still couldn't understand why anyone as handsome and intelligent as Robert would need to offer anyone money to marry them.

I wrapped myself in the robe that hung on the bathroom door and made my way out to the kitchen for something resembling breakfast. Robert was sitting on a tall stool at the kitchen counter, a cup of steaming coffee by his side.

The sight of him took my breath away.

I had a flash of memory of his head between my legs. I could feel the heat of desire coursing through me. I hadn't said a word to him. I simply stood, watching the way his long fingers caressed the keys of his laptop and thought about the way they felt when they travelled across my skin last night.

Robert lifted the tumbler that held his coffee to his lips and I thought about the way they felt when they touched mine.

Soft. Yet firm and demanding.

I could feel my heart beating faster and faster. I wore nothing but a bathrobe and I felt incredibly vulnerable stood in front of this man who screamed money, elegance and grace.

Just as I was debating whether or not I should say something, Robert glanced in my direction. When he saw me, a beaming smile lit his face.

"Good. You're awake. Did you sleep well?"

"I did, thank you."

He looked at his watch. "We'll be leaving here in twenty minutes. Your clothes are over there," he pointed in the direction of the door where my skirt and blouse sat freshly laundered and under a long plastic covering emblazoned with the name of the local laundry service.

Robert looked at me, with a glint of mischief in his dark hazel eyes, "And since I made such a mess of your panties last night, I arranged with Stacy for these to be delivered this morning." He pushed a small box with the now familiar lettering of *Olive's* on the lid.

"Thank you," I said picking up the box, but unable to look Robert in the eye. The champagne had made me bold last night, but this morning, my confidence had left me.

Robert continued on as if it was the most natural thing to do, giving a stranger a box of underwear first thing in the morning. He lived an unusual life. How would I ever adapt?

"And now that our engagement has been made public," even hearing the words coming from his mouth made me nervous, "there'll be an expectation around what you wear and how you behave. So I've arranged for Stacy to put together an appropriate wardrobe for you."

Then it dawned on me.

This was purely a business arrangement.

No matter that Robert smiled at me this morning. No matter, he had his head between my legs last night. This was a business arrangement, pure and simple.

I needed to treat our dealings together as purely professional. Otherwise I'd be destroyed.

Robert looked at his watch again.

"You best get dressed and have something to eat," he said. "I've a meeting in the office in twenty minutes and I'm never late to meetings."

He stood up and put his tumbler in the dishwasher. He closed the lid on his laptop and his perfectly attired derriere was the last thing I saw as he walked out of the room and left me to my own devices.

I could feel the tears beginning to well in my chest.

I don't know what I was expecting from this man.

Some kind of acknowledgement of what had happened last night?

The only reference had been our *official engagement.*

What about everything else?

I grabbed a piece of fruit from the well stocked fruit bowl and made myself a cup of tea. I took them both back to my bedroom, at least I felt safe there.

I found my phone and it was filled with text messages and missed calls from my mother.

Demands of *ring me* and *oh my god, you're engaged! Why didn't you tell us that was why you were going to Auckland?* And other such ridiculous messages.

Flicking to my news feed on my social media channels I was assaulted by multiple pictures of me in the red gown. Some on Robert's arm. Others by myself.

Headlines screamed: *Who is this mystery woman? Redfern Tycoon to Wed. Surprise Engagement.*

People I hadn't spoken to for years were making comments about my life. Suddenly claiming to be my best friend.

What the fuck?

I couldn't breathe.

The room began to spin.

What the hell had I done?

CHAPTER 11

*R*obert

I needed to keep my mind on the job at hand.

We arrived at the office and the entire floor stood and clapped as Hannah and I entered. Instinctively, I reached for her hand. The protective streak that had overcome me last night resurfacing with a zeal that equally terrified and thrilled me. Hannah brought out feelings in me that I'd never experienced. I wanted to hustle her to safety, not leave her out here for the staff to cross-examine.

I held up my hands and the staff all fell quiet. My receptionist, the woman who sat at the helm of my corporate ship day in and day out was the first to speak.

"We saw the news last night and we just wanted you to know that you have the full support of all of us. Congratulations," she cooed. I'd not seen her so animated in years. I liked her being the face of my floor, with her sharp, angle bob cut hair and her perfect corporate presentation.

I didn't need the congratulations of the staff and I could tell all ready that Hannah was uncomfortable. I'd thrown her in at the deep end and I needed to make sure that she kept swimming. Until I had her signature on the contract, she could back out of this deal and I wasn't about to let that happen.

"Thank you all very much," I said, "but really, it's just work as usual. We don't expect there to be any kind of considerations. Hannah's come to work with me because she's the best person for the job."

I'd have to be blind not to see the way that half the female staff were staring daggers at Hannah from across the room. I'd managed to avoid dating so many of them by espousing my *I don't mix work with pleasure* philosophy on life. I might be an intelligent man, but I'd been pushed into a corner and now I had to deal with the implications of having a fiancée and an EA as one and the same person.

I ushered Hannah into my office, my first meeting could wait.

"Have you seen the news this morning?" she asked, a sense of panic in her voice. "Half of the people in southland that I might have said a single word to in my lifetime are suggesting that they're my lifelong friends." I could hear the rising panic in Hannah's voice.

"Look," I said, "you need to calm down."

"I am calm." Hannah spat at me.

"I know calm and you are not it." I said.

My next sentence was cut off as my receptionist arrived with black coffee for me and a mochaccino for Hannah.

"Thank you, Cynthia," Hannah said with a tight smile.

"Jonathan's due shortly," I said to my receptionist, "will you please give him my apologies and offer him something to drink. I'll be with him as soon as I can."

"Certainly," she said as she broke out into a smile directed at Hannah, before she headed for the door.

"Oh," I called after her.

"Yes, Mr Redfern."

"Please make sure in the future that anyone wishing to make an appointment with me, or see me is referred to Hannah. She will be managing my business diary as well as my home diary from now on."

"Of course," she said, as she closed the door behind her.

I'd never let ultimate control of my diary out of my hands before.

"Sit down," I said to Hannah. I needed to make sure that she understood what I'd just done.

The radiant woman who'd peered out at me this morning from the social pages and the internet news sites looked nothing like the seething woman who sat in front of me now. If the truth be told, on some level I think I preferred the seething woman sitting in front of me to the self-conscious girl who stood by my side last night.

There was something about the set of Hannah's jaw. The way she angled the side of her body towards me while she sat staring at the mochaccino as if it were the enemy.

Is that how she was going to be looking at me for the next six months?

"By giving control of my diary to you, I've indicated to the entire staff that you're to be taken seriously."

"How can anyone take me seriously, really?" she asked before she took a sip of the coffee. Hannah screwed her face up at the taste and I wanted to laugh. But I stopped myself. I still needed the papers signed that my solicitor had brought to the office this morning.

Hannah continued, "I arrived yesterday a nobody and suddenly I'm your fiancée. How does that work?"

"It doesn't matter how it works. I could have known you from anywhere in my past. The details don't matter."

"The devil is in the details," Hannah said. Putting the coffee back down on the table.

"Let my receptionist know what kind of tea you drink and she'll bring you one of those instead next time."

I watched the pained expression almost leave Hannah's face.

"Her name's Cynthia."

I waved my hand in the air.

"My solicitor, Jonathan Hawke is outside. He has the papers that we need to sign. Are you ready?"

I thought I saw a flicker of hesitation cross Hannah's face, but then it was gone. This was her last chance to back out of our deal and I still wasn't entirely sure that she'd sign on the dotted line.

Hannah stood up, a look of defiance painted on her pretty face. She lifted her chin in the air and said, "I'm ready." She picked up her coffee, "I'll give this to *Cynthia* and send your solicitor in, shall I?"

"Yes," I said and then added, "I want you to sit in on the meeting. I don't want you thinking that there are things being said that you're not a party to around this deal."

Hannah simply nodded and walked out of my office.

The sooner we got this out of the way and all the loose ends were tidied up, I thought, the better.

A few moments later, Jonathan swept into my office, threw his briefcase down on my desk and made himself at home.

"Robert," he said as he unclipped the brass clasps of his briefcase and pulled a large manilla folder out of its depths, along with his signature red glasses and his silver pen.

"Jonathan," I reciprocated his greeting. We'd been through plenty together and Jonathan had as good a handle on the business of the Redfern group as I did.

"You've met Hannah?" I asked as Hannah seated herself in the other chair next to Jonathan.

"Yes," Jonathan said as he closed the briefcase and set it

down on the floor beside my desk. "I've acquainted myself with your fiancée."

Jonathan looked at me over the top of his glasses before pushing them firmly against the bridge of his nose and sitting down. He looked across at Hannah and said, "No offence young lady." Then he turned his gaze back to me, "You've had me document some interesting business deals in the past, but this one..." Jonathan shook his head. "I don't know where to start advising you on this one."

I leaned back in my chair and took a deep breath. "I'm not asking you to give me advice, Jonathan. I'm asking you to document a straight-forward business transaction between two consenting adults.

"Ending in marriage," Jonathan said.

"Ending in marriage." I repeated his words.

Jonathan turned to Hannah, "Hannah, I really need to discuss a few things with Robert, do you think you could leave us alone?"

Hannah went to stand up.

"Sit down," I barked.

She returned to her seat.

"Anything you have to say to me," I said to Jonathan, "you can say in front of Hannah. I don't want her going into this deal thinking that there's anything going on in the background that she's not aware of."

I could tell by the flustered look on Jonathan's face that he wasn't happy.

"Does the Relationship Property Act mean anything to you?" Jonathan asked.

"It's not an issue," I said.

"I can assure you that it's an issue," Jonathan countered. "And if you're dead set on this course of action, then I'll need you to sign a disclaimer acknowledging that you're signing this document against my advice."

I looked him straight in the eye. "Don't have an issue with that."

"Fine," Jonathan said as he handed me a two page document and he handed a copy to Hannah. "You both need to read this, initial the bottom of the first page and then sign by your name on the second page. Two hundred thousand dollars will be paid into your bank account as soon as you supply me with the details, Hannah."

I'd read the contract, Jonathan had emailed it to me this morning. I cast my eyes through the short paragraphs, initialled the first page and then signed the second.

I watched with interest as Hannah began to read.

"Hannah," Jonathan interrupted her reading.

"Yes." She looked up at him and I noticed that the contract shook in her hand.

"You're entitled to obtain independent advice from another solicitor. You don't have to sign this document in front of me, but if you do, you're acknowledging that I've told you to obtain independent advice."

Hannah nodded and then turned her gaze directly at me.

"Get another lawyer's advice," I said to her, "I'll pay for the best in Auckland."

"It's okay," she said, her green eyes boring into mine, "I trust you."

The weight of Hannah's words sat like an undigested meal in my gut.

I was a man of my word and I wasn't going to let her down. She'd be paid and she'd be paid well for what she was doing. But there was something about the tone of Hannah's voice when she said those words.

That sense of protectiveness that she stirred in me came to the surface again. I didn't want to feel this way about Hannah. In fact, I didn't want to feel anything around her.

But every time she looked at me another tiny piece of my hardened heart seemed to thaw.

I couldn't get involved with this woman on anything other than a business level.

I'd been stupid last night.

Drunk too much champagne and indulged myself with her.

I needed to keep this relationship purely business, or I'd find myself in far too deep.

I didn't do deep and meaningful.

I was married to the job and that was the way I intended things to continue.

Hannah chewed the end of Jonathan's pen as she continued reading.

Jonathan agitated in the chair opposite me. I knew how much he loved that pen, but to give him his due, he didn't say a word about the fact that Hannah might be putting teeth marks in the metal top.

When she was satisfied, Hannah signed the document and handed it back to Jonathan. He waited for her to return the pen.

She looked at him. "Have I done something wrong?"

"Jonathan wants his pen back," I said saving him the trouble.

"Oh, yes of course," she said handing the silver pen back to him.

We both watched as Jonathan scrawled his indecipherable signature on the documents and dated them.

"I'll keep the original copies with me," Jonathan said as he put the folder back in his briefcase and stowed his glasses and pen at the same time. "Do you want me to send an electronic copy to you both?"

"No." I didn't want anyone else getting hold of a copy of the contract. "Courier them to the apartment."

"Certainly," Jonathan said as he stood up. He offered Hannah his hand first, "Nice to meet you, Hannah."

"Likewise," Hannah said.

"Here's my card." Jonathan pulled a small business card from his top pocket and handed it to Hannah. "Email me your bank account details and I'll have the funds deposited before the end of the day."

"Robert," he said to me and he shook my hand.

"Hannah, will you stay here please," I saw Jonathan out of my office and waited until the door was firmly closed before I turned my attention back to Hannah.

CHAPTER 12

*H*annah

My mind was in a whirl. I couldn't believe that it had been that easy to secure two hundred thousand dollars for myself.

A simple signature on a piece of paper.

What the hell would my mother say if she knew what was really happening here?

"Are you okay?" Robert looked down at me, concern etched across his features.

I took a deep breath. "Of course," I said trying to behave as if I signed contracts every day that made me richer than I could even imagine.

There was enough money going into my bank account this afternoon to buy my mum and me a nice house down south.

I could do that for her now. If I wanted to, I could go home and I wouldn't have to live with my brother and Trudi.

The pull of the familiar was strong.

But then Robert put his hands on my shoulders.

"You're shaking," he said.

"It's that damn coffee you keep making me drink." I knew it wasn't and I think Robert did as well, but he didn't press me on the point.

"I won't make you drink anymore of it, okay?"

I nodded.

"Come and sit down, over here by the window. It's one of my favourite places to sit when I'm feeling unsettled."

I couldn't ever imagine Robert being unsettled. Every situation I'd seen him in so far he'd dominated his surroundings and the people around him.

The idea that he might need a moment to compose himself, seemed bizarre.

"Make sure you send Jonathan your bank account details," Robert said as he sat on the couch beside me, "I want to be sure that money's out of his trust account and in your bank account by the close of the day."

"I will," I said and I heard the crack in my voice.

I looked out at the view from Robert's office. The large floor-to-ceiling windows gave the impression that we were sitting out in the harbour itself. The sense of spaciousness and the pale blue of the ocean began to calm my swirling insides.

"The money disturbs you, doesn't it?" Robert slipped his hand over mine and I looked down at the large, strong fingers with their perfectly manicured nails and had an immediate memory of those hands roaming my body.

An involuntary shiver set my body trembling again.

"It's all right," he soothed.

"It's not the money," I started to say. "Well, it is the money. Well, it's not just the money. Everything's happening so fast." I was babbling.

All the while, Robert stroked the top of my hand.

I could cope with his presence when there was a desk or a

kitchen bench between us. But I couldn't cope when he sat close to me like this. Or when he touched me.

As much as my head told me this was nothing more than a business transaction, my body was telling me another completely different story.

"Money's not an issue," Robert said as he looked out the window to the view of the northern beaches and the inner islands beyond.

"It's not for you," I said, "but it is for someone who's come from where I've come from."

"What I mean," Robert said as he turned his attention back to me, "is that money's not something you should be scared of."

It wasn't money that was terrifying me right this moment. I'd rather that Robert looked out the window. My heart beat raced every time he turned his attention on me. At this rate, I'd be in coronary care before the week was out.

There didn't seem to be a sensible way to express my concerns around money. Robert was so at ease with it all. I mean I only had to look at where we were sitting now to know how at ease he was with everything.

"I don't think you'd understand," I said hoping to change the subject.

"Try me," he said letting go of my hand and leaning back into the couch, as if he had all the time in the world to sit here and listen to me.

I knew what was waiting for Robert. The emails in his inbox. The staff waiting with impatience outside the door for a few minutes with him. The fact he was putting all that aside to listen to my insecurities touched me more than the physical connection of his hand.

A long silence hung between us.

"Shall I tell you what money means to me?" Robert asked.
I nodded, "Yes."

"Nothing."

Now I was mad. "You can say that when you've got millions."

"Billions," he corrected me.

"Millions, billions I'm not splitting hairs. It's all right for someone like you to sit up here in your ivory tower and say that money means nothing to you. You should trying living without it one day and see how easy it is."

Robert remained completely unmoved by my outburst and calmly picked a stray strand of something off his Italian suit.

"Money is simply the result of my passion for running these businesses. That's what motivates me to get out of bed in the morning, not the money that I earn."

That surprised me.

"So you tell me, Hannah," he said as he turned his cool gaze back on me again, "What motivates you to get out of bed in the morning?"

I still didn't know what to say.

Robert reached over and ran his fingers down the side of my face. I sucked in a sharp breath.

He couldn't touch me in the office. There were staff out there.

"You can't touch me like that here," I said.

"Where can I touch you like that then?"

I stood up and faced the large picture window and took a few deep breaths. Robert was toying with me. Pulling me in and then pushing me away. Two could play that game. I waited for my heart beat to slow before turning to face him again.

"How do you know I'm not just going to give my bank account details to Jonathan, wait for the money to go into my bank account and then up and leave?"

He put his arm up on the back of the couch, caressing the

smooth leather. Something inside of me tightened. I wanted his hand to be caressing my skin the way he stroked the top of that couch.

"I don't," he said looking up at me.

Everything about Robert Redfern in that instant radiated a calculating calm that I'd not seen before. "But I've done a few business deals in my time and had a number of them go off the rails." He flicked his arm off the rear of the couch and took a moment to readjust the gold cufflink by his wrist.

Robert turned his attention back to me. "But I'm of the firm opinion that I haven't backed a runaway bride in this deal."

He'd piqued my interest. "How can you be so sure?"

A slight smile crossed Robert's perfect features. The first smile that I'd seen today. "The way you moaned last night when I made you come."

I could feel the flare of heat as it radiated up my face.

"This is going to sound silly," I mumbled looking down at my feet to hide my embarrassment.

"Nothing you can say in front of me is silly, Hannah I can assure you of that."

My gaze returned to Robert and in the heat of his stare, everything about me screamed for him to touch me. I swallowed and said, "I thought our arrangement was going to be purely professional."

"That's the way I'd like it to be," Robert replied, "but I have to admit to finding you incredibly attractive."

"You don't have to sound so disappointed about that." I couldn't hold my tongue.

Now Robert let out a laugh. A genuine belly laugh. The sound reverberated through me, setting my senses alight with longing.

"You see, Hannah. There you go again giving me another reason to like you."

"You don't like women?"

"I don't understand women," Robert said his tone neither dismissive nor aggressive. "I haven't had time for them and quite frankly most of the women who want to spend any time with me haven't got a lot of interests other than trying to find ways to spend my money."

"I find it hard to believe that a man like you who understands the ins and outs of acquisitions and mergers could find women such a difficult subject."

Robert returned to his desk. "Well I do." He looked at his computer screen. "And as much as I'd love to continue this fascinating conversation with you, we both have work to do."

Now he was dismissing me?

Taking charge.

The man turned his feelings on and off at will.

I was in way over my head.

I made my way towards the door of his office.

"Hannah."

The commanding tone made me stop in my tracks and turn to face him again. "Yes?"

"Make sure that you send your details through to Jonathan and we will continue this conversation this evening, at home."

Yes.

Over my head.

In way too deep for my own good.

CHAPTER 13

*R*obert

The rest of the morning vanished in a maelstrom of meetings and urgent emails.

I'd eaten at my desk and took a moment to reflect on how well the meeting with Jonathan had gone this morning. Even if the man did make me sign that bullshit disclaimer. If he spent as much time looking after my business affairs as he did covering his own arse he'd be a billionaire by now.

Jonathan had just sent me an email confirming that he'd paid the money into Hannah's bank account. I'd sent Hannah on her way with another box of files and I guess she'd find his email on her return to her desk. I'd been pretty sure this morning that she wouldn't take the money and run. She'd done nothing in the following four hours or so to make me change my mind. In fact, if anything, Hannah seemed more committed to the job and our arrangement since she'd signed the contract.

There was something about having her working in my space that I found distracting in so many ways.

But still, I found myself taking surreptitious glances in

her direction. Wondering if the underwear that I'd purchased for her this morning fitted her body in the way that I expected it would. My mind kept dancing to the vision last night of her legs splayed in front of me.

Even now, I could feel my cock getting hard at the thought of her soft, luscious skin and the sweet scent of her body.

Fuck.

I was screwed.

If I didn't keep my mind on the work at hand, we weren't going to meet our due diligence obligations and I didn't intend to let that happen.

The buzz of my phone in my pocket dragged my eyes away from the door. I was gazing at Hannah like a love-struck school boy.

"Grandmother."

The sensible greeting of my Grandmother Mary settled the unfamiliar feelings coursing through my body.

"Robert, I just wanted you to know how well the evening went last night." I heard the rattling of paper and knew Grandmother was surveying the morning news. "I'm also pleased to see that your engagement has been received well by the press."

"I'm pleased that you're pleased."

"I've decided to delay my departure for Sydney by another week. I'd like to have lunch with Hannah before I return home and I also think that it would be a good idea for a formal engagement function."

I could feel my blood pressure rising and this time it was for all the wrong reasons.

"Neither Hannah nor I want a formal engagement party."

Grandmother sighed on the other end of the line. "I thought you may take that attitude, Robert especially with the sudden nature of the engagement." I wasn't going to take any notice whatsoever of that comment. "So I'm prepared to meet you half way. I'll arrange for a photographer to come to your apartment later this week. I'll liaise with Hannah over the date and I'd also like Edward and Nicki to attend. Your brother didn't get a chance to welcome formally his new sister-in-law into the family last night."

It was useless trying to avoid anything like this. Grandmother had been organising family photo sessions for the media for years. Hannah and I would be all over the local women's magazines in no time at all. The money paid for the story, of course, being donated to Grandmother's favourite charity.

"Now, you do have an engagement ring, don't you?"

I didn't, but I wasn't going to tell Grandmother that. "Of course I do, it's with the jeweller being sized."

"Good." Grandmother sounded pleased with herself.

"Now give me Hannah's cellphone number and I'll call her."

Shit! I didn't have Hannah's cellphone number.

"She's right here. You can speak to her yourself," I said as I bolted for the door to put Hannah on the phone.

"It's for you," I handed the phone to a dumbstruck looking Hannah and somehow managed to man-handle her into my office and close the door.

"Hello?" she said with a confused look on her face.

I stood in front of the clear glass of my office door, making sure that nobody entered the room while Hannah was engaged in conversation with my Grandmother.

"Well, I'm working that day and I only get an hour for lunch," I heard her say.

"Take as long as you need," I whispered but I don't think that Hannah heard me.

"Oh, well as long as you think that will be okay."

Hannah was glaring at me now, but her voice remained

perfectly composed. "Fine. I'll look forward to it. Goodbye."

She glanced at the face of my phone before she handed it back to me.

"I don't remember seeing a cat at your apartment."

She was referring to the picture I had of my Tabby cat on my phone.

"Silo went to the Rainbow Bridge last year. I'd rather not talk about it." I slipped my phone in my pocket, then thought better of it and pulled it out again. "You need to put your cellphone number in my phone."

"I'm here all day with you and apparently I'm going home with you tonight. Why do you need my cell?"

"Grandmother asked for it."

"And what Grandmother wants, Grandmother gets," Hannah replied in a sharp tone as I watched her key in the numbers. When she was done, Hannah handed me my phone and said, "She wants to discuss how we met and she says she's *really looking forward* to hearing about our plans for the wedding."

I closed my eyes and pinched the bridge of my nose.

"Any thoughts on what I should be telling her over lunch tomorrow?"

"We'll talk about it tonight," I said as I swung my office door open so Hannah could get back to work.

I had a business to run. I really didn't need these kinds of distractions.

*H*annah

I loathed the way he dismissed me.

All logic told me that he had businesses to run and I was employed to look after his office and him. Organise his files and generally make sure that his business life ran smoothly.

But the way he dismissed me like this.

It was becoming a theme.

From leaving me unceremoniously in the bedroom to shutting the door on me now. It wasn't something that should bother me, but for some strange reason it did.

It reminded me of the way that my brother dismissed me —as if I didn't have anything sensible to say. It was clear even this early in our professional relationship that Robert's office wasn't going to run well without me.

Managing his calendar was a full-time job. Then there was the task of arranging the files in some semblance of order for the audit of the businesses that he was considering purchasing. The name of the dairy factory down home had come up on a couple of pages. Something about that put me on edge and I didn't quite know why.

I'd spent an unproductive hour down in the copier room this morning. Trying to motivate an unmotivated seventeen-year-old who would rather have been permanently attached to her cellphone than feeding documentation into the scanner made me grind my teeth. Explaining the care required to make sure that Robert received information in his preferred format was like talking to a goldfish. The young lady wouldn't last long here if she didn't improve her standards.

Seething with unreasonable resentment, I sat down at my computer.

An email from Jonathan.

Evidence that $200,000 had been deposited to my bank account.

I stared at the screen.

It seemed surreal.

I found myself furtively checking around me to make sure that no-one else had seen the email. Hurriedly, I forwarded it to my personal email and then checked my online bank account.

There it was staring at me. A bank balance large enough to purchase a home, without a mortgage in my hometown. Not only a home, but one of the better homes in the town.

I'd been in Auckland just over a week and I had enough money to go home and never worry about having to find a man to look after me.

But I didn't want a man to look after me, I reminded myself.

That was the entire reason that I'd come to Auckland in the first place.

My hands started to shake.

I closed down the bank website and then turned around in my chair, trying to compose myself.

Robert came into my line of view.

I never believed that he'd go through with it. Even after we signed the contract this morning, there was something inside of me that refused to believe that he'd actually put that much money in my bank account.

Now, I didn't know how I felt.

I did know how I felt—but I didn't want to admit it to myself.

After last night, I felt like a whore.

I wrapped my arms around myself. Suddenly the air conditioning seemed colder. Had someone turned the thermostat down?

I took a deep breath. I had to get a grip. I watched Robert working away. A deep line of concentration marking his perfect brow.

His deep hazel eyes scanning the computer screen in front of him. Dark stubble had begun to form on his face, giving him a more masculine appearance.

He was impossibly attractive.

That perfect man had just wired two hundred thousand dollars to my bank account, so I'd agree to marry him.

Why did someone as perfect at Robert Redfern need a little nobody like me from the south to pretend to be his fiancée?

I hadn't even thought that through last night. I was so overwhelmed by the 'occasion'. I'd been a greedy little girl and look where it had gotten me now.

Two hundred thousand dollars richer. The sensible voice in my head said.

But you still want him to fuck you. The horny voice chanted.

I told the sensible voice to piss off.

The horny voice—well, I wasn't sure how I was going to deal with the horny voice.

It spoke the truth.

Whenever I spent any time around Robert, my ovaries went into overdrive.

Who could blame them after the way he wound my body up and down last night.

Finding two hundred thousand dollars in my bank account though, that had put a different spin on how I was feeling about everything.

I didn't want to feel like a paid whore.

Maybe Robert was right.

Maybe it was important that we keep this whole relationship professional.

I took a deep breath and lifted the lid on the most recent box of files that I'd brought to my desk.

It was probably best that he'd sent me out of his office to sort through them. My concentration levels were shit when we were in the same room.

Was it the same for him, I wondered?

I needed to keep my mind on the job at hand. As long as we stayed professional and kept some distance between the two of us, we'd be fine.

I hoped.

CHAPTER 14

*R*obert

It wasn't until I looked up as Hannah walked into my office to collect another box of files that I realised we were the only two people left on the floor.

I checked my watch. It was after 7pm.

"Have you had anything to eat since lunchtime?" Hannah jumped at the sound of my voice.

"No," she said, "I've been busy."

"You have." I was pleased to see that most of the boxes had gone from my office and the space had regained some of its aesthetic beauty.

It was important to me that the spaces I spent my time in were uncluttered. It had rattled me. Being surrounded by chaos for such a long time.

"You don't know how grateful I am that you've sculptured some order back into my workspace."

Hannah beamed under the praise.

I hadn't looked at her properly since we signed the contract this morning—every time I studied her, all I wanted to do was undress her and make her come again.

She would be the undoing of me if I wasn't careful.

"We'll pick up something to eat on the way home," I said, "you've done enough today and I can work later tonight."

"I've got to meet your Grandmother for lunch tomorrow," Hannah reminded me.

"I hadn't forgotten. We need to come up with a sensible story around how we met."

"I hate lying," Hannah said, "can't we just tell her the truth?"

"No!" I didn't mean to shout and I made Hannah jump again.

"I don't mean about the money," she squeaked, "I mean about the engagement being very sudden."

"I think she gets that," I said. I couldn't help sounding cynical. Then I took in the crushed look on Hannah's face and a pang of guilt rolled through me. I was being an asshole. It wasn't Hannah's fault that I'd gotten myself into the situation I'd found myself in with Grandmother.

"Maybe I'll just cancel lunch," Hannah said, as she stuffed documents into another storage box with enough gusto to rip the pages to shreds.

I sighed and closed my laptop. This was why I didn't get involved with women. I didn't know how to deal with emotion.

Contracts I was good at.

Emotions. Not.

"Look, Hannah," I took my voice down an octave, trying to sound as if I was some kind of reasonable human being, not the ruthless bastard who cut companies up and spat them out again in saleable portions. "I know this is difficult. I've not navigated this sort of relationship before either. It's been a long day. Let's get something to eat and talk about it, okay?"

She looked at me with big green eyes, her pale face framed with auburn hair and nodded her consent.

It was never much of a walk home. I hadn't had time today to exercise and I wasn't accustomed to walking with someone else beside me. All the way, I could hear the impossible clip-clopping of Hannah's shoes on the concrete.

"What shall we cook for dinner?" I asked as I manoeuvred Hannah into the corner store, come delicatessen that I relied on for fresh ingredients if I decided to cook.

"You decide," she said.

"Is there anything you don't eat?"

"Seriously. You're asking me that question after everything you fed me last night?"

Why did she have to bring last night up? Whenever I thought about last night, I thought about the way her full breasts fell out of her gown. I thought about the milky white of her skin. The way she shuddered when I made her come.

I turned my mind back to ingredients for dinner. I picked up a couple of pieces of chicken, fresh coriander and a few pine nuts. I'd stuff them with cheese and make us a nice rice risotto to boot. I'd need to get up early to run the meal off, but I could get an early start in the morning. Hannah could make her own way to the office.

I found Hannah admiring a pale pink orchid strand at the end of one of the small aisles.

"I've always loved these," she said. "They're so delicate and the flowers have perfect formation. Look at the way they all sit so beautifully on the stem."

"Pick it up, we'll take it home," I said.

"It's too expensive," she said airily.

"Hannah, you need to spoil yourself. Besides, money's not an issue now that you're engaged to a Redfern."

I picked it up and carried it to the cashier.

She stood beside me as I paid for the purchases. I handed

her the orchid as we made out way out the door and on towards my apartment.

"You need to start spoiling yourself," I said.

"I'm not used to it," Hannah mumbled as she clip-clopped alongside me, the tip of the orchid bobbing in time with her steps.

"Well, get used to it." I said as we arrived at the security gate for the apartment. I punched in the key code and the gate buzzed letting us in. "You need to get in touch with the building manager. You'll need a code for the gate and a key for the apartment."

"I could just go and live at my bed-sit."

As much as having Hannah around was going to be a distraction, I didn't want her living at her bed-sit.

"No. I want you here where you're safe and where I can keep an eye on you. There's all kinds of nutters around this town and you'll be a target for them now."

"A target. What kind of target?"

"Don't argue with me. You're not going back to your bed-sit and that's the end of it. You can give your landlord notice."

"I'm not giving my notice."

"Suit yourself, it's your money you're wasting. But I guess you don't have to worry about that, now you're a woman of your own means."

I could tell by the scowl on her face that she wasn't happy with me. I didn't even know why I let the last sentence out of my mouth. Maybe if I made her hate me, then I wouldn't have to deal with the way I was feeling.

"I need to go home," she said, "I've got nothing to wear. All my things are at my bed-sit."

"You don't have to worry about that. I had Stella pick up everything that you need. I'm not having you go back to that bed-sit on your own."

"What!" Hannah looked at me as if I'd grown another head.

"You heard. It made sense. She had your measurements. There's an entire wardrobe waiting for you upstairs." I swiped my security tag and pushed the button for the penthouse.

"You know you're an arrogant, over the top pig, don't you?"

I didn't care. I wasn't going to let anything happen to Hannah.

All ready I knew I was in far too deep to let that happen.

CHAPTER 15

*H*annah

I put the orchid down with a resounding thud on the chest of drawers opposite the bed.

Angry didn't even begin to describe the way that I was feeling right this minute.

Then I felt bad and apologised to the beautiful plant. It didn't deserve to be treated this way. It wasn't the poor plant's fault that I was feeling like a whore.

True to his word, Robert had taken care of my every need.

I pulled the top drawer out and it was full of brand new underwear. All in my size. All not too dissimilar to the lace ensemble I'd been presented with this morning.

The wardrobe was filled with a range of clothes in colours that would do nothing but accentuate my own colouring. From shorts, skirts, t-shirts and blouses, to tailored suits for the office and an assortment of dresses and gowns.

There was a leather jacket in an outrageous shade of orange. A long tailored blue coat that I couldn't even begin to imagine where I would wear it and a beautiful velvet black jacket that I immediately fell in love with—but hated myself for doing so.

I walked through the long thin, wardrobe running my hand along the racks of clothing. How much had this all cost?

I counted sixteen pairs of shoes, sandals, strappy heels and boots. Who wore this many pairs of shoes?

The bathroom was filled with every kind of cosmetic from make-up remover to translucent powder.

There were fourteen shades of lipstick. I'd only ever owned one lipstick at a time in my entire life. I wasn't sure where to start with all of this.

I needed help.

I needed my mum.

Picking up my phone with a shaking hand I dialled the number of my brother's home.

"Scott residence," I recognised the sound of my mother's voice in an instant.

"Mum," I stifled a nervous sob.

"Hannah, sweetheart. Are you okay, is everything all right?" Just the sound of her voice eased the terror that had stolen over me. If it all turned to crap, now at least I knew I could go home to mum.

"I'm just a bit tired. A bit overwhelmed, I guess."

"Oh, I'm not surprised. You've been all over the papers. They keep ringing, wanting to know things."

My stomach fell. "You're not telling them anything are you, Mum?"

She laughed and I couldn't help smiling. "What's there to tell?"

Of course. I'd not had a chequered past. I was a nobody from the south. They could dig as much as they wanted, what were they going to find out? My most heinous crime had been that I scratched my name on a new driveway in Arrow Street when I was thirteen. Hardly tabloid fodder.

"How are you doing, Hannah?"

"Good, Mum," better now that I'd heard her voice. There was something settling about the sound of the voice of the woman who'd raised me. Raised me to be a wife and a mother, but probably not the kind of wife that I'd signed up to be this week.

Even though I knew I didn't want to go back home, there was something calming about knowing that I could purchase a house if the shit hit the fan and I couldn't manage things here.

"A new job and a man. I always thought that you were so dead set against getting married and here you are, engaged."

I didn't want to talk about *my engagement*. In the cold, harsh light of sitting here in Robert's guest suite, I wasn't sure any more about whether or not I was going to be able to pull this off. The thought of lunch tomorrow with Robert's grandmother terrified me.

"It's as much of a shock for me as it is for you, Mum," and I wasn't telling a lie.

"Well, I want you to know that I'm very pleased for you and I'm so looking forward to meeting Robert."

Fuck!

I hadn't thought about my family meeting Robert's family.

The idea was enough to bring me out in hives.

"How soon do you think you'll be down?" The hopeful tone of mum's question brought a lump to my throat.

"I don't know, I'll have to talk to Robert and see when we can come."

As much as I didn't like the idea of going back down south, the thought of Robert sitting in Daniel and Trudi's lounge filled me with some kind of strange glee. The idea of

Daniel knowing that I had enough money sitting in my bank account right this moment to buy his house out from under him gave me even more of a strange sense of superiority.

Then I remembered how I came about that money and the superior feelings fled.

I didn't ever want anyone to know how I earned that money and now that I'd taken it, I had to go through with this bizarre charade.

"Let me know as soon as you can come, dear," mum said, "I'm looking forward to welcoming Robert into the family."

The idea of welcoming Robert into the family when I'd be shipping off overseas as soon as I could after the wedding didn't sit well with me.

Maybe I needed to renegotiate the wedding part of this agreement.

Perhaps I should rethink the entire prospect of Robert meeting my family. If they didn't meet him, then there would be no issue when we got our fake marriage dissolved.

"I'll let you know when we can come down," I reassured my mother.

The duplicitous way I was living my life was all ready taking its toll.

I needed to have dinner with Robert so that we could get our story straight before I met with his grandmother tomorrow. I had no idea what kind of a story he'd spun her.

I was going to need a spreadsheet just to keep a track of the lies I was telling.

The idea didn't sit well with me at all.

"I have to go," I said to mum, "Robert's cooking dinner."

The rudiments of a plan was beginning to form in my head. If I was going to be married to Robert and he was going to force me to live here while we were engaged. Well, why shouldn't I enjoy myself.

Time to throw caution to the wind and *sex this thing up*.

CHAPTER 16

*R*obert
I'd unpacked our small bag of groceries and was well into preparing our dinner by the time Hannah appeared back in the kitchen.

The scowl on her face told me that things weren't going well.

"Here," I said trying to lighten the mood, "let me pour you a glass of wine." I knew she wasn't happy with me not letting her go back to her bed-sit. She had no idea the idiots that she'd have to keep an eye out for now that she was engaged to me. She'd be on the radar of every crackpot in the city. I didn't want to have to worry about her safety. If necessary, I'd put a round-the-clock surveillance team on her tail so I knew that she was safe.

"Thank you," she said as she took a sip of the chardonnay.

The lines on her face disappeared. "This is nice."

"It should be," I said as I took a sip from my own glass, "it's one of the best from the region."

"Do you always have the best of everything?" she asked.

I stopped my food preparation and thought about the

question. "I suppose I do. I've never thought about it before. It's what I've grown up with." I went back to my food preparation. "You can help with the meal if you like." I was hoping that Hannah might stay in the guest suite. She'd shed her work clothes and put on a pretty floral skirt and a bright green t-shirt that brought out the intense colour of her eyes.

"I don't cook."

I stopped what I was doing again and looked at Hannah. Surely she was having me on. "What do you mean, you don't cook?"

"Exactly that." Hannah smiled and sat down on one of the tall stools in front of the kitchen bench. She twirled her glass of wine around in tiny circles, the crystal base scraping against the stone of the bench top.

"My parents were training me to become the perfect wife, so I avoided the kitchen at all costs."

I couldn't imagine anyone not knowing the first thing about preparing a meal. I found food preparation relaxing. It was one of the things that I missed when I spent too many hours at the office. Phoning in a takeaway meal wasn't the same.

"I never got past the onion and garlic stage," she said as she took another sip of her wine and watched me dice onion with ease. "As soon as those two ingredients were placed in the frying pan, I found a good reason to exit the kitchen."

"Well, you're not going to find one now," I said. "If we're going to live together during our engagement, then the least I can do is make sure that you learn how to cook." All of a sudden I was determined that I could teach this woman at least the rudiments of throwing a meal together.

Hannah cocked her head to one side, looking at me as if she were assessing the enemy. She took an almighty swig of her wine, almost emptying the glass and then a small smile began to creep across her face.

"What are you thinking?"

Maybe the wine was having more of an effect than I imagined, but the hell cat who had left me in the kitchen as soon as we arrived back from the office seemed to have vanished.

I felt sure I was looking into the eyes of a woman who had her sights firmly set on me.

When did the hell cat turn into a sexual predator?

Hannah tipped her chin in the air and said, "We need to discuss exactly how we met." She hopped off the tall stool she'd been sitting on and sauntered towards me.

Yep. Definite huntress. I licked my lips. I almost wished that the hell cat was back. At least I knew I wasn't in danger of ending up naked with Hannah when she wanted to kill me.

The way her hips swung from side to side as she walked towards me was hypnotic. By the time she'd walked a half circle around me and run her fingers across my back I knew I was in serious trouble.

"I think I could make sure that we're both out of the kitchen prior to any other ingredients being added to the pan," Hannah purred, a look of pure mischief on her face.

"And how do you mean to achieve that?" As if I didn't know and why the hell was I flirting with her? I should be shutting this down. Right now. Before it got out of hand.

Shortly after the words were out of my mouth, Hannah had her hands around my waist. I could feel the soft caress of her breasts beneath my shoulder blades.

"Stop that." Even I didn't think I sounded convincing. Hannah simply ignored my instructions, her hands continuing to explore my body. When her fingers threatened to find their way under my shirt, I held my breath.

I was powerless.

One hand full of onion and the other holding a sharp

knife. If I didn't take care I'd end up cutting my finger off, or stabbing Hannah.

Either way—she wasn't playing fair.

"I mean it." The words came out as a strangled sigh. "Please, Hannah. Stop," I said abandoning the cut onion and putting the knife down on the cutting board.

By the time I'd rinsed the juice off my fingers, Hannah's had found their way under the cotton of my shirt.

I sucked in a breath.

"I do hope this wasn't the method you used to get out of cooking when you were down south?" I spun around and pulled Hannah's hands out from under my shirt. The silly grin she wore on her face told me that she thought she was clever.

"You told me you were hungry not more than ten minutes ago."

"Not hungry for food," she said her eyes never leaving mine.

"You and I said that we weren't going to do this." How the hell I was supposed to keep our relationship professional when just being in the same room with her shot my desire sky high, I didn't know.

Besides the warnings my lawyer insisted on issuing over and over ad nauseam.

"A girl's allowed to change her mind," Hannah said as she reached up around my neck. Her hands were warm and soft and the way her breasts pressed themselves into my chest made my cock twitch.

Never mind what looking into her eyes did to my insides.

This was me. Robert Redfern.

I didn't do relationships with women.

I had sexual encounters. Preferably anonymous sexual encounters. If I felt like spending time with a woman, I picked one up in a bar, took her back to a hotel room. Fucked her and then came home.

What the hell was I doing here in my apartment, cooking dinner for a woman who seemed hell bent on taking me to bed?

"Hannah," I lowered my voice, trying to be gentle, "we can't do this. We agreed."

She looked at me with those bright green eyes and it was as if all the fight in her suddenly vanished. Her body went limp, her face fell and I saw the edge of her lip begin to tremble.

"I'm sorry. I'm an idiot to think that you'd actually find me attractive." She turned from me and went to walk into the other room.

Now I felt like a prick.

"It's not that," I said as I reached out and held her arm, preventing her from leaving.

"What is it, then?" she asked as she turned around and swiped a tear from the side of her face.

Her vulnerability was the undoing of me. Despite my own misgivings, I pulled Hannah into my arms. "It's that you're far too attractive. I'm not used to having someone here with me. I don't do this," I whispered as I slipped my lips over hers.

I'd wanted to kiss her all day. As her lips parted and her mouth surrendered to my insistent tongue, I felt the rest of her body yield to my touch.

I was in way too deep this time.

CHAPTER 17

*H*annah

This was what I thought I wanted. Robert's hands were all over my body. I could feel the length of his thick cock as it pressed against my belly.

Anxiety fought with desire as my body surrendered against the hard length of Robert's.

His hands were in my hair and he moaned as he continued to kiss me.

My breath came in ragged pants.

Fear.

Longing.

Desire.

All came together in one massive tumultuous rush.

When he pulled his lips from mine and looked down into my eyes, I could scarcely see where the dark of Robert's pupil ended and the brown of his eyes began.

"I've wanted to kiss you like that all day," he said, "we can eat later."

He picked me up and walked me through to the other

side of the penthouse apartment. This area had been off limits this morning when Robert gave me a tour of his home.

Robert's bedroom suite was twice as big as the one that I was residing in—it could easily have been an apartment proper all by itself. It had its own adjacent bathroom, wardrobe and dressing room. There was also another adjacent room that housed an exercise bike and what looked like a small home gym. Robert would easily be able to exercise and take his mind off what he was doing by watching the boats on the harbour. On the other side of the room a huge flat screen television filled the entire wall, with a designer chair and footstool sat opposite it. Robert had no need for the rooms that we'd just come from. He could easily live in here if he ordered take out food for the rest of his life. Unfortunately for him, it appeared that he enjoyed cooking far too much.

The bedroom's huge floor to ceiling windows looked out across the harbour as well. It felt as if we were sitting at the top of the world. Robert pressed a button by the side of the bed and block out blinds slid down the windows. He pushed another button and the lighting illuminated the far crevices of the room, adding to the sense of intimacy.

At the press of a further button, the soothing sound of relaxing music filled the huge expansive space.

As Robert turned his full attention back to me and began to peel my clothing from my body, it was clear that no expense had been spared in this part of his home either.

A sudden attack of doubt made my stomach clench.

"I'm not sure that we should be doing this," I murmured around Roberts lips as his mouth found mine again.

"You don't interrupt me while I'm cooking and then start having doubts," Robert said as he pulled my bra away and his lips found my tight nipple.

I sucked in a breath as a shot of pleasure ran through my

body. I wanted him, there was no doubt about that and it was clear from the insistent way he was rubbing his cock against my thigh that he wanted me as well.

"We're two consenting adults," Robert said as his lips trailed their way down my stomach. It felt as if every hair on my body rose to meet his breath.

"But the contract and the money," I managed to mutter between breaths.

Robert had begun to slide my panties off my body. He'd be able to tell how wet they were.

Who was I kidding?

I wanted him.

He had the good grace to stop and sit up.

I lay in front of him, almost naked, my panties still in place—but only just.

A shocking sense of abandonment slammed into me.

Robert had undone his shirt. When?

My eyes fell to the flat plane of his stomach. The enticing line of black hair that ran from his belly button down to the top of his trousers.

I wanted to follow that line with my tongue.

"We need to get this straight. Right now," Robert said as he ran his hand through his thick, black hair. "You need to forget about the money and the contract. All I want to know is whether or not you want me."

I didn't quite know what to say.

"Hannah," Robert took a deep breath. "I'm trying to keep this," he waved his hands around madly in the air, "thing between us professional. But I want you. The way you touched me in the kitchen, I thought you wanted me too."

"I do," I squeaked.

"Well what's the problem then?"

"It sort of feels…" I wasn't sure of the word I was looking for.

"Wrong?"

I nodded. "Yeah, wrong."

Robert looked away from me as if he was composing his thoughts. I couldn't help stealing another glance at his body.

Dear god he was beautiful. I wanted to lick every inch of him.

I wanted his thick cock in my mouth and I wanted to hear him moan when he came. I wanted to watch the carefully constructed persona that was Robert Redfern fall apart because of me.

I wanted to know what he sounded like when he let go.

I didn't want to leave this bedroom without making the man sitting in front of me come.

What the hell was my problem?

CHAPTER 18

*R*obert

     I looked at Hannah lying there, almost naked. I knew she wanted me and yet she'd effectively told me to stop.

Maybe I should stop.

Maybe the best thing for me to do was to give her back her clothes and send her to live at her bed-sit until the day of our wedding.

Then I looked at the way her auburn hair lay across my pillow and I knew I wasn't going to do that. But I needed to take it slow. To make sure that I had Hannah's consent every step of the way.

"You want me to stop and you want me to give you back your clothes so you can get dressed. Is that what you're telling me, Hannah?"

She screwed her nose up in that adorable way she had while she was thinking.

I could smell her arousal from where I sat. If I was a betting man, I'd say that the odds were one to one hundred of her telling me to get her clothes.

"I'm worried about the contract."

She kept banging on about the bloody contract.

"If I'd brought you back to my apartment and no money had been paid into your bank account today and we hadn't signed a contract this morning," I said with all the earnestness that I could muster, "would you still want to be here?"

There was no hesitation, "Yes."

I didn't understand, "Well, what's the issue then?"

"For an intelligent man, you can be quite stupid," she said simply staring at me.

And then I got it.

"Nobody is ever going to know about the contract between us," I said, "unless you tell them."

"You won't tell a soul?"

I made the grand gesture of crossing my finger across my chest. "Cross my heart."

That made her smile.

"But what about your solicitor?"

"He's bound by ethics. He'll take to his grave what he knows about me, don't you worry your pretty little self about him."

I could see that Hannah was mulling this new information over. I ran my fingertips along the soft flesh of her hip and she sucked in a breath.

I wanted to fuck her so bad. But I wasn't ever going to force myself on her. I'd never force myself on anyone who didn't want me, that wasn't my style.

"So no-one will ever know that you paid me to be your wife?"

"Not unless you tell them, sweetheart."

"Why do you need to pay someone to be your wife?"

Did we have to talk about this now?

I lay down on my side next to Hannah and began to trace my fingers around her belly button. Her skin fluttered under my touch and my cocked twitched in response to the call of her body.

"It's complicated." I didn't want to talk about this now, so I decided to change the subject. "We have to make sure we get our story straight before you have lunch with Grandmother tomorrow."

"What am I going to tell her?"

I'd come up with a cunning plan.

"The files that you've been sorting through for me relate to the acquisition of a dairy company."

"Yes, I saw mention of the factory near where I lived down south."

I couldn't hide my grin. "Exactly. You come from dairy farming country. So we'll tell Grandmother that we met when I came down to look at the factory."

"Did you?" Hannah sat up. I loved the way that her breasts bounced when she moved suddenly like that.

"I did, don't look so surprised. I am capable of setting foot outside of Auckland and I do, quite often."

"I didn't know that the dairy factory was for sale." A frown creased Hannah's perfect brow. "I know a lot of people who rely on that factory for their livelihoods."

"It's not the factory itself that's for sale." I shook my head a little as I thought it through. "Technically I suppose the factory is for sale, but it's the over-arching company structure that I'm interested in. I'm busy doing due diligence around the whole operation. I have until the end of the month to decide whether or not we'll proceed with the purchase of the companies and all of their assets."

"And what will you do with them if you decide to proceed?"

"What I always do, pull them apart. Work out which ones are profitable. Maybe keep them, or simply sell them on."

"What happens to the ones that aren't profitable?"

"We don't want to talk about business, right this minute do we? Now that we've decided how we met." I couldn't resist the lure of Hannah's almost naked body for another moment.

"Where did you work down south?" I asked as I ran butterfly kisses down Hannah's stomach.

Her breath hitched as she said, "In the superette on the corner of the Main Highway and Wilson Avenue."

"Perfect," I said as I slipped my thumbs under the thin lace of Hannah's panties and pulled them off. "I stopped by, it was a scorching hot day and I needed an ice cream."

I licked my way up the inside of Hannah's thigh and she shuddered.

"We have fourteen flavours of ice cream," she sighed.

My fingers found their way to Hannah's slick, wet folds and she shuddered as I stroked her hot, swollen lips. "I ordered choc-mint in a waffle cone." I slipped two fingers inside Hannah and her body arched in response. "You're so wet for me, Hannah. Do you want me to fuck you now?"

"Yes," she moaned.

We didn't need to talk about anything else.

*H*annah

I lay on the bed and watched as Robert removed his clothes and then reached across my body to the table at the side of the bed. He rolled a condom down his thick cock with the same level of concentration that I'd watched him use in the office.

It made sense now why I'd seen the name of the dairy factory on the documents I'd been sorting.

Robert was looking at the financial viability of the dairy factory.

What kind of impact would that have on the people that I knew and loved?

Could I even worry about that right at this minute?

Did I have a right to worry about that, having abandoned them all and come up here to Auckland?

I didn't want to be thinking about those things now. In fact, I could barely think straight at all.

Robert's naked body slipped against mine. The skin-on-skin contact sent a searing shot of lust through my body, wiping all rational thought from my mind.

All I wanted was to feel the immense width of Robert's cock inside of me.

He flipped onto his back and pulled me astride him. I thought he was going to impale me on his huge cock, but instead he looked at me with a wicked grin.

"Come sit on my face," he purred, "and let me make you come."

Robert's huge hands cupped my backside and he pulled me up to his lips.

I hadn't done this before. I found myself caught between feelings of mortification and intense pleasure.

As I surrendered to the pleasurable sensations and allowed Robert to guide my body, the tension I'd been carrying with me all day began to fade.

My mind went blank and all I could focus on was the intense sensations rolling through my body.

Robert didn't let up for a second and I found my body vibrating with my first orgasm.

Limp as a rag doll, he flipped me over onto my back.

"Now I'm going to fuck you until you scream my name," Robert growled. I could taste my own come on his lips as he slipped his tongue into my hungry mouth.

I moaned around his tongue as he filled me with his thick cock.

"Shit, you're so fucking tight," he whispered as he pushed himself further inside me.

When I thought I couldn't take any more, Robert pulled out and then thrust back inside me.

Over and over Robert slammed into me. I hooked my feet around the back of his thighs and hung on for the ride.

My body thundered towards another screaming orgasm.

My breath came in fast and hard pants.

"Say my name," Robert ordered. "I want to hear you say my name when I make you come again."

I groaned. My body was on fire.

Robert pushed into me over and over again.

He was on the cusp of coming. Tiny moans escaped his perfect lips. Lips still covered with my come.

Tiny drops of perspiration clung to his hair line.

His eyes were black.

"Hannah," he breathed, "come for me."

It was my final undoing.

My body shuddered. "Robert," I moaned as I surrendered again to the pleasure of him.

Robert rode my orgasm, pushing me to peaks that I didn't think I could reach and then surrendered to his own pleasure.

When the shaking subsided, he pulled the covers up over the two of us and held me in his arms.

I drifted on a cloud of contentment. I tried not to think about lunch with Robert's grandmother or what I'd learned about the dairy factory back home.

CHAPTER 19

*R*obert
　　　I opened my eyes as the bedroom filled with the early morning light of another Auckland day. I'd heard the familiar buzz of the blinds as the timer lifted them to let in the dawn light. Hannah stirred in my arms, let out a tiny, contented sigh and then rolled over and fell back into a deep sleep.

In all of my 31 years I'd never woken with a woman in my arms before. As I watched Hannah sleep, a strange tight feeling constricted my chest. I'd avoided forming attachments to anyone. If I wasn't attached, then I couldn't feel pain.

Hannah and I had a clear arrangement. She'd become my wife and once my position within the company was secure, she'd be leaving. I couldn't afford to become attached to her in any way.

What the fuck was I thinking letting her stay in my bed?

The logical side of my brain was screaming at me, but the part of me that had enjoyed waking with her in my arms— the part now that I could feel all constricted in my chest—

that part was telling me to keep watching the rise and fall of her body as she slept. It was reminding me of how warm and soft she felt in my arms last night. It spoke of the scent of her hair that lay in swathes of red across the pillow this morning. It whispered sweet nothings and made me want to keep this gorgeous, sexy woman in my bed all day.

Logic said she couldn't stay in my bed all day. Hannah had a luncheon appointment with my grandmother today.

I needed to clear my diary for this morning and make sure that Hannah was properly briefed before her appointment with Grandmother.

Now, first thing though, I needed to clear my head.

I slipped out of the bed without disturbing Hannah and put on my running clothes.

By the time I'd made it downstairs and out onto the Auckland waterfront the seeds of another plan were beginning to form in my head.

The familiar asphalt path along the waterfront was devoid of humanity at this time of the morning. Gulls whirled overhead and the ferries and water taxies that would transport Auckland's workforce from their homes to the city were still tied to various wharfs, bobbing against their tethers.

I loved my early morning run. The only people I was likely to meet were others like myself who took the time to pound the pavement, or the rubbish disposal teams who cleared the city's refuse from the day before.

This was the time that I used to sort my way through my latest acquisition and disposal project. But this morning the only thing I could think about was Hannah.

No matter how I tried to turn my mind to business, it always came back to Hannah. The colour of her eyes. The way she wrinkled her nose when she thought about something.

The little mewing sounds she made last night when we made love.

I'd never been affected by a woman this way before and it terrified me.

Running should have calmed me down and zoned me out. Feelings weren't things that bothered me.

I didn't have time for feelings and emotions—I had businesses to run.

Instead, as I pounded the pavement, I found myself daydreaming about the woman I left in my bed. The further I ran, the more I wanted to get back to my apartment and back into bed with Hannah.

As the miles began to stack up and I continued to suck in the clean, salt-laden air, a clear plan for my future began to emerge from the scrambled recess of my mind.

There was something about the connection to the sea and the endorphin rush that sparked my brain. Almost three quarters of the way into my morning run, this was the time when my best ideas emerged from the depths of my mind.

By the time I returned to my apartment and hit the shower, I knew the way forward.

All I had to do was ensure Hannah saw things the same way that I saw them.

She'd awoken feelings in me that I'd long thought buried.

Ordinarily, I wasn't a betting man.

But I wondered how hard could it be for me to seduce Hannah into staying with me after the wedding?

I knew I'd have to tread lightly. But if I could convince directors of companies to let me acquire and disseminate their life's work, how hard could it be to convince an innocent girl from the deep south to stay here in the city with me?

*H*annah

I'd slept so well, I didn't even hear Robert leave his room to go for his morning run.

It didn't seem right to shower in his bathroom, so I collected my clothes from where he'd thrown them last night and padded my way back across the apartment to my suite of rooms.

Standing in the shower, under the heat of the running water, I couldn't help but think about Robert's hands on my body last night.

In fact, I'd rather think about Robert's hands roaming my body than turn my mind to the dreaded thought of lunch today with his grandmother.

The limited discussions we'd had about our supposed meeting down south might have sounded plausible last night with a couple of glasses of wine on board, but this morning in the cold, harsh light of day, I was beginning to have my doubts.

I learned a long time ago that if I wanted to spin a lie to anyone, then the best course of action was staying as close to the truth as possible.

Unfortunately, there was little truth we could hang the entire charade of our engagement upon.

Maybe I'd just stick to talking about my family and his grandmother would be happy.

Wrapped in a towel, I knew that I wanted to think about the upcoming lunch, because then I didn't have to think about the way I felt waking up in Robert's bed this morning.

I didn't want to get emotionally attached to this man.

We had a business arrangement.

Surrendering to him last night may well rank up there as one of the most stupid things I'd ever done in my life. Second only to letting myself be talked into this ridiculous fake marriage arrangement in the first place.

Why did sex have to change everything?

Why couldn't I have an encounter with a man, chalk it up as an excellent experience and then keep on moving?

The thought of Robert naked. The wonderful way he touched me last night. It still sent a warm, lazy coil of heat to my insides.

I'd never tried to have a no strings, non-emotional arrangement with a man before. I didn't know what made me think that I could pull it off now.

Being in Auckland had made me bold.

The price that I'd pay for that boldness—aside from a large sum of money in my bank account—might be an inability to extricate myself from the arrangement without getting my heart smashed.

I didn't want to think about that now. I had far too many other pressing and terrifying things to think about.

Not the least was Robert's grandmother, Mary.

At least I could try to make myself look respectable.

I'd give Robert his dues. Between him, his home and the state of my new wardrobe, I found myself surrounded by beauty.

I busied myself pulling outrageous price tags off the new corporate wardrobe that Stacy had chosen for me.

Was she one of the many women in Robert's past?

Why did that thought pop into my head? Was I determined to drive myself into a tailspin of jealousy?

I needed to get a grip.

I couldn't remember seeing Stacy's photograph with him on any of the gossip sites that I'd started trawling since I'd entered into this ridiculous arrangement.

Why was I thinking like this? Robert's past had nothing to

do with me. *The same way that his future had nothing to do with me either,* a tiny voice in my head whispered.

I told it to shut up!

I pulled on an a-line dress in a beautiful shade of green that I thought would be suitable not only for the office, but also to meet Grandmother Mary. There was a lack of dark clothing in the assortment that Stacy had chosen for me. Colour seemed to be her trademark style. I didn't recall seeing a huge number of brightly dressed women in Robert's office.

Resigning myself to standing out from the crowd, I picked out a pair of simple black court shoes that didn't have too high a heel on them. They complimented the bright green dress. I located a simple black jacket in the wardrobe in an attempt to make me look less like a lime green Christmas tree. The bonus, it also made the entire outfit pop.

I took one last look at the room I was living in. The pale pink orchid that Robert had insisted on purchasing had dropped one of its flowers overnight. I picked up the perfect bloom, cradling it in my hand. It didn't look like a living thing—its pink petals could have been made of plastic. I couldn't bear to throw such an exotic flower in the rubbish bin, so I sat it on one of the large green leaves at the base of the towering spike of blooms.

Something else caught my eye on the floor. Another bloom, perhaps? When I investigated, I found a small plastic ball, with a silver bell inside. It was the same kind of toy that the old farm cat batted around the kitchen at home.

Did Robert have another cat? I hadn't seen any sign of a cat anywhere. I popped the small ball beside the potted orchid and made a note to discuss it with Robert later.

My room still resembled the suite of a large expensive hotel. That didn't ease the feelings of displacement that bubbled inside of me as I prepared myself to meet again with Robert.

The intimacy of last night pulled us closer together, but the arrangement that we had in place continued to keep us apart.

No matter how normal our interactions appeared to the outside world—I had the knowledge that everything we presented was an untruth. How I was going to cope with this and my growing attraction to Robert, I couldn't fathom. A growing attraction that was now cemented deep inside of me. I closed my eyes and took a deep breath trying to calm my increasing anxiety.

All I could see in my mind's eye was Robert, naked and wanting me.

How the hell was I going to continue with this charade?

CHAPTER 20

*R*obert

I'd been at my desk for more than three hours struggling with the figures from the dairy factory.

By the time the thought of Hannah had entered my mind for the fourth time, I knew I was in serious trouble.

The sight of her lying in my bed this morning continued to replay in my head, feeding my growing desire. I didn't want to admit, even to myself, that when I got back from my run, I'd been disappointed to find her gone from my room.

When she walked out ready to head to work, looking at her was like taking a sucker punch to the stomach.

I'm certain she had no idea of how attractive she looked. I had to remember to thank Stacy for the colourful array of clothing that she'd arranged for Hannah.

I always made sure that I thanked the people around me who did a good job. It was the best way to keep people motivated.

That's what brought my mind back from Hannah to the baffling figures in front of me. The forecasts and outcomes didn't make sense.

I couldn't imagine how a supposed profitable dairy factory, in the current market, wasn't turning the kind of profit that I'd expect.

My gut feeling on first glance, was to cut this millstone of a factory from the rest of the profitable portfolio and sell it off—or even close it down.

I'd looked at a similar factory not too far from this one and caught under the same commercial umbrella.

Maybe a trip down to Hannah's home town might be in order after all.

Pity we couldn't make it before she had lunch with grandmother—so our story wouldn't be too far from the truth.

I looked up and caught Hannah looking back towards me through the glass partition that separated our working spaces.

I couldn't help myself—I smiled and was immediately rewarded with a beaming grin from Hannah.

I cocked my finger and summoned her into my office.

She stood up and I caught a glance of her gorgeous, shapely arse—one sumptuous arse that refused to be hidden under the dress she wore. I had a sudden flash of memory of her naked body. I closed my eyes, took a deep breath and remonstrated myself. I wasn't going to be able to continue to work with her if I didn't get my head under control.

I'd never been affected by a woman like this before.

I had sex and then moved on.

I didn't seem to be able to shut down my head—or my body for that matter—around Hannah.

Something would have to change, or I was never going to be able to get any work done.

I'd lose everything that I'd worked so hard to build and I wasn't going to let that happen. No matter what.

"Yes?" Hannah asked, having closed the door behind her and clearly pleased to be in my office, alone with me.

"Have you got the balance of those accounts for the dairy factory scanned yet?" I knew she had, they were sitting in my inbox. I had no reason whatsoever to call her in here.

She took on a stricken look. "Has that girl not finished them yet? I swear, I'll swing for her. She's had all morning."

I turned my attention to my laptop, feigning surprise.

"Oh no, don't worry. They're here."

A look of relief flooded Hannah's face. "I was beginning to wonder what she did down there all day."

"Sit down, Hannah."

She complied with my direction and crossed her shapely legs. Another flash of the milky white of her flesh filled my mind. While she was here, I may as well try to find out what, if anything, she knew about the local dairy industry.

"What do you know about the dairy factories down in your home town?"

Hannah shrugged.

"Not a lot. They're where everyone ends up working. I didn't want to go there, so I got out." She explained further, "Came up here, to Auckland."

"You mean the entire town relies on them?" I didn't like the sound of that. It was one thing to hock off a factory, but quite another to take away the commercial lifeblood of a community. Especially the community where Hannah's relations and friends resided.

She nodded. "Yeah, pretty much. Unless you're share milking like my brother. If we didn't have the milk factories we wouldn't have a town."

Things were pretty much how I knew they would be. I didn't need Hannah confirming economics 101. Any rural town in the country that built itself around the dairy industry would be dependant on how well the factories were managed and run. Looking at the figures for these particular properties and taking into account the downturn in the local economy—from a commercial point of view, there was only one sensible thing to do. To close one of the factories.

But what to do when I found myself engaged to a woman with ties to the local area? If I was seen to be responsible for shutting down one of the unprofitable dairy factories while engaged to a local—all hell would break loose.

Our spin-doctors could have easily dealt with my engagement to Hannah. But after last night I very much wanted to remain on the positive side of Hannah's ledger. If I single handedly took away the livelihood of half of the town and probably half of her family into the bargain, then I didn't think I had much chance of remaining on the right side of anything at all.

Business remained cut and dried for me. It was what I'd been doing for the whole of my adult life. Relationships, however, they were another story.

I thought I'd been smart. Making my relationship with Hannah a business decision. What I hadn't counted on was finding myself becoming emotionally involved with this woman.

Lunchtime was upon us. I turned my mind to more pressing matters. "Have you heard from my grandmother?"

At the mention of Grandmother Mary, I watched the colour drain from Hannah's face.

"Yes," Hannah looked up at the line of clocks that I had above my desk—each one set for a different time zone in the world. "She wants to meet for afternoon tea. Something about she'd double booked lunch. I'm due to meet her at the hotel down the road at 3 o'clock." It wasn't like Mary to double book anything. What was going on? Hannah looked up at me with what could have been described as hope in her eyes. "You sure you wouldn't like to come with me?"

"And crash my Grandmother's party?" I shook my head, "No way. You'll be fine, just stick to the story that we discussed last night." Besides, I didn't want to spend too much time around Mary until I was certain that my plan was firmly in place. The way my head was behaving today, I could scarcely be certain that I could remember what time they were both going to meet.

The thought ran through my mind that if the meeting took place in another two weeks or so, the story Hannah and I had conceived last night wouldn't be too far from the truth.

I wondered if Mary would disclose to Hannah the reason for our sudden engagement. Maybe I needed to circumvent that kind of discussion.

"On second thoughts," I said as I checked my electronic diary, "I'm clear after 2pm. I'll make sure that I'm available to come down with you."

It was worth changing my plans to see the look of relief on Hannah's face.

*H*annah

Robert and I walked in companionable silence through the crowded and hot streets to the foyer of the grandest hotel in Auckland.

"You've obviously made an impression with Mary," Robert said as we were shown to our seats in the foyer of the hotel.

"Why's that?" I was genuinely perplexed as to how he could make that kind of assumption.

"She's summoned you here for high tea. It isn't like my grandmother to double book herself, she's decided that you're worth treating." Robert seated himself next to me in a plush armchair, while the black-clad staff arranged a third on the other side of the small, circular table.

I watched as Robert pulled his phone from the inside of his jacket to check the time and silence the device. He was so at ease in the plush surroundings.

I on the other hand, still felt as if I was way out of my comfort zone. On the plus side with the revamp of my wardrobe, at least I no longer looked like a country bumpkin who had come to town.

Sitting here with Robert in his beautiful Italian suit and me in my newly acquired designer clothes, I was aware that for anyone on the outside looking in, we fit.

I thought about my father's words, 'How things look on the outside doesn't always mean that's how they are on the inside.' I was a sitting cliche and I wasn't sure that I liked that prospect.

My heart thumped in my chest as I took another look at my surroundings. My gaze crossed from the tall palms that adorned the edges of the eating area, to the vaulted height of the floors of the hotel balconies that towered above us. The glass atrium that formed the roof of the hotel encased us in a glass bubble of luxury.

Miniature chandeliers hung from large beams and discreet staff in regulation black and gold padded softly across the marble floor.

Colourful flowers bloomed from pristine pots and the entire area had the feel of sitting inside some kind of sumptuous, tropical greenhouse.

Like everything I'd been exposed to since I met Robert I couldn't begin to put a value on the extreme opulence.

The other people who were here enjoying high tea, picked tiny morsels of food from floral china towers and drank tea from fragile cups and saucers.

I saw Robert's grandmother from across the room even before she was brought to our table.

"Robert, I wasn't expecting you to be joining us." Mary

said as Robert stood up to assist his grandmother to take her place at our table. "Couldn't stand to be away from your bride-to-be for more than a moment?"

Robert pulled at the tie around his throat. "I didn't think it was fair to expose Hannah to your scrutiny until she'd been to a few more family functions," Robert replied, throwing me a genuine smile. It went some way to ease the nervous fluttering that had started up inside of me from the moment that I'd spotted Mary.

Mary and Robert's interactions appeared to be a strange mixture of formality and genuine affection. I watched with keen interest as Robert kissed his grandmother on the cheek. As she settled herself down into the chair opposite me, the scent of flower blossom washed across the perfectly set table.

Once Mary had done with greeting her grandson, she turned her attention to me. "You really didn't need to bring a bodyguard, dear." An authentic smile lit up her warm features.

"He needed some time out from behind his desk," I said, "and I think the walk uptown has been good for him."

To my horror, Robert reached for my hand and squeezed it, "Always looking out for me, that's why I love this girl."

He'd used the L word. What the hell?

I tried not to react too slowly, but I thought I might have been a few too many seconds behind when I replied, "Always keeping an eye out for my man."

I gazed into Robert's eyes as I said the words and it felt as if the entire universe had dropped away from around the two of us. Despite the milling staff and Grandmother Mary, we were the only two people in the room. An intense desire curled in my stomach, whispering to me again of the time that Robert and I had spent together.

Naked.

I could feel the heat of my desire pooling inside me, it began to uncurl and travel through my body.

Robert's pupils dilated almost erasing the hazel of his eyes as his own body responded to the sexual call of mine.

Time stood still.

Nothing in the room meant anything except this moment of connection with Robert.

All I wanted to do was to escape with him, back to the expanse of his luxurious bedroom and feel the heat of his body caressing mine.

Grandmother Mary coughed. "I hate to interrupt what is clearly a moment for the two of you," she said, her blue eyes bright and another sincere smile on her pastel features.

Robert removed his hand from mine and I felt as if I'd been unplugged from the national grid. The electricity that flowed between the two of us when we touched was unlike anything I'd ever experienced.

I tried to compose myself by turning my attention to the small bound leather menu that sat on the table in front of me.

"We should order something," Robert said the deep tone of his voice reverberating through my body and having the same effect as if his hands had been stroking my skin.

I closed my eyes and took a deep breath.

What was happening to me? Why was this man having such an unexplainable effect on me?

The sensation was equal parts terrifying and enthralling.

High tea passed in a blur of Earl Grey tea and tiny cucumber and cheese squares. I listened with rapt attention as Robert retold Mary the story we'd concocted the night before. It still sounded ridiculous to me, but listening to Robert spin the tale, I began to understand why he was so good at what he did.

How he convinced people to part with their life's work and never look back.

He even had me believing our own bullshit by the end of the hour or so that we chatted with Grandmother Mary. I couldn't resist the tiny chocolate dessert morsels, with their candied pieces of orange and lemon peel, served with sweet cream. I closed my eyes, letting out a small moan of delight as the velvet treat melted on my tongue.

Grandmother Mary nodded her approval, "It's so lovely to spend time with a woman who enjoys good food."

"It's a shame that she can't cook," Robert teased.

The comforting feeling of having eaten and the facade that we'd convincingly woven for Mary made me bold, I reached out and traced a tiny circle on the top of Robert's hand. "But there's no need for me to cook. Between your culinary skills and the hours we spend in the office."

Robert looked at the pattern my finger traced and then turned his hand over and held mine as if it were the most natural thing in the world for him to be doing.

With a softness to his tone he turned to me and said, "We'll be ordering in food bags. You'll learn to cook in no time and then you can do your fair share."

"I don't know," Mary piped in, "why you simply don't hire a live-in housekeeper. You'll need one when the children come along."

I'd just put another sweet treat in my mouth and I nearly choked.

Robert let go of my hand and simultaneously slapped me on the back and handed me one of the thick linen napkins from the table.

I smothered my coughing and when I'd recovered my composure took a drink from the tall glass of sparkling water that sat beside my empty cup and saucer.

"I think I speak for us both," Robert said, "when I say that we're not planning on having children right off the bat. We prefer to have some time together before we look at starting a family."

"You can't leave it too late," Mary said, as she concentrated on folding up her napkin and collecting the large blue, square handbag from beside her chair. I wondered if she found it difficult to locate accessories in the exact same shade as her dress and jacket. "You know how long it took for your brother's wife to get pregnant. Women are just leaving it too long these days," Mary said wagging a finger in Robert's stunning looking face.

"Quite." Robert said in a tone that left no-one in any doubt that this conversation had come to an end.

He almost clicked his fingers in the air and a staff member appeared at his side. "Our account."

"I've got this," Mary said, "it's my treat."

I expected Robert to object, but he acquiesced, then stood up and buttoned his jacket. I guess this was my cue to follow. I went to stand up and Mary reached across the table and held my arm. I hesitated and remained in a half standing half sitting position.

She looked into my eyes, hers sincere and as blue as the dress she wore. "He needs a strong woman in his life. You make sure that you stand up to him and don't let him win all the arguments. His mother took that stance with his father and theirs was a marriage built on a strong foundation."

I looked across at Robert, expecting fury to be pouring out of his entire body, but instead his eyes were on his Grandmother and the look on his face spoke of nothing but love and adoration.

"I'm sorry mum couldn't get to meet you," he said as he reached his hand out with the expectation that I'd take it.

I did.

Robert pulled me to his side and slipped his arm around me as if we'd stood together like this forever.

"She'd have liked you," he said and he held my gaze.

"Yes she would," Mary said. What could I hear in his grandmother's voice? Regret, despair, longing? I couldn't be sure. But I deduced from the tone of voice that Robert's mother must have been some kind of special woman.

Mary stood up, and hooked her handbag on her arm, as if the movement snapped her back into the present moment. "Now, I've arranged for a photographer to meet us at your apartment tomorrow evening for the formal engagement photographs."

"Will Edward and Nicki be coming as well?" Robert asked.

"Yes," Mary said and then turned her attention to me again. "I thought it would be nice for you to meet formally with Edward and Nicki."

"Of course," I said wondering how many more difficult family meetings I'd have to deal with this week. If I was finding it tough now. How was I going to cope with everything the closer we came to the wedding date?

CHAPTER 21

*R*obert

I'd ushered Hannah back to her desk for the remainder of the afternoon.

Things had gone well with grandmother and I had to be grateful for that. Aside from her coy suggestion at the end of the meal that Hannah should stand up to me.

If I could pull this ridiculous marriage idea off with Mary, then I knew that it would be an easy call with the rest of the family. Besides, Mary wanted me married.

I knew she didn't want to admit it, but we all knew that Edward wasn't capable of running the company, no matter how much Mary threatened to cut me from the position.

I'd had my lawyer go over the constitution of the company.

There was nothing in there that said I had to remain married—or for that matter provide an heir. The only ridiculous stipulation was that I had to get married.

The first thing I'd do as soon as humanly possible would be to have that part of the company's constitution changed.

An antiquated requirement that no longer fit with the philosophy of business today.

Although, even I had to admit that if I hadn't been pushed, I would never have been looking for someone to marry and I certainly wouldn't have found Hannah.

Turning my mind back to the figures in front of me for the two dairy factories down south, it became even more apparent that one of them would have to go.

Whether I sold it off for what little I'd be able to get for it, or simply closed it down, I wasn't sure yet which way to go. Ordinarily, a simple cut and run decision that I'd made hundreds of times in the past, became clouded with a feeling of obligation around Hannah's home town.

One thing was certain, though, I wouldn't be keeping it as part of the portfolio of companies that would sit within the umbrella of the organisation we were going to acquire.

"Hannah," I'd gotten into the habit of yelling for Hannah. Truth be told, I liked the sound of her name when it came out of my mouth.

There were so many things about Hannah that I liked. I particularly enjoyed watching her squirm with my grand-mother this afternoon. I might have crashed their party, but I think it was a good job I'd been on hand. I could tell by the way my grandmother interacted with Hannah that she enjoyed the company of my fiancée. Mary was many things, but she wasn't disingenuous with her praise.

Mary approved of Hannah and that was half the battle as far as I was concerned.

"You can message me, you know," Hannah said as she walked into my room.

"What do you think about a trip home?" I watched with horror as the colour left her face.

"You mean down south, home, not apartment home?"

I nodded, "Yes."

"Why would we go there?"

"You don't want to take me home to meet your parents? You're ashamed of me."

"No," she stammered, colour filling her cheeks, "not at all."

"What then?" I thought she'd jump at the chance to go back to see her family.

"I've only just left there. Why would I go back?"

"It's a good job one of us has thought this through," I said. "Because you only left to be here with me. Like we told Mary today. We met and you came here to be with me and we can't wait to get married."

Hannah gave up pretending that she was just my EA. She dropped herself down on the chair opposite my desk. For the first time I saw that she was tired. A lot had happened in the last few days and maybe she wasn't able to deal with the pace of life that I'd been living for as long as I could remember.

"You're tired."

I looked at the clock. "Shit. When did it get to be past 7pm?"

She shrugged. "I don't know. Don't you notice when everyone else has left the office?"

"No." I didn't. "You're exhausted. You should have gone home. Got yourself something to eat."

"It's not my home," Hannah said with all earnestness, "it's your home."

"You've got to stop thinking like that, or you'll wear yourself out. Did you organise a key and code with the manager?"

"Yes." Hannah pulled at the hem of the green dress she wore. I'd spent all day fantasising about peeling it off her body.

"Well, then you can go home at any time you want."

"What about you?" She looked up at me with huge eyes

almost the same colour as the dress that she wore. "And what about dinner? You know I don't cook."

I tipped my head to the side, "So. You want me to come home and cook you dinner?"

"Maybe."

I knew exactly what happened when we tried to cook dinner the last time and so did Hannah. The spacious room filled with an intensity that suddenly made it feel cramped and small.

I loosened the tie at my neck. The thought of going home with Hannah again eclipsed the complicated puzzle of the dairy factories that stared back at me from my computer screen.

The figures could wait.

"Get your things," I said, "I can always do some more work at home." Not that I thought it likely tonight.

*H*annah

Robert didn't even make a pretence of trying to cook a meal tonight.

We were scarcely inside the door of his apartment before we were in each other's arms. As soon as he touched me, I wondered how I'd managed to keep such a cool and calm exterior for the entire day.

I pulled his jacket off him.

His hands were in my hair, freeing it from the tight little band of elastic that had held it in an appropriate corporate bun.

Robert buried his face in my hair. "I've wanted to do that all day," he moaned, "you smell divine."

He leaned away from me enough for me to get a hold of the end of his tie and tear it from his throat, the soft silk slipping easily from around his neck. It made me wonder what it would feel like to have my hands tied by the smooth material.

Then I decided I'd rather have my hands free so that I could explore Robert's strong body.

"We should take this to the bedroom," Robert moaned as he relieved me of my green dress and I stood in front of him in nothing more than matching underwear and a pair of high heels. "But on second thoughts," he growled as he picked me up and carried me across the room to the leather sofa near the large picture windows, "I think I'd quite like to take you here, again."

He put me down on the sofa and I gasped as the cool leather hit my body.

Robert ran his thumbs along the top of my breasts. "I love it when you take a deep breath like that…" The balance of his words were lost to me as he buried his face between my breasts.

I lay back on the soft leather and allowed Robert to explore my body.

As he butterfly kissed his way down my stomach and across the fine lace of my underwear, I could feel the heat of desire that had been buried inside of me all day coming to the fore.

By the time Robert had carefully removed my shoes and I lay in front of him in nothing more than my bra and soaking wet panties, I was ready to beg him to take me.

He began to unbutton his business shirt. A look of complete determination painted on his face. If I wanted him to stop—which I didn't—I was certain that it would take a mammoth amount of negotiating to deter this man from anything he'd set his mind on.

Right this minute, his mind was set on me and that made me the happiest woman in Auckland.

I wasn't going to think about the consequences of having

sex with Robert again. I was determined that I would remain in the moment and enjoy this experience as much as possible before it all came to an end.

Robert dropped his shirt on the floor beside the sofa and shucked off his shoes and socks before dropping his expensive suit trousers on top of the heap.

In nothing more than his boxers, he slipped between my legs and lowered the weight of his body down on top of mine.

At the touch of his heated flesh an involuntary moan escaped my lips.

I could feel his thick erection pressing down onto my pubic bone. Every inch of my body screamed for him to be inside of me as he slid that hard cock up and down. Teasing and taunting me with the promise of pleasure to come.

Robert slipped the lace cup of my bra from my breast and suckled my impossibly hard nipple. A rush of pleasure shot through me.

"I want you inside of me," I moaned.

"Soon," Robert purred as he looked down into my eyes.

"I can't just lie here," I whined, "I at least need to touch you."

Robert sat back on the couch, "I'm all yours," he said with a confidence that I might have found distasteful if it were anyone other than Robert saying the words.

I hadn't had a chance to explore Robert's body last time so this time I was going to make sure that I explored every delicious inch of him.

I slipped between his knees and onto the floor in front of him. I'd never been this bold with a man before. There was something about the way that Robert's eyes roamed over my body—as if he were devouring me—that gave me the courage to proceed.

I slipped my hands up the side of his face and felt the

rough scrub of his dark stubble on my palms. My body shivered.

"Cold?" Robert asked.

I shook my head, "No."

He tipped his head to the side and raised an eyebrow, "Must be excitement then."

I looked down at his boxers and took a long and drawn out moment to survey the state of his erect cock. "You're pretty full of yourself for a man sat there with a raging hard on."

"It's all your doing," Robert said with complete sincerity.

Then he sucked in a breath as my hands began to travel down the firm muscle of his pecs. I could feel the tension in his body as my hands moved lower, over the hard muscles of his belly and to the elastic waist of his boxers.

I hooked a thumb on each side of his hips and pulled down. Robert's body reacted as if it were on automatic pilot. He lifted himself enough to allow the thin cotton to slide down the muscle of his long, toned legs.

"What now?" Robert asked, with a growl in his voice that called to the sex siren who had lain idle inside of me for far too long.

I licked my lips and watched in awe as Robert's entire body quivered in response. It dawned on me that I didn't even have to touch him—but where would the fun be in that?

"Now I get to taste you," I purred as I took my time positioning myself comfortably between Robert's outstretched legs.

I thought about the first time he made me come, right here on this leather sofa and my desire for this man soared.

I began to lick the velvet head of Robert's cock and was rewarded by the sound of soft moaning from above me. As I settled myself to my task, I took Robert's cock into my mouth and closed my eyes. The sweet scent of his body, its undertones of musk and pine, filled my senses as his cock filled my mouth.

As I slid my hands and my mouth up and down Robert's cock in a steady rhythm, the scorching heat of my own desire began to build.

Robert wrapped my hair in his hands and cradled my head as I continued to bob on his cock.

"I can't stand too much of this," Robert moaned as he held my head still. "If you keep this up, I'll come in that pretty mouth of yours."

He pulled me up on top of his hot, hard body and plundered my mouth with his tongue.

"Wait here," Robert barked as he flipped me back onto the leather sofa and then stood up and walked out of the room.

A sense of abandonment flooded through me. What the hell had I done wrong now?

CHAPTER 22

*R*obert
Damn that woman and damn my cock that stood in front of me like a piece of steel. I scrubbed my hand through my hair as I walked naked through my apartment to my bedroom in search of a fucking condom.

I wasn't the kind of guy who carried condoms on him when he set out for a day at work. I should have just carried Hannah back to my bedroom, but there was something about taking her on the couch in the middle of the apartment that appealed to me in a way that I didn't understand.

If I'd let her suck my cock any longer, I'd have bent her over the couch and rammed myself inside of her and I wasn't that kind of guy.

Scrambling through the drawer at the side of my bed I found a condom and then marched back to the living room.

"What's the matter?" Hannah leaned up on one elbow, eyeing me with suspicion from across the room. The angle of her body, the sweet way the curve of her breast moved when she lifted herself up to look at me made my cock stand right back at attention.

I waved the square foil packet in the air and she laughed, the sound filling the room.

"I guess I should be pleased that you're not taking condoms to the office."

As I slipped my body back across her again I said, "Damn grateful. And now I'm going to show you how grateful I am that you stayed right here like a good girl."

"Mmm… That sounds nice…" The balance of her words were lost as I covered her mouth with mine. I had a sense of coming home whenever I kissed Hannah. It was a feeling that I hadn't even realised I'd been looking for until this minute.

"I'm going to fuck you now until you can't move a muscle," I said as I unclipped Hannah's bra and dropped it on the floor. The sight of her full, milky white breasts with their pale pink nipples reminded me why my cock was so hard.

I nipped at one of the hard pebbles of flesh with my teeth and pinched the other.

Hannah arched and moaned and I felt her fingernails dig into the tight muscle of my back.

Unable to wait any longer to be inside of her, I slipped off the tiny scrap of lace that covered her pussy and licked the inside of her thigh.

My fingers found my way into her sopping wet heat and Hannah arched against my hand.

"What do you say?" I asked as my fingers began to tease her swollen folds.

"Please," Hannah sighed the word uttered on a heavy breath out. My fingers continued to tease and she began to pant.

"Please what?" I insisted as I ripped the condom from the packet and rolled it down the length of my iron hard cock.

"Please fuck me, Robert. I want you in me now. I've waited all day. Don't make me wait any longer."

The sound of her plea and the sight of her open and waiting for me was more than I could stand. I plunged my cock into Hannah. An overwhelming feeling of coming home took a hold of me.

I closed my eyes so I could concentrate on the sensation of having Hannah's body surrendering to my own.

If I wasn't careful, I'd come in an instant and that wasn't what I had planned. But then nothing had gone to plan where Hannah was concerned.

"This is too good," I muttered as I flipped Hannah's languid body up on top of my own. At least with her on top I might have some modicum of control.

"You're so deep, this is too good," Hannah echoed my words as the beginnings of an orgasm began to roll through her body.

She raked her teeth across the side of my neck and moaned in an incoherent fashion as she shuddered to a climax.

This was too damn good. I slipped my cock out of Hannah to give myself a chance to catch my breath. While she recovered from her orgasm, I lay her across the sofa, the cheeks of her arse begging me to take her again.

I twisted her hair in my hand and pulled her back up towards me. "You ready for some more, my good girl?" I growled as I sank my teeth into her shoulder.

"Yes," she moaned as I plunged my cock back into her.

Hannah pushed herself back onto me. She met me stroke for stroke and didn't let up for a moment. The plane of her back and her lush curves were all too much for me.

Faster and faster I slammed into her, our bodies slick with heat and sweat. Hannah's moans escalated in volume as I found myself in that in between place, teetering in the brink of orgasm.

"I'm going to come," she eventually screamed, "come with me, Robert."

At the sound of my name on her lips it was all over for me.

I came in a shuddering orgasm that sucked the air from my lungs and made the surrounding room disappear in a flash of blazing lights.

When I could think again, I pulled Hannah into my arms and crushed her body to mine. I would never let this woman go—no matter what the future had in store for us both—she was mine and I was going to make sure that once we were married, she never left my side.

*H*aving satisfied my appetite for Hannah and having satisfied our appetite for food, I thought it was time to bring up the plan for the day tomorrow.

"You know we've got the official engagement shoot tomorrow with Grandmother."

Hannah stood by the kitchen sink rinsing off the dishes and loading the dishwasher. Despite my protestation that she should leave these things for the housekeeper, she seemed to want to look after the small domestic chores. Somehow, her presence in the apartment made it all seem like a strangely perfect domestic scene. It felt as if I'd walked into someone else's life somehow. I didn't wish to admit it to myself, but I was enjoying the change in pace and more than anything, I was enjoying watching Hannah's curvaceous body move with impeccable grace in the confines of my apartment.

"Can't be any worse than lunch today," Hannah said, throwing me one of her smiles. There was something about the way her face lit up when she smiled. Something deep inside of me wanted that smile to be reserved only for me from now on.

I pulled a small box out of my pocket that I'd been carrying around with me for most of the day. In fact, I'd pulled the tiny package from my pocket on a number of occasions simply to gaze at the piece that sat snug inside.

"Hannah, come sit with me." I patted the leather cushion beside me. "I have something for you."

I watched as she wiped her hands on the towel and then hung it with care inside the kitchen cupboard. Everything that Hannah did she did with care. It was something that I was coming to love about her. The care and attention to detail.

"What is it?"

I reached for Hannah's hand. It was warm and soft and I could smell the scent of the lemon detergent that she'd been spraying with vigour around the kitchen surfaces.

"We can't have an engagement shoot without a ring," I said as I passed her the box. "This belonged to my mother and now I want you to have it."

The three carat diamond solitaire ring sparkled when Hannah opened the box. The ring had been sitting in my safe since it had been recovered from my mother's body.

She gasped, "It's too much, I can't possibly accept this."

"I want you to have it," I insisted as I slipped the ring over Hannah's now shaking hand. "It's been sitting in the safe since my mother passed and," I paused for a moment, a large lump making it difficult to speak. I loved my mother and I never thought I'd feel the same way about another person. Hannah with her uncomplicated nature and down-to-earth attitude had found a way through the hard, impermeable shell that I'd constructed around myself. For the first time in my life, I found myself unable to speak.

Hannah clasped her hands over mine, the large diamond caught the light again and sparkled, the same way it used to do when my mother moved her hand. An overwhelming feeling of connection and love surged through me.

Terrifying me.

"You don't have to explain," Hannah said, her own voice sounding as if it had an unnatural quiver.

I coughed, clearing my throat. "I feel that I do."

She looked up at me, large green eyes hooded with long auburn lashes. I felt sure Hannah had no idea of her own beauty.

"Thank you," Hannah whispered as she leaned forward and touched her lips to mine in a gentle kiss.

An overpowering feeling of ownership and possessiveness coursed through me. I slipped my arms around Hannah and crushed her body to mine.

My hands found their way into her hair and I crashed my lips against hers. My tongue plundered her mouth and Hannah's body arched into mine as she allowed me to take control.

"I can't get enough of you," I moaned against the soft nape of her neck.

"The feeling's mutual," Hannah moaned as my hand found the peak of her nipple and gave it a squeeze.

"We should take this somewhere more comfortable," I said as I slipped Hannah's clothing away and sucked her nipple into my mouth.

"Yes, please," she sighed.

I didn't need any more encouragement. I picked Hannah up and carried her to our bedroom.

*H*annah
"I don't know why I let you talk me into this," I said as I tottered on a set of heels between the long roots of an aged fig tree.

"This wasn't my idea," Robert grumbled, "Grandmother arranges for a number of family occasions to be marked by photo shoots."

"Smile you two love birds." The photographer who had been commissioned by Grandmother Mary to take the photographs didn't seem to mind my discomfort, or my fear that I'd twist an ankle as I tried to make my way to the third and final spot for the photographs.

"What's with photographs under this tree, anyway?" Why we couldn't have simply arranged for all the shots to have been taken in the comfortable confines of Robert's apartment I didn't know. We'd all ready spent the late afternoon perched on precarious volcanic boulders at an ancient lava forest at the waterfront. Granted, the photographs would be spectacular and I'd had an unexpected and informative tour of the seafront, but now I was tired and I'd had enough. I was also on my third change of outfit. I guess the dress designers who had made their wares available to me would be pleased in any event.

"It's one of the oldest trees in the city," Robert replied, "the magazine's going for the angle of the family's history in Auckland."

That explained the long drive over the Auckland harbour bridge to the petrified lava forest in what was quickly becoming rush hour traffic.

"Hannah, dear you're screwing your eyes up again," the photographer continued to give me directions from behind the large lens. My thoughts were that this particular lens had followed my every move for far too long now. Exhausted didn't even begin to cover my feelings.

"Sorry," I'd spent most of the photographic shoot apologising, "the sun's in my eyes."

"Maybe if you turn more towards each other and, Robert you could help Hannah over that large root."

"This is ridiculous," I whined, I'd had enough. "I can't walk across here in these shoes." I'd nearly broken an ankle more than once while we were navigating our way across the dark lava boulders on the North Shore. I stopped and bent down and removed the strappy sandals with the tall heel and stood on top of the fig tree's root in bare feet.

"Actually," the photographer called, "that's a perfect shot. Robert, take Hannah's hand and lead her to the spot we chose and then stop there." At least we were doing something right. "I want one more of the two of you," she said the sound of the shutter going off at staccato speed. "Hannah," she barked more orders, "put your arms up around Robert's neck."

"How much longer?" I muttered to Robert as we took up the required pose. My stomach grumbled reminding me how long it had been since I'd eaten last. I wasn't good when I was hungry and I'd forgotten to bring anything to snack on. I had no idea we'd be this long with a silly little photo shoot.

"We'll be here until dawn if you don't remember to smile and look like you're in love," Robert said with infinite patience. Something about the tone of his voice made me smile in any event. It seemed all Robert had to do these days was open his mouth and say something and I had a sense of being wrapped in a soft, warm blanket.

"I don't know how models do it." I said gazing up at Robert as the hair and makeup lady rearranged my hair for the hundredth time this afternoon.

"That's it," the photographer called. "Hannah, darling. Can you move your left hand to Robert's shoulder? We want to be able to see that beautiful engagement ring."

I still hadn't become accustomed to wearing the large stone on my left hand. Aside from the fact that I felt as if I should be followed around by an armoured guard every time

I went out the door, Robert's assurances that it was insured and I should relax didn't make me feel any better.

He'd given me something that belonged to his mother and to which he clearly had a huge emotional attachment. I hadn't overlooked the way his emotions had gotten the better of him last night.

Our lovemaking had been soft and gentle.

He'd caressed my body with a reverence that had touched me so deeply. Far more deeply than the fact that I wore hundreds of thousands of dollars worth of jewellery on my hand right now.

I knew I was in trouble. Robert and I had a professional arrangement and somehow, both of us were breaching the contractual arrangements we had with each other.

As I looked up into the deep brown of his eyes, under this century old fig tree I knew I had become invested in this relationship far more than I'd ever intended when I said "yes" to the ridiculous arrangement.

He must have been reading my mind, for that moment Robert leaned down and kissed me. A kiss full of sweet promise and tenderness.

"Perfect," the camerawoman yelled from across the way. I'd almost forgotten that she was there I'd lost myself so much in the moment with Robert. "I have what I want here and just in time, we're about to lose the light. We'll meet you back at your apartment for the formal family shots."

"There's more?" I asked, our foreheads still pressed together after the intimate kiss.

"You know there's more," Robert soothed. "Grandmother will be waiting for us at the apartment with Edward and Nicki."

"I'll need something to eat," I whined. There had been so much going on in the last few days, I'd been struggling to keep Robert's diary straight, let alone keep my newfound family side of our life in order.

I shivered. The sun had gone behind some large clouds and the grounds of Auckland's Domain had taken on an early evening chill.

"Here," Robert took off his jacket and draped it around my shoulders. "I can't have my wife-to-be going down with pneumonia on the engagement shoot. And I sent Sally an email this afternoon and told her to make sure that she caters for everyone this evening. The family will likely stay for a bite to eat since Grandmother's going back to Sydney tomorrow."

Surrounded by the scent of Robert, the cool touch of the silk from the inside of his jacket reminded me of the intense pleasure I'd experienced with him last night.

"Thank you," I said as I wrapped the elegantly tailored jacket around my body. The jacket alone was probably worth more than the photographer was being paid for this entire engagement shoot. "Who's Sally?"

"She's my part-time housekeeper come family events manager."

Robert opened the passenger door of the car and his driver instantly came to attention. I liked Graham and it wasn't just for the fact that he'd been my quasi tour leader for the short time that he'd been driving me around Auckland. It had come to my attention that there was very little about the city on the isthmus that Graham didn't have some sound knowledge.

With Sally on the pay roll I began to wonder how many people it actually took to manage the life of Robert Redfern and how many more I'd yet to hear about. No wonder he didn't like to see me in the kitchen clearing up. He had an army of staff to take care of our every need.

"Where to, Sir?" Graham asked.

"Home thanks," Robert said. "And I'd be grateful if you could stay for the evening. Grandmother will need a lift back to her hotel."

"No problem," Graham said, as he started the motor and began to pull us out into what had become rush hour traffic. It seemed that we weren't the only ones who were enjoying the early evening at the Domain. The park was filling with people who'd finished work for the day. Some were jogging through the winding roads and others were setting up blankets on the large expanse of lawn just below the roots of the huge trees that we'd been standing in.

The imposing columns of the war memorial museum came in to view. Behind the majestic grey of the stately building sat a modern looking flying saucer shaped extension. Looking at the two buildings, they reminded me of the new hitching a ride on the old. A metaphor for my relationship with Robert, perhaps?

"It's a beautiful building," I sighed, "and the grounds here are spectacular."

"If you like it so much," Robert said, "we could get married in the courtyard between the Wintergardens and have our reception in the museum atrium, if you wanted."

Even though we were on our engagement shoot, the thought of actually marrying Robert hadn't entered my mind all afternoon.

The harsh reality of what we were doing suddenly struck home. As much as I knew I was falling in love with Robert, somehow I had cloaked myself in a sash of denial about our impending nuptials.

My appetite vanished.

I was on my way to be formally introduced to his brother and sister-in-law. This meant I was becoming a member of the Redfern family and all of a sudden, the reality of the situation hit home.

The sexual allure of a stunningly handsome billionaire.

The touching gift of his mother's engagement ring.

Being treated like a supermodel on a photo shoot.

These things were part of an elaborate fantasy.

The reality was that I'd taken money and agreed to marry a stranger.

What the hell was I doing?

More terrifying was the fact that I knew that I had fallen in love with Robert. The longer we continued on with this pretence, the harder it was becoming to think about what would happen after we'd said our "I do's".

My plan had always been to leave New Zealand—I hadn't bargained on falling for a billionaire.

CHAPTER 23

*R*obert
Normally I hated these kinds of family occasions, but with Hannah by my side, spending time with grandmother and my brother and sister-in-law was almost bearable. In fact, I'd even describe it as downright pleasant.

I watched Hannah deep in conversation on the other side of the room with Nicki and Ed. Nicki had her hand sat protectively across the swell of her stomach. I knew that another generation of the family grew inside of her and for the first time I wondered what it might be like to have a child of my own.

The baby must have been moving, because Nicki took Hannah's hand and placed it high, on the side of her stomach. I watched with fascination as Hannah's face lit up. The joy of feeling a new life inside of someone else had a profound effect on her.

Ed slipped an arm around his wife and she turned and met his gaze with a beaming smile. The perfect family scene had never affected me in any way before, but tonight, there was something about the way Hannah sat with the two of them. Ed and Nicki were on the cusp of creating a real family.

I had a sudden and overwhelming urge to make that happen for Hannah and me.

"She looks like she'd make a wonderful mother," Grandmother Mary said as she arrived at my side. Grandmother had an all knowing look about her. As if she'd caught me out doing something wrong. It was the same look I remembered as a child when she caught me with my hand in the cake tin. *It's just between you and me and I'll let you get away with it, even though we both know it's wrong,* kind of look.

Grandmother Mary took a sip of champagne and then said, "Considering the speed of the announcement of your engagement, I did wonder for a while whether or not you might be ticking the boxes to ensure that you remained at the head of the company." Her eyes shone with understanding as she took another sip of her champagne. I knew it was the same glass that we'd poured hours ago for the official photographs. Unlike my brother, Ed who was somewhere between the first and second bottle, Grandmother like me, always kept a clear head around family matters.

"You must have something more interesting to do than sit here watching me," I said as I put my glass down. The uncomfortable realisation that Grandmother had her finger on exactly what we were doing unnerved me. I wasn't going to allow anything to come between me and my intended place at the head of the family business.

"We both know where my interests lie, Robert," Grandmother Mary said in a tone that confirmed she knew exactly what was unfolding in front of her. "The company is extremely important to me and I believe that you have that same passion for the business."

No matter where she took the conversation, there was no way I would allow my defences to drop. Until I had a wedding ring on Hannah's hand I knew that my position within the company wasn't safe.

I needed to be careful.

I couldn't allow my newfound feelings around Hannah to jeopardise in any way my ultimate goal of ensuring that I remained at the head of the Redfern group of companies.

"You know I have that same passion for the business," I replied, "and Hannah understands that passion."

Grandmother Mary cocked her head to one side, a glint in her steel blue eyes. I knew that those eyes had seen so much family history pass and that they were trained on the future of the company and the family.

"And of course," Grandmother said as she held my stare, "that's why she's the perfect match for you in the matrimonial stakes. Don't think for a moment that I can't see what's going on here, Robert."

"There's nothing going on, Grandmother." I don't know why I even tried to defend myself.

"You may have anticipated when you came to whatever arrangement you came to with Hannah that nothing would be going on," Grandmother said at the same moment Hannah looked across the room and caught me watching her.

The smile that Hannah shared with me was like a punch in the solar plexus. The woman could take the fight out of me with a single glance.

"The way she looks at you and the way you held yourselves for the photographs this evening," Grandmother continued, "those things can't be faked, Robert." Grandmother Mary searched my eyes for some kind of acknowledgment. I wasn't giving anything away. She tried again. "I know how much your mother's engagement ring means to you."

I couldn't be sure I wanted to hear this.

For what seemed like an age all ready, I'd been trying to tell myself that Hannah and I were enjoying a friendship—some kind of contractual relationship with benefits. The idea that we might be falling in love—that we could have a future together—for some reason that thrilled and terrified me all at the same time.

To have Grandmother Mary pointing out to me what I didn't even want to admit to myself. Well, that sat way up there in a swamp of denial.

"You'll get your family marriage," I said in a calm tone that didn't befit the turmoil that threatened to break free from my composed exterior.

"And a rightful heir?"

"The company constitution said nothing about a rightful heir." I kept my tone calm despite the rising tide of emotion that raged inside of me. I brought over a decade of contractual negotiations and boardroom chess games to the fore. For the first time in my life, I found myself unable, or maybe even unwilling, to share my true emotions with my beloved Grandmother.

My loyalty had passed to Hannah.

Ahead of my Grandmother and, it suddenly dawned on me, ahead of the company.

I couldn't be sure whether that was a good or a bad thing. All I knew was that for the first time in my life I was unsure of my next move.

*H*annah

I stood in the bathroom, so tired I was surprised I was still on my feet. The woman who stared back at me in the mirror resembled an exotic, pampered stranger.

Sally had put on a wonderful banquet meal for the family. In fact, she'd excelled herself. She had the ability to glide around the room, clearing tables and keeping everything running smoothly. No-one seemed to even notice her presence.

I'd marvelled at the way anyone could simply fade into the wallpaper. I'd been practising hiding in the background for a long time and in the last short while, I'd found myself in the limelight, being the centre of attention and I wasn't so sure that I liked it.

I struggled to find the energy to remove the thick make-up that still adorned my face.

If this was what it would be like being Robert's wife, then maybe I would be better off sticking to my plan and escaping the country as soon as possible after we'd been through the farce of a wedding.

Then I thought about the times tonight I found myself looking across the room at him.

He'd catch my eye a certain way. Or I'd watch him dealing with his Grandmother. The gentle way he touched her arm as if he were caressing a fragile flower and the love inside of me that I kept trying to deny would grow a tiny bit stronger.

But then I'd seen Sally, the way she breezed around the room. It seemed as if no-one except me took any notice of her. An air of expectancy seemed to dominate. This family were used to being waited on. They were used to having their every need met in an instant and I wasn't from that kind of home.

I cleaned up after myself and I made sure that the needs of everyone else were met before my own. I still couldn't fathom how I would ever fit into this strange, cloistered world of drivers, maids, makeup artists and women who wanted to decide what I should wear.

"You looked as if you were enjoying yourself tonight." Robert arrived in the bathroom totally naked. Having dealt with the makeup, I was struggling to remove the multiple pins in my hair. Portions of it still felt like the straw that my brother would feed out to the cows in winter.

I took a deep breath and swallowed the lump in my throat. I wasn't used to standing in such an enclosed space with a naked man. Never mind a man as beautiful as Robert.

I tried to concentrate on removing the last of the clips from my hair, but my eyes continued to stray to the expanse of hard muscle and flesh that stood so tantalisingly close behind me.

Robert reached around me and placed a small glass of strong smelling liquor on the marble vanity.

"What's that?"

"I like to keep a clear head while I'm dealing with family matters," he said, "but now that the family have gone, I thought it was about time you were rewarded for being such a good girl today."

All ready I could feel the heat of his body through the thin material of the final dress that I'd worn for our official engagement shots.

He threw back the contents of the glass in his hand and encouraged me to do the same.

"Come on, indulge me," he teased. "It's been a long day and you survived the entire Redfern family. You deserve a drink." His fingers traced down the side of my neck and lingered above the swell of my breast.

My nipples peaked in immediate response to his touch.

I could feel the hard outline of Robert's cock nestled in the small of my back.

Then I watched in the mirror with fascination as Robert's lips followed his fingers. Light butterfly kisses. When he looked up again, the fire that burned in his eyes spoke a promise of desire that sent a surge of lust through my body.

With a shaking hand, I picked up the glass of liquor and threw it down.

All caution left my body as the burn of the liquor and the driving force of my own desire mingled.

Robert slipped my dress from my shoulders and I stood and watched as, with intense concentration, he explored my body with his strong hands, leaving a trail of heat in his wake.

"I want you," Robert said, the deep baritone of his voice reverberating around the marble bathroom, "I want you beside me and I want you to be a part of my life."

As I leaned back against his hard body, I was taken by an overwhelming desire to never leave this spot.

"I want you too," I whispered.

When this man had his hands on my body, everything felt right.

I surrendered to my desire and allowed Robert to pick me up and carry me to our bed.

As he lay me down, for some strange reason I thought of the tiny cat toy I found in my room.

"Do you have another cat besides, Silo?" I asked.

Robert froze. "No. Why do you ask that?"

"I found a little ball with a bell in it on the floor in my room."

He straightened up and I watched a flicker of pain cross his face.

"Tell me about, Silo," I prompted. Trying to get Robert to open up to me.

"I bottle fed Silo from when he was a kitten," he said the flicker of pain easing. "Ed and I found him one day on our way home from school." Robert's face softened at the memory. "I was about fourteen, I think. Mum said we could keep him and we kind of grew up together. He went everywhere with me."

"What happened?" I asked, watching the hard curve of Robert's muscles as he climbed back on the bed beside me.

He pulled me into the curve of his body, his lips touching my hair as he continued on with his story.

"He got old and bit blind and senile. He adapted quite well to living here, but one day he managed to get out. I'm not even sure how." Robert's voice went very quiet. "Little bastard didn't have any kind of road sense. It was inevitable that he'd get bowled on the road."

"I'm sorry," I whispered.

"Don't be," Robert said, "he had a good life."

"You've never gotten another one?"

"It wouldn't be fair," Robert replied, his hands circling my stomach. "I spend too much time at the office, I couldn't leave a little guy alone up here all day."

Robert flipped me over onto my back, a wistful look on his face and said, "I didn't bring you in here to talk about Silo. There's only one kind of pussy I'm interested in at the moment." His fingers found their way inside of me as his lips covered mine.

Over and over again I surrendered to the pleasure bestowed upon me by the intense and complicated man I was engaged to marry.

CHAPTER 24

*H*annah
It didn't take more than a couple of days for the engagement photographs to go viral.

We'd been the toast of the social scene, but thankfully, Robert had been too busy to accept many of the outrageous number of social invitations we'd received.

I couldn't be sure whether I was happy to be avoiding the limelight, or whether I'd become bored with what seemed like a routine that you could call mundane.

In the last two months, Robert's focus remained firmly on the company and the acquisition that appeared to be becoming more problematic by the moment.

More and more I saw the names of the local milk manu-facturing plants coming up in correspondence. They were named in telephone discussions Robert had with his team of advisors. I thought often about what could happen to the livelihoods of the people I knew back home.

Between the photo shoots, requests for interviews from various journalists and invitations to become the patron of numerous charities around the country, I didn't have much time to worry about whether or not I was making the right decisions around my intended nuptials.

Our days started at dawn and I couldn't remember the last time I'd left the office in daylight.

Sally left meals for us at the apartment and quite frankly, there was no time to think about any kind of physical relationship. If Robert wasn't working in the office, he was locked up in the office he had at the apartment.

The relentless daily grind was beginning to take its toll and I struggled to remember what it was that I'd found appealing about Robert or the job.

Most of my time was taken with trying to keep abreast of the charities and women's groups that Grandmother Mary insisted that I become familiar with. She'd somewhat taken me under her wing and seemed dead set on schooling me on the ways of being a Redfern wife.

There's been a Redfern woman at the head of these charities for decades. Grandmother Mary reminded me whenever I tried to object about my latest assignment.

It had almost become necessary for me to have my own assistant. An assistant at least would give me someone to confide in. There were a number of occasions that I'd thought about phoning home. Then I looked at my bank account balance and wondered again how I'd begin to explain the loneliness of being Robert's fiancée. The newspapers, magazines and internet gossip sites were touting the elaborate and exclusive lives of *RoHannah* as we'd been dubbed by the popular press.

Now I had a real understanding of the old adage, *don't believe what you read in the newspapers*. Fact checking didn't seem to be a requirement for anything written about either of us.

"Hannah!" It had been at least the third time in the two hours since we'd arrived at work that Robert had called me into his office. I looked at the raft of unanswered emails in my inbox and sighed.

"What now?" I struggled to keep the irritation out of my voice. With the workload that I'd acquired from Grand-mother Mary since our official engagement, I'd begun to feel as if Robert needed a new assistant.

"Book the company jet. I want to be down south before lunchtime," Robert said without looking up from his computer screen. He'd also used a tone that I knew he reserved for the hired help.

I swallowed hard and reminded myself that I was the hired help in the office. But there was something about the way he spoke to me when we were here that had begun to grate.

My mother used to say that familiarity bred contempt and I guess that's what I was beginning to feel.

For all the suggested advantages that my new position had given me, all I could see was an endless juggling match of corporate crap and social situations that Robert refused to be a part of.

I felt as if I'd been thrown in the deep end and now I just had to keep on swimming. There appeared to be absolutely no let up from the continued demands on my time from people that I didn't even know.

"For just you?" I asked Robert trying to keep a civil tone.

He looked up as if I'd just suggested that he walk naked down Queen Street. "No. I'm going to Gore, your home town," he said, "how would it look if I arrived there without my future wife?"

My hands began to sweat. A clenching fear that I hadn't anticipated feeling at the thought of returning home gripped my insides. Nausea washed over me.

I didn't need to look at my diary, I knew it was chock full

of interviews that I didn't want to attend. "I can't come. I have an interview tomorrow with the Women's Institute."

"Cancel it," he said, "and make sure that you book us into the best hotel in the town. I'm not staying in some flea pit."

I decided immediately that I'd book something online. There wasn't a hotel in the district that would meet Robert's exacting standards. I'd worry about his expectations later.

"The Women's Institute have been trying to see me for the last two weeks, tomorrow was the only day that I could do."

Cold eyes stared back at me. "Well, now you can't do it. Reschedule. I'm not going down south without you. That's the end of it." He turned back to his laptop. Conversation at an end.

Only the conversation wasn't at an end.

"How many nights?"

"What?" He didn't even look up again from his computer screen.

Through gritted teeth I asked, "How many nights are we going to be down there?"

"One. Tell the pilot to arrange catering for dinner tomorrow night for the two of us. We'll eat on the way home."

On trembling legs, I turned and made my way back to my desk. With any luck, we wouldn't have time to catch up with my family.

"And one more thing," Robert's tone of voice sent chills through my body. I stopped in the doorway and turned to face him again. At least this time his gaze met mine.

"Yes?" I tried to keep the animosity that coursed through me out of my voice, but I guess I didn't from the way he cocked his head.

"I thought you'd be pleased to be going home," his voice softened. I didn't know how to cope with being here anymore. Or how to cope with my escalating feelings around Robert.

"It's complicated," I replied, all too aware of the clipped tone of my voice.

My discomfort didn't seem to phase Robert for a moment. He dropped the corporate persona and with a heartwarming smile said, "we can talk about it on the way."

"I might not want to talk about it." The thought of Robert being anywhere near my family brought up issues for me that I hadn't contemplated ever feeling.

I could feel my stress levels climbing the more I thought about him trying to have a conversation with my brother and sister-in-law.

How my mother would behave didn't even bear thinking about.

Robert's concentration was back on his laptop. "Is there anything else?" I asked. If I didn't sit down soon, my knees were going to give out and I didn't want to fall down in a stressed out heap in Robert's doorway.

"I don't want anyone knowing why we're in town," he replied without looking up from the computer screen.

"What?"

"You heard me." I felt as if I'd been slapped across the face. He went from being sensitive fiancé to corporate businessman in a nano-second. "There are still confidentiality clauses around the disclosure part of the due diligence enquiries."

"What the fuck am I supposed to tell my family?" I gripped the doorframe, closed my eyes and took a deep breath.

"There's no need for that kind of language," Robert said eventually looking up from his computer screen. "You can tell them we're in town on business, but you're not to tell them what kind of business."

I don't know what irked me more, being told I had to keep quiet, or the look on Robert's face and his reprimand about my language. Ever since the engagement shoot things had been different between us. I couldn't put my finger on exactly when things changed, but there was a controlling element creeping into the way Robert interacted with me and I didn't like it. I didn't like it one bit.

"This is all a bit too cloak and dagger for me," I muttered as I turned on my heel and left Robert's office.

By the time I sat back down at my desk, I could scarcely hold my mouse because my hand had become so wet. I pulled up the details for the company's corporate jet and, with a feeling of the world spinning around me, booked return flights for the two of us out of Auckland Airport to Invercargill.

With a shaking hand I pulled my phone from my pocket and pressed the number for my mum. I'd contemplated simply going home and not telling any of my family. But the thought that someone else would tell my mother that I'd been back in Gore and I hadn't contacted her filled me with such shame, I couldn't do it.

"Hello, stranger." The familiar voice of my mother, the voice that should have settled my nerves simply sent them into orbit.

"Hi Mum," I tried to keep the edge of fear out of my voice.

"Are you okay, you sound stressed?"

Really, she had no idea. "I'm coming home," I squeaked.

"When?" I could hear the excitement bubbling down the line.

I wanted to vomit. Instead, I took a deep breath and tried to tell myself that everything would be okay. "Around lunchtime today." How did I explain this sudden, unexpected visit?

She sounded surprised. "But there are no flights until tonight."

"Robert has his own plane, so we don't need to rely on the airlines."

The stunned silence did nothing to ease my mounting anxiety levels.

"Mum, are you still there?"

"Yes, dear. I'm here. Why would anyone need their own plane?"

I had no idea how to answer that question, so I decided to ignore it. I had an inkling there would be a lot of questions that I'd have to ignore on this trip home.

Robert

My focus had been on all things business for the past two months.

I didn't like the way the due diligence enquiries were panning out, so I'd had to arrange an extension to the deadline. There was something sour about the way one of the dairy factories had been operating. Hannah was the perfect person to help me solve the riddle.

I had misgivings about taking Hannah back to her home town. I'd have preferred to wait until the ink had dried on the marriage certificate and I had a wedding band on her finger, but time was running out on this business acquisition and it was unlikely that the vendors would agree to another extension. I had to get to the bottom of why things didn't add up.

Inside knowledge, in my experience, was the key ingredient when it came to unravel whatever unorthodox methods had been employed to make something look like something it was not. I knew that Hannah may well be the key to that inside knowledge, so she had to come with me.

I'd flown many times on the company jet and I'd forgotten the thrill that Hannah exhibited when we boarded the sumptuously appointed plane. The main cabin where we were now seated had been set up much like a conference room. Hannah sat across the table from me, buckled into a comfortable leather seat. To the rear of this cabin was a well appointed sleeping area and further on, a full bathroom facility. The flight crew had their own separate galley area and a comfortable place to relax when we were on long journeys.

I eyed Hannah carefully as she continued to tap away at the tiny tablet keyboard. The frown of concentration on her face as she pecked away at the keys made me want to touch her. I'd been so focussed on the work I had to do with the company acquisitions that I'd somehow managed to overlook the curvy and stunning woman who'd been by my side for the past months.

An overwhelming urge to undo the seatbelt, spread Hannah across the table and take her right there in the middle of the cabin had me adjusting my fast hardening cock.

Once we had this acquisition sorted, I decided that I'd take some time away from the company. Take Hannah somewhere nice and spend all day fucking her senseless.

Why wait?

I folded the papers I'd been looking at and put them back into my briefcase.

"You ever thought about joining the mile high club?" I asked.

Hannah's head jerked up from her work, her fingers stopping in mid-flight above the keyboard.

"What?"

"You heard me." I watched as a tiny blush began to crawl its way up her throat.

"Here?"

I indicated with my head to the bedroom cabin beyond. "No, through there."

Hannah looked behind her and for a split second I thought I might be losing my touch and that she might turn me down. I didn't like anyone saying no to me.

"What about the hostess?"

"She'll be up the front reading a book."

I watched a small, sly smile spread across Hannah's beautiful face. My cock responded by throbbing.

"Aren't we supposed to stay in our seats with the belt fastened while we're in flight?" Hannah teased.

"I can arrange the appropriate restraints."

The shudder of Hannah's response was all I needed to see.

I wasn't waiting any longer. I unbuckled my lap belt, helped Hannah out of her own restraint and pulled her into my arms.

My hands tangled in her hair as I pulled her lips towards mine. My tongue plundered her waiting mouth and my other hand found its way to the curve of her arse.

"Come on," I said my breath ragged.

I nearly pulled her to the rear of the plane. I knew we had just under an hour before the crew would prepare the plane to land in Invercargill. That was enough time to make sure that Hannah knew exactly how much I needed and wanted her in my life, permanently.

I managed to let go of Hannah long enough to close and lock the door before I pulled her back into my arms. She was like a drug. Now I'd tasted her again, I couldn't get enough.

"You're sure this is okay?" Hannah whispered, her breath warm on the side of my neck.

"Absolutely," I growled as I pushed Hannah down onto the crisp sheets.

"How many women have you had here?" she asked

leaning up on her elbows, taunting me with the soft swell of her breasts.

"Only you." I said.

It was the truth.

I took in the glorious sight of Hannah laid out in front of me for the taking. I swallowed. A knot of desire shooting through my body like nothing I'd experienced. Hannah's short skirt had ridden up when I pushed her down on the bed, revealing a swathe of pale inner thigh.

Until Hannah had come along, my entire focus had been on business matters. I still had files in the forward cabin I should be looking at in anticipation of the meetings that we'd set up. Instead, here I found myself, on my knees sliding my hands up the softest flesh I'd ever encountered.

My lips followed my fingers, hunting out the musky scent of Hannah's mounting desire.

Her body began to tremble the closer I got to the heat of her.

Hands found their way to my head and began threading through my hair.

I bit the small scrap of satin that lay between my mouth and Hannah.

She moaned, pulling her fingers tighter in my hair.

As I slid back up Hannah's body, I took her small wrists in one hand and pinned them above her head.

"Now, I think you'll find that the captain has the seatbelt sign on, so I'm afraid I'm going to have to restrain you for your own safety."

Before Hannah had a chance to object, I stripped her shoes, skirt and panties from her body. Now naked from the waist down, I slipped a sleeping belt across her stomach and pulled it tight.

"What the hell is this?"

"Safety for sleeping." The wicked grin on Hannah's face

and the way she wriggled, trying out the belt around her midriff, told me that she liked the idea. "I can't have you hitting the ceiling if an unexpected air pocket comes along, can I?"

"And what about you?" she asked as she tipped her head to one side.

"I'm a big boy, I think I can take a few more knocks than you."

Hannah reached for the bulge between my legs and rubbed my hard cock through the fabric of my suit trousers.

"I think it's best we get this big boy out to play," she said as she began to undo the buckle on my belt.

As the buckle came undone and Hannah continued to work to release my cock from the confines of my clothing, I sucked in a breath. I wanted to fuck her until she moaned my name incoherently.

I slipped the belt free of my pants just as Hannah's cool hands hit the swollen flesh of my cock.

"Come here," I moaned as I pulled her hands from me and wrapped the soft leather of my belt around her wrists. "I don't want you moving your hands from above your head, do you understand?"

"And if I do?" Hannah asked.

"Then you'll be punished," I growled. "There's nothing more I'd enjoy than to tan your arse."

Hannah shivered in response to my words, relaxing her arms and leaving them bound in my belt above her head.

I took a deep breath. Now I had her exactly where I wanted her and I was going to take my time making sure that she was well satisfied before we hit the ground.

*H*annah
Bound and buckled I should have felt helpless

165

and out of control. Instead, I had an unexplainable and overwhelming sense of power. Robert's attention and care, the way he looked at me and the sight of his erect cock—all for me—ramped up my excitement to an unexpected level.

I forgot all about my fears. My frustrations of the last couple of months and simply kept my attention on Robert. He was worse than some kind of drug and I was addicted.

I couldn't say no to him.

There was something dirty about what we were doing that turned me on more than I'd ever been turned on before.

I lay there motionless and silent. Aware only of the slight movement of the aircraft and the hum of the engines.

Robert never took his eyes off me.

Naked from the waist down—he may as well have strung my legs from the ceiling of the aircraft—the sensation of exposure wouldn't have been any less.

Dark hazel eyes raked over my body.

I shivered.

"Cold?" he asked

"No," I shook my head.

Robert threw a self-assured smile my way as he removed his shirt and tie with meticulous care. I watched with mounting anticipation as he hung them both on a hanger inside a small alcove.

Picking his trousers up, he laid the creased edge of each leg together with excruciating accuracy and then hung them on another hanger. With his back to me, I watched the long muscles of his toned body contract and relax. I could feel the wetness of my overwhelming desire seeping from between my legs.

Whatever game Robert was playing, it was working.

If he didn't hurry up and come to me, I knew I was likely to start begging.

The thought crossed my mind that it might be worth moving my hands just to enjoy the promised spanking.

Then he turned around.

I glimpsed a bead of pre-come sitting atop his hard cock.

I couldn't help licking my lips and was rewarded by the sight of a smile breaking across Robert's beautiful face. I still found it hard to believe that a man who travelled around in a private jet wanted anything to do with me at all.

And yet. Here he was, those perfect hands spreading my legs, that beautiful, flawless mouth about to…

All coherent thought left me as Robert's fingers and mouth began to work their magic.

I closed my eyes and arched up into the pleasurable sensations.

As my body shuddered to its first orgasm, I heard myself moaning Robert's name. At the sound of his name, he redoubled his efforts, tongue and mouth driving my body to climb higher.

When I didn't think I could take it any longer, suddenly Robert appeared in my vision. I didn't even care that he must have brought a condom with him.

Hell. We were going away for the night, I'd be upset if he hadn't.

"I hate using these," he said.

"Don't," I whispered, "I'm clean."

He threw the packet over his shoulder, unopened and I felt every inch of him as he slid his hard cock inside of me.

"I want to touch you," I moaned as I tried to wriggle against the confines of the belt around my waist.

"Move those hands," he warned, "and you'll wear the mark of my hand on your backside afterwards."

His words were too much. The feeling of him inside of me.

Robert leaned forward, clamping his teeth against my neck as he thrust inside of me faster and faster.

I couldn't stand it any longer, I threw off the belt around my wrists and raked my fingernails down Robert's back. If he was going to hurt me, then I was going to hurt him first.

He erupted, howling as a roaring orgasm tore through his body.

My own answered the call and I clung to him as another shuddering tremor took me.

Robert collapsed beside me, released the belt from around my waist and then pulled my languid body on top of his own.

He rested his lips in the dip of my shoulder and said, in a menacing tone, "You're going to regret that last move. I always keep my promises."

CHAPTER 25

*H*annah
No more than fifteen minutes later, we were seated at the board table in the middle cabin waiting for clearance to land at Invercargill.

I couldn't imagine the necessity for any kind of clearance —it wasn't as if there were aircraft circling the airport waiting to land. Maybe they had to find some ground crew to deal with the jet.

I'd only ever flown into the airport by my home town once before—after a trip to Wellington. Looking back now, it had probably been the reason for my wanderlust. Seeing the capital city, enjoying the vibrant cafes and soaking in the special atmosphere of Wellington. The only reason that I hadn't run from my hometown to Wellington, was because it wasn't far enough away.

As the jet continued to circle the small airport, I struggled with my feelings. It had been two months since I'd left Gore and now we were about to land in Invercargill and head back to my home town. At times like this, especially since I'd agreed to marry Robert, I felt as if my life had taken a strange turn. Being back here in the deep south was the very last thing that I'd expected. But I didn't have a lot of time to worry about that at the moment.

I pressed my thighs together.

I could still feel the heat of Robert's strong body between them. He cast the odd, almost arrogant, glance in my direction as the small crew readied the plane for landing. I hadn't been able to look a single one of them in the eye since we'd returned to the main cabin. I didn't even want to think about what must have been going through their minds.

There would be no missing what Robert and I had been doing when the sheets were changed on the bed in the back cabin. He seemed completely unperturbed by what others thought about him. I wished sometimes that I had the presence to be able to feel the same way. But that wasn't the way I'd been brought up and it didn't fit in with my philosophy on life. How I'd come to have my own strange philosophy on life, I couldn't be sure. But I knew that I'd come up against so many barriers since I'd been involved with Robert and somehow, he continued to find a way to push me beyond my own idea of decency.

"Mr Redfern," the hostess, like so many other people in his life addressed Robert in such a formal way. I noticed that she'd barely been able to keep her eyes off him every time she walked into the cabin. I guess as far as she was concerned, I was just another woman on another plane trip—never mind that I was the future Mrs Robert Redfern. It dawned on me that a lot of people might not be pleased that I was to be the future Mrs Robert Redfern. It explained the cool air of disdain that so many people had been treating me with since the announcement. I'd been so caught up in the hoopla of family, photography, press and charity engagements that I hadn't had a chance to notice how real people reacted to my engagement news.

Robert acknowledged the presence of the hostess without taking his eyes off me. "Yes?" A single word, but the tone of voice he used when he said it spoke far more than those three letters of that universal word.

The tone spoke of the overwhelming control Robert exercised across everyone around him. That control now extended to me. There was no doubting it—the way I'd surrendered to him in the back cabin—the way his will had somehow crept with stealth into all areas of my life.

"We'll need to stow your briefcase, we're coming in to land."

"Of course," Robert's dismissive tone and the way he paid the poor woman little attention made me feel some sympathy for her, sympathy that wasn't reciprocal.

"You need to stow your laptop as well, Miss Scott." I didn't miss the sharp tone of the hostess' voice and I noted that the smile on her face didn't reach her eyes. She certainly wasn't looking at me with the same kind of respect she showed Robert.

Coming back here with Robert could be a huge mistake—but he'd been so insistent that I should accompany him and I couldn't work out why.

I may be coming home, but I was coming home a completely different woman than had left a couple of months ago. Most of that change came down to the simmering, billionaire sitting across from me.

As the runway came into sight and the familiar landscape of the rugged coast flashed by my window, my body began to tremble—and not in the way Robert had made it tremble less than half an hour ago.

I'd left this town for a good reason.

Returning with Robert, didn't seem like the smartest idea I'd had in a long time. Now, facing the fact that he would be meeting my family, agreeing to marry him didn't seem like such a smart idea either.

The plane hit an air pocket and my stomach rolled in protest. I plastered my hand over my mouth, but it was too late.

Robert somehow managed to produce a sick bag and the contents of my stomach made a hurried escape from my mouth.

"It's okay," he soothed as waves of embarrassment flowed through me and fought with the waves of nausea. "First time flying in a small jet can do this to you."

My anxiety had nothing to do with my first time in a small jet and everything to do with what I knew waited for me once we disembarked.

Robert

"This is the best that they've got in this god-forsaken town?" I couldn't hide the irritation in my voice.

"At short notice, yes," Hannah bristled under the onslaught of my criticism. "It's got everything we need. Internet access and somewhere to sleep. This isn't Auckland, or Sydney. If you don't like it, I'm sure we can get straight back on the plane and go home."

"Isn't this your home?"

"No," she snapped in an indignant tone. It made me wonder what had happened to drive her away from here and into the arrangement we'd made.

Not that I was complaining about the arrangement. Hannah was the single largest distraction I'd had from work.

Ever.

Even now, my mind wandered to the interlude we'd shared aboard the jet on the way down here. I looked at the not-quite-large-enough bed that sat in the middle of the shack someone at this end of the country dared to call 'accommodation'.

"You sure that you couldn't find anything better than this?"

"Not without spending a fortune." Hannah's face flushed. "You wouldn't have cared how much it cost," she said, her voice trailing off to a whisper. I watched as Hannah scrunched up her face in what had become that familiar way when she thought about things.

"That's why we have an expense account." As much as I wanted to be, I couldn't be angry with Hannah. I knew she was having trouble adjusting and I hadn't given her a fair chance, especially as she hadn't wanted to come back here in any event.

"I'll find something else," she offered.

"No," I shook my head. "Time is my currency." I walked over to her, crossing the small space between us in a moment. I took her in my arms and stroked her, soft red hair. "I think I can rough it for one night."

I felt the palpable relief as it washed through Hannah's body.

The rustic cabin wasn't too bad.

A converted railway house, with a verandah tacked on the front. The entire space looked as if it had recently been refurbished. The internal walls had been demolished, creating one large modern open space. A long kitchen ran across the wall opposite the bed. A doorway to the rear housed the bathroom beyond with its faux 19th century bath, shower and tap ware.

Original kauri timber floorboards had been varnished and I was certain I could feel the cool southern air rising between the cracks in the boards. The entire room had been furnished in what could only be described as rustic, country.

A far cry from the metal, polished stone and floor to ceiling glass of my usual haunts in Auckland.

I'd have described it as homely.

I wasn't a homely kind of guy, but for Hannah I was prepared to make an exception. Just for one night.

"You shouldn't have brought me here," Hannah said as she broke free of my hold on her body. I loved touching her curves, feeling the weight of her breasts in my hands. Hannah had been my only obsession aside from business for such a long time. I didn't understand her emotional reaction to being here. It didn't make any sense to me.

"Rubbish." I wasn't going to allow her to wallow in her anxiety—whatever the reason for it. "I need a local tour guide and you're the perfect person for the job. The first thing we need to do is to meet with your family."

Her eyes flew wide open in surprise. "I thought the reason we came down here was for you to look at the factories."

"It is, but I want to meet my future wife's family. That's important to me."

I watched as what little colour Hannah had in her face drained away and her hand flew to her mouth.

"Are you going to be sick again?"

"No," she said as she took great gulps of air.

"Then why do you look so stricken at the mention of your family?"

"You haven't met my family."

"They can't be any worse than mine?"

Hannah laughed, the sound bouncing around the stark walls of the room. "You haven't met my mum and my brother."

"They're just people," I said. "You're good with people. Anyone who can get my Grandmother in the palm of her hand," I shook my head. "She likes you a lot."

"She'd like anyone she thought you were going to marry," Hannah teased.

"You might have a point." I was tired of this conversation. "Ring your mother. Tell her we'll be there in an hour. We'll spend an hour with them and then I'll arrange a tour of the factories."

I pulled my computer from its satchel and sat down, following the instructions to connect to the local internet. At least they had internet. It might not be as fast as I was used to, but it was adequate.

In fact, everything about this place was adequate. Maybe Hannah hadn't done such a bad job after all.

I could hear her talking to her mother on the phone. I tried not to listen in. She sounded tense. I knew there was something about the reason she'd run that she wasn't telling me.

Or maybe someone like Hannah shouldn't be living her life out in a backwater.

Not that I had anything against the rest of the country. Huge portions of my businesses relied on entire towns similar to this one. Perhaps an insight into the people who lived and worked here might not be such a bad thing.

But there was still a reason why someone like Hannah didn't want to stay and that, more than anything, intrigued me.

Or was it simply that everything about Hannah intrigued me?

CHAPTER 26

*H*annah

We pulled up the dusty, gravel drive to arrive outside my brother's front door in the latest Audi. At the last minute, Robert had insisted that Graham travel with us. How Graham had found a car like this, I had no idea. Arriving in the latest Audi with a driver wasn't going to make my 'coming home' any easier.

It occurred to me that the car I sat in was probably worth more than the house that we were about to enter.

"You okay here?" Robert asked Graham.

"You're more than welcome to come inside," I offered. The more strangers I could fill the house with the better as far as I was concerned. I wanted to take the focus off me and Robert any way that I could.

"I'll be fine here, Miss Scott," Graham replied.

Robert offered me his hand and helped me out of the car. I stood in my brother's driveway on shaking legs. I wasn't sure what was wrong with me. I'd never felt so emotionally out of control. Being here shouldn't be doing this to me.

The old blue door flew open and Mum stood in the open space between us and the house.

She flung her arms open and, for a reason that I couldn't fathom, I fell into the familiar and secure embrace of my mother. It took everything I had inside of me not to burst into tears. What had happened to the carefree and capable woman who'd left this town only eight weeks ago?

"Look at you," Mum said as she pushed me away from her and held me by my shoulders at arms-length so she could scan my body. "It hasn't taken long for you to become a real city girl."

Robert made a coughing sound behind me and I stepped back towards him. He took my hand, somehow making me a part of him, striking the maternal bond that lingered between me and my mother.

"Mum, this is Robert Redfern," I said wondering if I should have added, *my fiancé* to the sentence? "Robert, my mother, Karen Scott."

"I'm very pleased to meet you, Karen," Robert said as he shook my mother's hand.

Mum's fingers flew to her throat and I was amazed to watch a blush crawl across her face. "I've been looking forward to meeting you very much," Mum gushed, "ever since I found out that you and Hannah were going to be married."

It was then that I realised that Robert had this effect on all women. Mum couldn't keep her eyes off him. For the first time ever, I saw my mother as a sexual being, not just plain old mum. In fact, when I looked closely, I could see that she'd gone to quite some trouble with her makeup. Mum never wore makeup.

Could that be a new dress that she was wearing? I didn't remember ever seeing it before. Perhaps Robert coming to visit was more of an occasion than I thought. Not a lot happened in mum's life and I guess having your daughter bring home a billionaire was a good reason to buy a new dress.

"Where are my manners," Mum said clearly flustered in the presence of Robert. I understood the feeling. "Come on in." Mum turned her attention back to me. I could see how hard it was for her to pull her eyes away from Robert. Is this how it would always be when I went anywhere with him? People suddenly remembering that I was by his side. Some kind of second-class citizen wife? "Your brother's down in the back paddock fixing some fencing, but he should be back soon for afternoon tea. You know how much he likes to have something in his stomach before he tackles afternoon milking."

I'd have happily forgotten how life revolved around the daily milking schedule. I guess since I'd been up in Auckland, my schedule had revolved around Robert. There really wasn't a hell of a lot of difference. Women making accommodations for men's schedules. That seemed to be all that I'd done for most of my life.

We walked through the familiar hallway, past the bedrooms that sat at the front of the house and down towards the living area at the back. The whole back half of the house had been renovated, so now the kitchen, dining and living area were open to the north-facing sunshine. A large covered verandah ran across the back of the home, with a view of the rich, green farmland beyond. I could see the small dot of my brother, in one of his familiar check shirts, out working on the fencing. The milking sheds sat to the right of the property and the late afternoon sun glinted on the steel rooftop. A few of the herd—which Dan had invested heavily in—had already begun to gather near the gate, waiting patiently for their chance to relieve the growing pressure in their udders.

"Hello, Trudi," I said to the woman stood in the kitchen. Trudi was kneading bread and barely acknowledged my presence. Saying a quick, 'Hi' before turning her attention back to the dough.

She looked tired.

"Trudi," Mum said, demanding the attention of the younger woman. "This is Mr Robert Redfern, Hannah's fiancé."

I almost cringed at hearing the words aloud. Not so much because I felt like a fake, but because of the proud way my mother announced Robert's arrival in Trudi's kitchen.

It hurt me knowing that I was going to let my mother down when I eventually walked away from Robert. I would have to leave the country after we annulled the marriage, there simply wouldn't be any way I could return to this small community.

The thought caught me off guard, almost as much as Trudi's reaction to Robert caught me off guard. She seemed completely unfazed by the fact that a billionaire stood in the middle of her living space.

Maybe there was something refreshing about that.

Maybe I'd underestimated Trudi.

"Dan will be in any time from fixing the fence," Trudi said as she laid the spongy dough out into loaf tins to rise, "I've baked a banana cake," she looked over the bench top in my direction, "because I know it's your favourite."

Trudi's sudden show of womanly solidarity thew me.

"Th-thank you," I stammered.

"We haven't got long," Robert said looking at his watch with more than a little impatience. Mother's face fell and I had the overwhelming desire to hit him—and not in a plea-surable way.

"Perhaps Hannah can stay with us while you go about your business," Mother suggested.

Robert shook his head. "No. I need her with me."

I glared at him, but my death stare didn't seem to be having any kind of effect.

At that moment, Old Thomas, the smokey grey farm cat made an appearance and snaked his way between Robert's legs. Ears ripped from one too many entanglements with an arrogant rat the fearless feline seemed to revel in the attention Robert bestowed upon him. We all stood and watched holding our collective breath, waiting for the teeth and spitting show. Robert leaned down and petted the gruff cat under the chin.

"Hello, fella, how are you?"

Thomas chirped a reply and reached his head up for another scratch under the chin, exposing the white of his bib.

"I'm sure we've got time to have a cup of tea and a piece of banana cake," I suggested, taking the opportunity to put the suggestion to Robert while he continued to pet the cat. Thomas might turn at any moment, but he seemed to have taken a shine to Robert. He gave Robert's suit legs one more circuit, thoroughly scenting the material, before heading for his favourite afternoon window seat. Leaving my defenceless billionaire unscathed.

Robert followed Thomas across the room and stroked his fur as the cat settled himself in the afternoon sun. I could hear the loud purring from where I stood on the other side of the room.

Then Robert looked at me and said, "I'll call ahead. Tell the factory manager that we'll be there an hour later."

I watched my mother's body straighten and a smile erupt on her face.

"That's settled then," she said aiming her smile at Robert. As mum made her way to the kitchen, she looked out toward the paddock where Dan had been fixing the fence. "Good timing too. It looks as if Daniel's on his way back." As she rounded the kitchen bench, she turned her attention to Robert. "It will be good for the men of the family to get to know each other."

The crashing reality of 'the men in the family' getting to know each other hit me.

Maybe I should have held my death stare and bolted for the factory. Damn that cat, coming in here and seducing Robert, he was normally all spitting teeth and claws with anyone new.

The idea that Robert and Daniel might have any common ground to come together on seemed insane.

What the hell would a dairy farmer and a billionaire company director have to talk about?

$\mathcal{R}$obert

Despite my immediate misgivings around the state of disrepair of the farmhouse and the aloof nature of Hannah's sister-in-law, I could see that Daniel and I had plenty in common.

We were both ambitious.

Neither of us had any time for fools and, most important of all, we both loved Hannah.

That had been apparent from the second Daniel had laid eyes on his sister.

True enough, Hannah's mother and her sister-in-law had real affection for the woman that I'd grown to love over the past few weeks, but there was something about the way that Daniel looked at his sister. The way he thew his strong, tanned arms around her when he walked into the house that told me more than words.

"Hey sis," he'd said as he dropped his wide-brimmed hat

on the kitchen bench top, "I've missed you. The house hasn't been the same since you shot up to the big smoke."

From the look on Hannah's face, it was obvious that she loved her brother as well. What could have driven her away from so much love?

"You need to come back more often," Daniel said as he eyed the large banana cake, dripping with icing. "Trudi doesn't go to the bother of making cakes like this now that you've gone."

"Really?" Hannah said in a disbelieving tone.

"Really," Daniel teased as he pulled his sister into his arms to give her another bear-like hug.

He'd turned his attention to me and said, "You've got yourself a good wife here." I couldn't help but nod in agreement. When Daniel had shaken my hand, his grip was firm and his palm hard from working on the farm.

"You're here to check out the dairy factory." He said between mouthfuls of moist, sweet banana cake.

News travelled fast. We'd barely been on the ground for more than a couple of hours. "That's right," I said as I watched Hannah wolfing down the sweet treat that had been made for her return to the family.

The way the woman ate still did things to me that I didn't have time to think about at the moment.

"Anything you can tell me about what's been going on there?" I asked.

Daniel shook his head in the negative and then took a moment to take a gulp of his tea. Hannah had poured us all a large mug of tea from the big yellow tea pot that now sat in the middle the scrubbed, pine table.

"Business as usual as far as I can see," Daniel said. "The tanker arrives on its regular schedule to collect our milk. That's it as far as I'm concerned."

I nodded. So the producers weren't being affected.

"There's no-one in the district making noises about being treated unfairly, or differently?" I took another mouthful of the moist cake, with its thick cream icing and wondered whether or not Hannah would ask for a second piece. Why that should concern me, I couldn't fathom. I was here to work out why one of the factories wasn't performing the way I'd expected, not to work out whether or not Hannah had a fetish for banana cake.

"Not that I'm aware," Daniel said. Tipping the balance of his mug of tea into his mouth.

"She makes a fine cup of tea," he said cocking his head in the direction of his sister. To my amusement, I watched the colour rise up Hannah's face.

"Mum taught me everything I know," Hannah replied to her brother's warm compliment and I watched as she slipped her hand down her mother's forearm.

They were clearly a close, loving family and nothing like I'd expected. If I had the time, I'd stay and watch Hannah interact with her family. The truth of the matter is that I could watch Hannah doing anything all day.

Maybe she had been right.

Maybe it hadn't been a great idea to bring her down here. Yet, now, as I watched her talking with her mother, their close, fond looks, the gentle and intimate way they touched each other, I felt a strange sense of belonging. A sense of belonging that had been sadly missing from my own family life for such a long time.

I envied Hannah a relationship with her mother.

It made me think of my own mother.

The flash of her ring on Hannah's finger. The ring that I watched Hannah's mother and sister-in-law now admiring. It brought up a sense of something—an emotion that I'd been suppressing for many years.

Grief.

I swallowed a lump in my throat.

As I watched these women together, I knew in that moment I'd do whatever it took to make sure that Hannah never left me.

CHAPTER 27

*H*annah
"We have to go," Robert said looking at his watch. "Get your things, Hannah."

I still couldn't understand why he'd brought me here and now he was dragging me away.

Fury rolled inside of me, threatening to turn the sweet taste of tea and banana cake to bitter bile. Something about the way that Robert wanted to control everything I did, everything I wore. Everywhere I went.

"You're sure she can't stay, just for the afternoon?" The disappointment in Mum's voice hurt.

"We'll be back again soon," Robert said.

It might have placated mum slightly, but it did nothing to calm the raging array of out-of-control emotions that threatened to erupt from inside of me.

Had it only been eight weeks since I'd left?

How could so much have changed?

"It's been great meeting you," Daniel said as he shook Robert's hand again. "We'll have to get you out milking the next time you visit."

To my complete surprise, Robert said, "Yes. I think I'd enjoy that."

I gave mum a quick hug and was surprised again at the warmth showed to me by Trudi. "We've missed you since you've been gone," she whispered almost as if she didn't want anyone else to hear what she said.

Maybe being away for a few weeks had changed my outlook. Or maybe there were things about the old farmhouse and the slow pace of life down here that I hadn't realised I would miss until I came back.

Robert put his arm around me, literally pulling me out of the house.

"Come on. We have work to do."

"See ya, Sis," Daniel said giving my hair a rub. It was a juvenile gesture and one that I'd have hated two months ago, but today, somehow, it just made me sad.

Robert and I sat in silence on our way to the first factory.

Mainly because I was too angry to say anything and he was pouring over documents on his laptop that I was sure he'd poured over a thousand times before.

"Why couldn't I have stayed with mum?" I eventually piped up.

"Because I need you with me," he said without taking his eyes off the screen in front of him.

I hated it when he behaved in this dismissive way with me.

Everything inside of me screamed in frustration. It was then that I realised that I'd moved away from my town a little girl and somehow, in the short time that I'd been away, I'd turned into a woman.

A woman who had needs that Robert was meeting, but also a woman who had the ability to assert herself. But somehow, I'd found myself in a relationship where I didn't feel that I could assert myself.

It was all down to the dollars sitting in my bank account.

I needed to give them back.

I needed to reclaim my independence.

Seeing my family today had reinforced for me the values that I'd been brought up with.

Hard work.

Honesty.

Integrity.

I'd abandoned those values when I'd agreed to Robert's ridiculous proposal.

On our way to the first factory, I decided that I didn't need his money. I could get another temporary job and I could save up and go overseas.

Getting away from his controlling behaviour would be the best thing I could do.

Then I looked at him.

His black hair begging me to run my fingers through it. His long black eye-lashes sitting over hooded, dark eyes.

The sensual pout of his lips. When I thought about where his mouth had been, I couldn't help but shudder.

He must have sensed me watching him because he looked up and his entire face softened as his eyes connected with mine.

Robert reached out with long, strong fingers, fingers that had played my body in the most sensual way.

"I'm sorry that I had to take you away from your family," he soothed, "but I do need you to come with me."

"Why?" I asked, trying not to allow the warmth I was feeling from his touch to dissolve my resolve to walk away from him.

"There's something about the way the accounts have come together for this factory that don't make sense."

"What about the other one?" I asked, a fleeting concern lodging itself in my gut. As we approached the factory that processed the milk from Daniel's herd, I had a sudden sense that something might not be right in my brother's world.

"Everything about it checks out. But nothing about this one does. For some strange reason, it's losing money."

"But that doesn't make sense," I said. "The industry's going from strength to strength. Dan's doing so well because they're paying him so well."

"Are they paying him over the going rate?"

"I don't know?"

"But you could find out."

I didn't like the sound of Robert's tone. I pulled my hand out from under his, instinctively cradling it in my lap. "What will happen if you buy the corporation?"

"We'll close the factories that aren't making money and concentrate on those that are making money," Robert said as the car rolled to a stop outside the large, white brick building.

The sense of dread I'd been harbouring ratcheted up a notch. I scolded myself for not taking enough notice of what was happening with Daniel's herd. What would happen to the farmers who were supplying milk to this factory if it closed down?

"Let's get this over with," Robert said as he stepped outside the car, doing up the button on his suit. He looked so completely out of place in this farming community.

I shivered as I got out of the car, despite the warmth of the sun on my back. I couldn't shake the sense that somehow I'd brought something evil home with me.

A sudden wave of nausea washed over me.

I couldn't do anything about it. I leaned against the side of the car and the contents of my stomach landed at my feet.

Robert was behind me in an instant. Holding my hair as a second wave of tea and banana cake hit the ground.

"I'm sorry," I muttered, "I don't know what's the matter with me."

"It's okay," Robert soothed. In a moment he was on the phone. "Karen, it's Robert Redfern here. Hannah's not well. Can I send her back to you while I complete my business?" How the hell did he even get my mother's phone number?

I didn't have time to worry about that as another wave of nausea swept over me. I didn't get sick. What the hell was happening to me?

"Great," I heard Robert say, "I'll send her straight back to you."

When I thought I had nothing left in my stomach, Robert tucked me back into the car, taking great care in making sure that the seatbelt was fastened.

"Will you stop fussing," I grumbled.

"You know I like to make sure that you're strapped down," he said, a mischievous twinkle in his eye. "And don't think I haven't forgotten about the promise that I made on the plane," he said as he pulled the belt tight enough to pin me to the backseat of the car.

The idea of being put across Robert's knee equally terrified and excited me.

He brushed his lips across my forehead. "I shouldn't be too long," he said and then he was gone.

I sat in the back of the car as we headed back to my real home.

A thought popped uninvited into my head. It was a thought that had been drifting in and out of my mind for a while, but one that I'd refused to pay any attention.

I leaned forward to attract Graham's attention. "Can you stop at the shops in the main street?"

"Certainly, Miss Scott," he replied.

There was something I needed to pick up from the chemist. Something I should have picked up in Auckland.

J sat on the toilet in the bathroom staring at the little screen on the pregnancy test kit and willing the lines not to be there.

How could this have happened?

We'd used protection. I was on the pill for crying out loud.

How had one of those little wriggling bastards managed to find its way up my fallopian tube and gotten me pregnant?

I'd lived on a dairy farm.

I knew the probability of impregnation.

What was the chance that Robert's sperm had found its way outside the confines of those horrible condoms and swam its way to my egg? Was I really unlucky enough to be one of those women whose birth control failed when she took antibiotics?

And yet, here was the evidence staring me in the face.

I wanted to throw up again, but I had nothing left.

It all made sense now. The cold I thought I had. Feeling so tired. The constant threat of nausea that I'd put down to numerous occasions of supposed food poisoning.

I closed my eyes. When would I ever get food poisoning with the delicious meals cooked by Sally?

After I'd hidden the evidence of the test kit in my handbag—one of the many that Robert had purchased for me and looked so out of place here at the farm—I washed my hands. I splashed some water on my face and wondered when the pregnancy 'glow' would arrive that I'd heard so much about? All I could see in the mirror was the pale colour of my skin. Pale because I felt so god-damn awful at the moment, or pale because of the shock I couldn't be sure.

I took a deep breath and dried my hands. I needed to go out there and face my mother. I certainly couldn't tell her what was going on. Hell, the idea of telling anyone, including Robert, that I was pregnant brought on another wave of nausea.

I sat down on the old yellow milking stool that sat beside the bath. My mother had sat on this very stool when she'd bathed me and Daniel as children. I could still see her, in her blue apron with the big pockets in the front, her hair pulled back in a scrappy, serviceable bun, the way she brushed the odd wisps away from her face with the back of her hand while she wrestled me and Dan into some kind of submission.

It dawned on me. I was going to be that woman. Sitting on a stool, not unlike the one holding me now.

A sense of overwhelming panic rushed through me, sucking the air from my lungs. I grabbed the big, green towel hanging from the rail beside me for support and took deep, calming breaths.

How could this be happening to me?

What was Robert going to say?

Did I even have the courage to tell him?

A loud rapping at the door and the familiar sound of my mother's voice brought me back to my senses. "Are you okay?" came the muffled call through the bathroom door.

"Yes," I called.

Lies, a tiny voice in my head said.

"You've been in there for ages, do you need anything?"

I could easily have laughed. How about a new life and another new start?

"No. I'm coming right out."

Generations of women before me had stood at this cross roads in their life. Surely as the sun would come up tomorrow morning, I knew I wasn't the first woman to find herself in this situation and I wasn't going to be the last.

I splashed some water on my face and pinched my

cheeks. Why I thought that would help, I wasn't sure. But I think I'd seen it in a movie somewhere.

I unlocked the door and walked straight into the arms of my mother.

The tears were pouring down my face before I had a chance to think.

"How long have you been pregnant?" she asked, her voice devoid of anything except the enduring support she'd always had for me.

"How did you know?" I asked her once she'd settled me down on the easy chair in the front room. I knew this was serious. We never went in the front room for anything. It was a room reserved for entertaining the likes of my husband-to-be. In fact, it occurred to me that mum had been remiss in not receiving Robert for his first visit to the house in this very room.

Mum closed the door, so we had some privacy and then took a seat in the green velvet chair opposite me. She'd put a box of tissues on the low walnut table that sat between us.

"I didn't know until I heard you being sick."

I could have had a stomach bug. I blew my nose and pulled another tissue from the box.

"You had a look about you that I've not seen since I was carrying you." Mum reached out and closed her hand over mine as another flood of tears fell down my face.

"Robert doesn't know," I sobbed.

"He'll be thrilled," Mum said as she stroked my hair. "It doesn't matter that you're pregnant before you get married."

In the panic of finding out I was pregnant I'd somehow forgotten about the wedding. What the hell was he going to say? He was paying me to marry him. I don't recall there being any discussion about a baby being part of the deal.

"I didn't know until just now," I sobbed. "I don't want to

be pregnant. I don't know the first thing about being a mother."

Mum soothed and stroked. "We all learn on the job."

"But I've already got a job," I wailed as I wiped my eyes and blew my nose for the fourth time.

A small mountain of sodden tissues sat on the little walnut table.

Mum sat opposite me with a look on her face that I recognised from my childhood. The look that said, *it will all be okay*, even though everything going through my head said it was never going to be okay ever again.

CHAPTER 28

*H*annah

Mum had done what she always did when I struggled to come to terms with whatever it was that ailed me. She'd sent me to bed.

I lay on the single bed in what had been my old room, a room I couldn't wait to get away from, but which now seemed strangely comforting.

Maybe it was the way the late afternoon sun shone through the nets at the window, or the simple scent of the bedding that I'd slept under for as many years as I could remember. The room had barely been touched in my short absence and I had a strange sense that if everything went terribly wrong with Robert, then at least I'd be able to come back here.

Trudi hadn't been so bad since I'd been back.

She'd brought me a cup of tea and a ginger biscuit and given me a knowing look. I'd sworn mum to secrecy, but maybe Trudi could tell by looking at my face that I was pregnant as well.

Had I joined some strange club and was there some kind

of female pheromone that my body excreted that I wasn't aware of? I couldn't be sure. But what I could be sure of was the fact that since I'd set foot back in the house, Trudi was treating me like an equal, instead of some annoying extra she had to put up with because she was married to my brother.

My phone rang and I looked at the screen.

Robert.

I wanted to throw up again.

Instead, I took a deep breath and tried to sound half decent. "Hello."

"How are you?" His tone of voice suggested that he was genuinely concerned and I found myself welling up. Crying wasn't going to solve anything either.

I lied. "Feeling better," I said trying to add a chirp to my voice.

"Look, I'm at the factory. It's as I suspected. There's something not right going on here. Can I talk to Daniel?"

"He's milking," I said.

"And?" Robert asked.

I forgot that Robert wasn't from a dairying family. "Nothing interferes with milking."

"Oh, right," he replied.

A silence hung between us. I was pregnant. How was I going to tell Robert? I couldn't tell him on the phone. But I needed to tell him.

"I'll talk to him when I come and pick you up."

"Okay," I replied. Then he was gone.

No doubt lost in the complications of business acquisitions going wrong.

A sense of doom clung to me.

What was wrong with the factory and how would it affect my family?

*R*obert

I told my driver to take me back to the farm. I could tell by the shadows cast by the long line of shelterbelt trees that evening wasn't too far away. We were going back to Auckland tomorrow—the sooner I got Hannah out of here the better as far as I was concerned. I didn't like the way she'd taken a turn for the worse since we'd been back in her home town. Something wasn't quite adding up, but I had too much to worry about with the factory to turn my mind to Hannah. As much as thinking about her seemed to be taking up a disproportionate amount of time in my head—I still had to get to the bottom of what was going on with this business.

The telephone discussion I'd had earlier in the day weighed on my mind. I knew something was up the moment I heard Hannah's voice. It sounded strained. But I couldn't be certain of the problem.

I thought back to the enticing idea of putting her over my knee and giving her a good spanking for moving when I told her to stay still.

Promising to follow through on that threat couldn't be it, surely?

Hannah needed to know that I wouldn't do a thing to her without her consent.

We needed to get this straight before we went any further.

Although, I had to admit that the sight of her welcoming arse turning bright red under my hand did things to me.

I turned my mind back to the short telephone discussion we'd had earlier. Not unlike the discussions I had with the manager at the dairy factory this afternoon, I had the feeling that Hannah too was keeping something from me. Like my business sense, my senses around Hannah had become finely tuned.

I had a large bullshit detector and, right this minute, it was flashing red.

The manager at the dairy factory had been evasive, confrontational and incredibly unhelpful. Anybody else that I'd dealt with while collecting confidential information would have stood on their heads to help me. I was trying to put a lot of money in that man's pocket and he didn't seem to want me around at all.

I knew it didn't have anything to do with the fact that I was from Auckland. It had more to do with the fact that, like Hannah this afternoon, he was hiding something from me and in both of their cases I had a sense it was something big.

As much as the business subterfuge disturbed me, my greatest fear was that now I'd seen Hannah in the bosom of her family, that she'd stay here and tell me that we were over.

She had a contractual obligation to me—not unlike the contractual obligation that the lying scumbag at the factory had to me—but the importance of keeping Hannah was of greater concern to me than losing the factory deal.

I wanted her in my life and I always got what I wanted.

We'd arrived at the farm and I'd instructed Graham to drop me just down the road a little from the milking sheds.

I spotted Hannah's brother as the last of the cows made their way back out to pasture. It never ceased to amaze me, the way they came in for milking—almost in an orderly line —and the way they exited the buildings again after milking.

Daniel didn't see me coming. Not that I wanted to sneak up on him or anything. When he caught sight of me, he adjusted the stetson that he was wearing and gave me the universal acknowledgement of greeting between men—a tilt of the chin.

"Didn't expect to see you darkening the doors of a milking shed," he said as he turned off the stream of water coming from the high pressure hose in his hand. "I thought your type were keyboard warriors at head office." The comment was made with an air of humour and kindness.

I'd managed to skirt a couple of cow pats as I made my way to the milking sheds, but the flood of effluent that stood between us now meant I would either have to walk through it or remain exactly where I was standing. Italian leather and cow excrement weren't the greatest of companions in my estimation.

I chose to remain rooted to the spot while a large grin crept across Daniel's face. He recommended washing the concrete in front of me, the droplets of water missing my shoes by inches.

"Any chance I can have a word to you," I yelled above the sound of the rushing water.

"No worries," Daniel answered. "Just let me finish washing up here. Or," he said with a wide grin, "you could grab a pair of gummies from over there," Daniel pointed to a stand of sturdy, white gumboots, "and give us a hand if you like."

"I could wait for you over here," I offered looking at the shade of a large oak tree.

"Yeah, you townies," Daniel said, "never happy to get your hands dirty, but happy to take the money off the back of the hard graft of others."

I'd have been an idiot to fail to note the challenge in the tone of his voice. Not one to back down from anything—not even cleaning up cow shit—I hung my suit jacket on the nearest fence post, unclipped my eighteen carat gold cuff links, stowed them in the pocket of the jacket and rolled up my sleeves.

"You got a size 12 over there?" I shouted.

Daniel stopped the hose again and nodded his approval. "Yeah, I think you'll find that the white pair on the end will fit you. Pressure hose is on the left."

CHAPTER 29

*ℋ*annah
     I'd spent the afternoon lying on the bed in what had been my old bedroom. I knew every single spot and stain on the ceiling and I was surrounded by the familiar scent of safety.

As much as I'd loved running away to Auckland and I knew I'd never have a chance of getting away from here if I hadn't left, now that I found myself facing the issue of a pregnancy—this seemed a safe place to be. I'd been convincing myself that no matter what happened, I didn't want to come back here.

No matter how much I knew Daniel would love to have me back, I still felt unsure of my new status with his wife. She'd been welcoming enough with the idea that I was here for a quick visit with my new billionaire fiancé, but how would she be if staying, with a baby, became a permanent arrangement?

Besides, there was still a part of me that had seen a completely different kind of life in Auckland and coming back here would be admitting defeat. Admitting that they were all right when they said I shouldn't go. I couldn't stand the idea of that.

Maybe I should go back to Auckland and get rid of this baby.

That thought, however fleetingly it passed through my mind, turned my stomach and caused me to succumb to another wave of nausea. I might be some things, but taking the life of my own child, no matter how newly formed, was not something that I could even think about or comprehend.

That wasn't going to happen.

It wasn't an option.

No matter the consequences.

I knew all ready, as I placed my hands protectively over my stomach, that I was going to nurture this new life growing inside of me with all of my resources.

I thought about the sacrifices that my parents had made for me. They hadn't had a lot, but they'd done their best for me and given me everything within their power.

They hadn't sent me to university and some days I found it hard to forgive them for that—but then I wouldn't have met Robert if I'd gone to University.

Robert!

The thought of telling him brought on another wave of nausea.

Maybe I could hide the truth from him. If I met my side of the contract we'd made, then I'd have enough money to set up me and the baby. That's what I needed to do.

I sat up and waited for the nausea to pass. If I continued to lie around in bed, Robert really would suspect that something was seriously wrong. He was such a control freak he'd have me in his doctor's office as soon as we returned to Auckland and then he'd know the truth.

I took a deep breath.

I had to continue on as if nothing was amiss, no matter how wretched I felt.

Then it occurred to me that mum knew what was going on and possibly my sister-in-law as well. Trying to hide this pregnancy was going to be impossible.

I dropped my head into my hands. How did I find myself in this intolerable position?

Maybe they were right, a tiny voice whispered in my head. Maybe I should have stayed home.

The ridiculous thought occurred to me that I was now in exactly the position I'd run away from here to prevent.

Engaged to be married and pregnant!

Not to a dairy farmer, but a billionaire. A billionaire determined to deconstruct the corporation that held the key to the livelihoods of everyone I'd known for my entire life.

I couldn't imagine Robert ever wanting a child. I couldn't imagine someone like him ever settling down. Wasn't the issue that he couldn't find a wife in the first place and that's how I found myself in this ridiculous situation.

What made me think that a man so averse to marriage that he had to contract someone to pretend to be his fiancée would ever be happy to have a child foisted on them?

All he ever wanted to do was take over companies—a child wouldn't even enter the equation. A little voice in the back of my head said, *but didn't he mention it once, when we were sitting with his family at the dinner after our engagement photographs?*

I had a flash of memory, but life had been such a whirlwind adventure since I'd gotten to Auckland, I couldn't quite remember. Maybe pregnancy hormones were making me delusional. I didn't want to think about it too hard in any event.

I pulled myself up off the bed and planted my feet firmly on the floor. I waited for my head to stop spinning and the overwhelming feeling of the world swimming before my eyes to settle.

I took a deep breath. I reminded myself that thousands of women had been here before me and thousands would follow in my footsteps. For the first time in my life that feeling of overwhelming aloneness left me. Those women managed to get on without falling apart and I could do as much.

I decided a walk in the fresh air would do me good. I would walk down to the milking sheds and spend some time with my brother. He'd be sluicing out the sheds by now. It was a job that we'd done together as children and one that I hated. There was something hideous about a milking shed after the herd had been through.

We'd talked out many problems over the years in the milking shed and maybe a part of me was looking for that familiar shoulder to help me through my current crisis.

I put on a pair of old sandals that still lay at the bottom of the wardrobe. I took myself off out the front door and down the familiar path to the sheds. I walked past blackberry patches that we'd struggled to control for years and marvelled at the tenacity of nature. No matter the amount of chemical warfare, the blackberry and thistles still had the ability to grow.

I wasn't too far away when I spotted Robert's jacket on one of the fence posts. I slowed my pace.

As I got closer, I saw him and then I did stop.

I couldn't take my eyes off him.

I'd never seen him looking like this before.

He stood there in a pair of white gumboots, a sleek hose in his hand. He was spraying the muck off the concrete, shoulder-to-shoulder with my brother.

They were just about finished and I didn't want him to know I was there, so I simply stood and watched. It was hard work, cleaning out a shed, and I'd never seen Robert do anything that resembled physical labour. The nearest he came to physical labour was pushing a mouse across a mouse pad.

The flex of his muscles through the thin business shirt he was wearing caught my eye. The easy grace he had as he handled the powerful pressure hose. He looked as if he'd been doing this kind of work for years, not minutes.

I heard the warm sound of his laughter as he shared some mutual joke with Daniel.

A sense of something bubbled up inside of me. An overwhelming feeling of connectedness and love. My hand fell to the tiny growing being that I knew was lodged inside of my body.

A part of him.

A part of them.

A part of the two men that I saw in front of me.

I felt the weight of generations sitting with me.

I wanted a future with this man, more than I wanted anything else in the world.

He was a good man.

A kind man and a generous man.

More importantly, there was a chance that he could be mine and, for the first time ever, I didn't want to let that chance slip away.

*R*obert
I hadn't been so dirty since I could remember. I also hadn't laughed so much in an age. I had a sudden insight into the kind of work the people of this town were doing and the kind of family Hannah had come from.

All of those insights continued to make me more determined to get to the bottom of what was happening with the factory. I thought I had an inkling of what was going on, but I needed to confirm something with Daniel first.

Daniel threw a towel at me. "You've got some shit on you, mate and my sister probably won't thank me for dirtying up her man."

"Thanks," I wiped my sweaty face with the towel and caught sight of the dirty, streaked material. "Can I ask you something about the factory? This is off the record and I want you to keep it between us."

"Yeah, sure," Daniel said as he coiled up the last of the hose and hung it on a peg on the wall above the line of gumboots. "Shoot."

"The factory," I said as I hung the towel alongside the hose, "where you sell your milk."

"Yeah."

"It's going well, isn't it?" We walked side by side on our way back to the fence line where my jacket hung under the large oak tree.

Daniel dragged his forearm across his forehead while he considered my question. "The rep came round last quarter and offered us an increase in price per litre if we went exclusively with him."

"Really?" This was news to me. With the declining performance that I'd seen over time with the factory's books, I couldn't imagine where money was coming from to acquire raw product at greater cost. But I wasn't about to share that information with Daniel.

"So the extra money's made a big difference for you?"

"Yeah, it's been steady increases and because of the money that we've got coming in, the bank have given me a loan and I'm contracted to purchase the land you're standing on. I haven't seen good news and forecast growth like this for years."

I scratched my head. So what he was telling me was that

he'd put everything on the line to buy the land on the forecasts given to him by the dishonest factory manager's representative.

"You've always wanted to purchase the land?"

Daniel nodded. "Yeah, I've been a share milker for years. Buying my own place has been my dream."

The look of pride on Daniel's face tore at my gut. Great, if I shut this factory down, I was going to make Hannah's brother and her family homeless.

"So, did he give you any reasons as to why the prices were going up? It seems against trend."

Daniel shrugged. "He said something about more efficiency in the factory and that they wanted to pay some of that back to the guys who had been doing the hard work out here in the sheds."

"Right. Okay." I nodded.

Now, I had a real sense of what had been going on. Daniel's confirmation that he was being paid more for product confirmed my suspicions. The factory manager was running the profits of the business down by redirecting funds back to the farmers. There must have been some dodgy accounting going on somewhere, but it wouldn't take me long to find that with a forensic accountant on board.

He must have gotten wind that a takeover bid was in the offing and he'd been systematically running the company down so that I'd let it go as unprofitable as soon as we completed the deal.

Then he and whoever was sitting behind him, would swoop in and pick up a profitable factory at next-to-nothing prices. I'd seen it happen before.

He'd been tying up all the local farmers on contract to him. What I knew and what Daniel didn't know was that the money he was being paid now was unsustainable. The business model didn't make sense.

The factory manager's investors were putting money up front now, for long term profit in the future. The people who were going to get squeezed down the line were honest men like Daniel. Men who'd relied on the increased prices and were going to find themselves unable to pay their mortgage once prices returned to a profitable level for the company.

I couldn't tell him that when he thought he was on to such a good thing.

"Owning my own land," Daniel said, "well, it's something I never thought I'd be able to achieve and something that I wish Dad had seen before he passed."

The words tore at my gut.

What was I going to do? I couldn't tell him the truth. I'd be able to find proof in the next week or so. Confronting the manager with the information would likely be enough to flush out his dodgy investors. What I didn't want to do was create chaos for my future brother-in-law and take out his dreams—and probably the dreams of a few other farmers in the area.

I picked up my jacket and wondered when I'd suddenly developed a social conscience.

Daniel walked beside me, on our way back up the path to the house. "Have you told Hannah about buying the farm?" I asked.

"No. I haven't had a chance," Daniel replied. "The news of you guys getting hitched has eclipsed pretty much everything. And, of course your other news."

"Our other news?"

I stopped dead in the middle of the path. What the hell was he talking about?

"Yeah, the baby on the way."

"Right that," I said acting as if I'd known all along what he'd been talking about.

Baby!

Fuck!

Hannah hadn't told me anything about a baby. What the hell. I could feel my insides constricting. How had I missed this news?

Daniel continued on walking ahead and I scrambled to keep up, catching a glimpse of his conversation here or there, a sense of something strange washing over me as the idea of Hannah being pregnant began to register.

"Yeah, that's why Hannah's been flat on her back all afternoon in her old room. All these women's issues." Daniel flicked me a wink, "you think we'd be used to it living on a dairy farm and all."

I had no idea what I was supposed to be *used to*. All I knew was that Hannah had been withholding information from me and I couldn't stand being treated in that way.

I had too much running through my mind to take much interest in the continuing conversation. I caught the odd sentence here or there, but all I could think about was Hannah.

Was she going to tell me she was pregnant?

Hell, when did she conceive. It wasn't as if we'd been at it every second of the day. I'd been too busy with work.

What did she think she was going to be doing about this?

How long had she been pregnant?

How long had she known?

Shit. So many questions. I needed to get back to the house and get her out of there so we could talk.

"It's been good having this conversation with you," I said to Daniel as we approached the house.

"Yeah, you'll be coming back a bit more often now you have the family on the way," Daniel said and he made to turn off the path to the house and head down to the implement shed. "We're really looking forward to the wedding." He laughed. "It's a good job my Dad's not around or our Hannah would be a shot-gun bride."

Daniel turned to face me. He stood not more than a few inches away from me, the bulk of his body encroaching on my personal space. We were almost nose-to-nose. "But seriously," he said his tone taking a stern edge, "I love my sister and if a big shot like you, from up in Auckland thinks of doing anything to hurt her, I may only be a share milker, but I'll kill any man with my bare hands who hurts my sister."

I took a step back and held my hands up in mock surrender.

"Mate, you got nothing to worry about. I love your sister and, believe me, I'm going to marry her and take good care of her."

"Yeah, well I know sometimes Hannah isn't the easiest person on the planet, but aside from Mum and my wife she's all I've got. And now, she's carrying the next generation of our family and we look out for our own down here."

"You made that pretty clear," I said.

"About the factory," Daniel said taking the conversation on a tangent that I hadn't been expecting. "You thinking of buying it?"

There had to be rumour about in this community. It was the only thing that made sense. Maybe I wasn't so clever at hiding my intentions as I thought I'd been.

"I'd rather you and I agreed that we didn't have any conversations about the factory," I said. "There's a few things that I need to tidy up and the factory is one of them."

"Yeah, well while you big guys are coming down here in your suits and tidying up, just remember that there's entire families like the one you're about to become a part of, who are relying on the money those factories bring into our district."

"I see that." I could see far more than Daniel at this time

and what I now saw clearly worried the hell out of me. "Don't concern yourself," I reassured him, "I'm not going to put your livelihood or your sister's happiness in jeopardy."

"As long as we're straight about that, then," Daniel said as he readjusted his hat. There were quite a few things that I was straight on after talking to Daniel. "I've a few things to tend to down the shed now the girls are done for the night. Will I see you back at the house later?"

"I have some business to deal with and I think Hannah needs some rest, so we'll be flying out tomorrow morning. But we'll be back soon enough, don't you worry."

Daniel wiped his hand on the back of his trousers and held it out to me. I took it and noted for a second time today the coarse texture of his skin.

"Just remember what I said." Daniel's eyes never left mine as he firmly shook my hand. "We look after our own down here."

"I get that," I replied.

I had the greatest of respect for Daniel.

He'd helped me realise how much I loved Hannah and how much I was prepared to give up to make us into a real family.

Thoughts tumbled through my head as I made for the door of the farm house.

CHAPTER 30

*H*annah

I could tell by the look on Robert's face as he walked through the door that something was up and I suspected it had more to do with me than the recent visit to the dairy factory.

"Hello," he said. The tone of his voice and the single word confirmed that the something had to do with me. I could see the sheen of muck and dirt on his face from the work he'd been doing down at the milking sheds with my brother.

"Look at the state of you," I said trying to deflect his mood, "what have you been up to?"

"I've been down at the milking sheds helping your brother to clean up. I understand from him that it's something that you and he used to do a lot together as children."

"Yes, that's right," I said with an increasing feeling of unease. I rearranged myself on the bed. I smoothed the old counterpane and picked a couple of stray threads. "Did you have a lot of time to chat?"

"We did," Robert said as he leaned against the chipped wooden drawers that housed my clothes only a couple of months ago. "He told me a few interesting things." Robert's eyes drilled into me from across the room and I had the overwhelming urge to vomit.

"Did he?" I said breaking away from the hold that Robert's eyes had on me and turning my attention again to the stray threads on the bed clothes.

"He did," Robert said as he began to pace from one side of the tiny room to the other. He reminded me of a caged lion and despite myself, I began to tremble. "He told me that you spent a lot of time in this very room."

Robert stopped pacing and I said nothing, waiting for his next move.

He came and sat down beside me. He looked so out of place. The bulk of his body taking up most of the tiny space on the bed. I felt trapped in so many ways and yet he looked comfortable, in control, even out of his environment.

He knows a small voice whispered in the back of my head.

I swallowed. Choosing to ignore the call of logic.

Robert threw his designer jacket across the end of the bed and it occurred to me that it was probably the most expensive item in here. Again, it showed me the difference between our backgrounds. But somehow, he managed to sit next to me looking completely at ease. I felt anything but at ease. I had a desire to crawl up the walls and get as far away from Robert as I could. The feeling seemed so out of place, considering earlier today we'd been holed up in a plane together and I couldn't get enough of him.

I decided my hormones must be playing havoc with my emotional stability.

He knew I was pregnant. I could tell by the way he looked at me. Something had changed. There was a possessiveness about him that I'd not seen before.

I wasn't another one of his companies to be acquired.

"Did Daniel help you with your enquires about the factory?" I asked. Still trying to pretend that nothing had changed since he'd left me this afternoon.

"He did," Robert said, "but that wasn't the most enlightening news I heard today. Apparently you have something to tell me." He let the words hang in the air then added, "Something that you've been keeping from me." The intensity of his gaze went up a notch and the deep hazel of his eyes was almost eclipsed by the black of his enlarged pupils.

I knew Robert well enough already to know that there was no point in trying to tell him anything other than the truth. I took a deep breath and held it, willing the trembling in my body to cease. I stared at my hands clasped in my lap. I wanted to cry.

Robert reached across and took one of my hands in his.

"You're shaking," he said the soft tone of his voice enough to give me the courage to look again into his eyes.

Instead of demanding intensity, I saw brown pools of concern.

He ran his finger across the engagement ring that I wore and said, "I never expected to see that on anyone's hand except my mother's."

"I wasn't trying to hide anything from you, Robert, I swear," I said. "I only found out I was pregnant this afternoon. After we left you at the factory, I stopped at the chemist and I picked up a pregnancy kit and it was the first that I knew about it."

"But you told your family before you told me." I could sense the hurt in his voice and in his body language.

"I didn't tell my mum, she knew."

He laughed. "Grandmother used to talk to me about that woman's intuition thing, I guess she wasn't bull-shitting."

I felt the edge of a smile curl my lips. "No, I guess she wasn't."

"I haven't told anyone," I said as I ran my finger in soft

circles in the palm of Robert's hand. "Mum must have told Dan."

Robert pulled me into his arms.

He smelled different. He smelled of hard, physical work. The farm. All the things that I'd known as I'd grown up in this town. I felt his lips on my hair.

"You don't have to worry about this, Hannah." I knew he was serious. He held me tight and I felt so loved and protected encircled by his strong arms.

"I am worried."

"I'll do the right thing by you."

"I don't want you to just do the right thing by me, even though I know you will."

"No, Hannah," he said, "you don't understand. It's only since I've seen you here, with your family. I've seen how much I love you. Your brother threatened to fucking kill me if I did anything to hurt you."

I pulled back in shock. "He didn't!"

"He did." Robert nodded, "With his own bare hands."

"He's not a violent man."

"It's how much he loves you," Robert soothed, stroking my hair, "and it's how much I love you. I want us to be a family. I want you to be a permanent part of my life. I don't want you to go overseas."

There was a long silence between us. I wasn't sure now whether Robert's declaration of love was what I wanted to here now that he'd voiced the words. I'd lay on this very bed this afternoon making plans for my escape. Working out how I and the growing life inside of me could manage on our own and now Robert was telling me that he wanted exactly the thing that I'd run away from here to avoid.

"Are you going to say anything?" Robert asked.

"It's a lot to get my head around," I squeaked. "The hormones, they're making me mad and strange." I could feel tears dripping down my face. I swatted at them in frustration. "I'm not one to cry," I complained, "but I seem to have been lying here crying all afternoon."

"I'm not going to force you to do anything you don't want to do," Robert reassured me.

He stood up and walked to the other side of the room.

Now that he'd left me I wanted him right back beside me.

"No, no it's not that," I said as I stood up and followed him across the threadbare carpet.

He opened his arms to me and I slipped against his strong body. It seemed so safe and warm and secure. I felt so loved in his arms and as his lips caressed my hair, I thought about the life that grew inside of me. The small part of him growing inside of me. Something that would always link me to him. I couldn't run away.

Robert lifted my chin with his finger and slipped his lips over mine. A soft gentle kiss that spoke of love and commitment and passion and a deep promise. When he eventually broke from me, he whispered, "I don't need an immediate answer. I know you have a lot to think about. Come on," he slipped his arm around my waist, "I think we need to get back to the cabin. We've an early start tomorrow and from what I hear it's going to take you quite some time to get on your feet in the morning." He smiled, a knowing smile, "And I'd prefer not to have a repeat performance of the air sick bag on the way home."

I giggled. "I think we need to stop and buy some ginger biscuits. Apparently, it's supposed to help."

Robert opened the bedroom door.

"I need to say bye to Dan," I said.

"He's down in the shed."

"He's always in the shed at this time of the day," I laughed.

"Of course," Robert said, "I forget that the routine around here is second nature to you."

"No different than yours in town," I said. "Let's go and find Mum and Trudi."

We found them where I knew we'd find all good farmer's wives, in the kitchen preparing dinner for Daniel.

Would life be much different for me in Auckland? Maybe Robert had a housekeeper who did dinner, but what would I be doing with a child to look after?

"It's great to see you on your feet," Mum continued to fuss. "How are you feeling, dear?" Then she looked at Robert and realised what she'd said and slapped her hand across her mouth and went bright red.

"It's okay," Robert soothed, "I know the news."

Mum dried her hands on a tea towel lying on the bench and said, "That's a relief." She threw her arms around us both. "It's not only great news to welcome you to the family, but the fact you now have a little one on the way. It's wonderful," she gushed.

I was hoping that it would be wonderful, but sometimes I couldn't be too sure.

I also knew something had gone down at the factory today that Robert was keeping from me. I guess my news had out shone everything. It also occurred to me that if Robert wasn't telling me what was going on, it was because he wanted to protect me. That single thought frightened me as much as being pregnant to him frightened me.

*R*obert

As Hannah walked shamelessly naked across the room, she was a welcome distraction from my turbulent thoughts. But it would take more than the curves of her body to untangle my frayed nerves after the news I'd received today.

I continued to watch the curves of her body as she moved

and thought about the growing life inside of her. The growing life that was a part of me and was going to change the shape of her body and, ultimately both of our lives.

Aside from the contract that we'd made and our intended contract with the coming wedding, we were now inextricably linked forever by that growing life.

Hannah lay down beside me, a smile curling her lips. The vixen. She knew exactly what her brazen show was doing to me.

"You're feeling better," I said as I found my hands drawn like magnets to her large and sensitive breasts. They were heavy in my hands. No doubt something to do with the hormonal changes that were going on inside of her body.

Hannah leaned into my chest. To hell with it, I thought, we both needed this distraction.

"The last time we were naked like this you moved," I said, "strictly against my instructions." I smothered the last of the words in a kiss. My tongue explored the depths of Hannah's mouth as she yielded to me.

"Are you really going to spank me?" Hannah asked her eyes wide with lust.

I couldn't resist. "Would you like me to?"

Hannah scrunched up her face and wrinkled her nose in that fascinating way I loved when she thought about something. "I don't know whether I'd like pain."

I leaned up on one elbow, running my fingers from the edge of her breast to the peak of her hip. "Well, maybe you won't know unless you give it a try," I said trying to keep the amusement out of my voice. The idea of having Hannah across my knee and painting her white arse pink with my hand turned me on more than I cared to admit.

I pulled her across my body and ran my hand over the cool flesh of her arse cheek.

Hannah shuddered.

"They would look so lovely painted pink," I said and Hannah shuddered again.

"If I hate it will you stop?"

"You just have to say the word."

"How many times do you think you'll spank me?"

I rolled my hands across her arse and then hit one cheek quickly. The sound echoed around the small room and Hannah jumped.

"Ow!"

I immediately rubbed the outline of the red hand print that was forming on her backside and then slapped the other cheek.

Hannah moaned.

I slipped my fingers between the cheeks of her arse and they were met with heat and wet.

"You're enjoying this," I said as I slid my fingers in and out and allowed Hannah to push herself back and forth on my hand.

"I might be," she said.

"I do believe that the lady is turned on," I said as I slipped two fingers down deeper into Hannah's wet folds.

Hannah groaned and pushed herself onto my exploring fingers.

I repeated the succession of slaps a couple of times and then slipped my fingers back inside of Hannah. Then I found her firm little clit and began to circle the nub of flesh with my wet fingers.

Hannah sighed, relaxing against me and opening herself fully to me.

"Enough," she groaned as she lifted herself off my lap and settled her body against the length of mine. "I want you inside of me, not just your fingers."

She'd spent the afternoon in bed feeling like crap. "Are

you sure you're well enough for this?" I couldn't help rubbing my rock hard cock against her soft thigh.

"I feel better at night," she said trying to reassure me. "And if you keep doing this to me, I'm going to come."

"That was the idea," I said as I circled her clit again and then dipped my finger back inside of her, moving the wetness around.

I slipped my mouth over the tight bud of her nipple, giving it a nip. Hannah's body shuddered at the beginning of an orgasm. I watched the heat creep up her face as she closed her eyes, surrendering to the pleasure I was giving her.

"I want you inside of me," she said as she scraped her fingernails down my chest.

Pain radiated from the sharp edges of her nails. "You need to be careful with those, they're lethal weapons," I said.

"No more lethal than your hand," she replied as she opened her eyes and smiled at me.

I didn't want to wait any longer and pulled Hannah astride my naked cock. "No chance of you getting pregnant, now," I teased.

"No," Hannah said with a moan as she slipped herself down my sensitive cock.

The sensation of entering her made me suck in my breath.

I gritted my teeth. Took another deep breath and took control of the situation by grabbing Hannah's hips.

"Slowly," I muttered. "If you keep that up it'll be over in a moment."

I plunged inside of her again and again and again.

The sensation was overwhelming. The most wonderful feeling of being inside of her. Flesh on flesh. Skin on skin. Nothing between us.

"This is how I always want it to be with you," I said between excruciatingly sensitive thrusts. "I want there to be nothing between us. I want you to tell me everything that's happening in your life. I don't ever want to be the last to know anything about what's going on."

I wound Hannah hair around my hand as I rammed myself inside of her over and over. "Do you understand what I'm saying," I said between urgent thrusts.

"Yes," she moaned.

I had a total need to possess Hannah.

I'd had a total need to possess her from the moment I'd first set eyes on her.

Nothing was ever going to come between me and Hannah.

Not her family.

Not my family.

Not a business.

Not a single thing.

I was going to make damn sure of that.

CHAPTER 31

*R*obert

Back in Auckland, I sat at my desk in front of my computer, with my solicitor, Jonathan Hawke. I watched with interest as Jonathan's face changed while he perused the bare bones of my offer. As he turned over another page, he peered at me over the rim of his red glasses and said, "Why are you purchasing that dog of a dairy factory?"

I said nothing and simply stared at Jonathan.

He continued. "You want to cut that one loose. Even if you buy it in this deal, you want to make sure that you've got an immediate purchaser for on-sale, while there's a market for it." Jonathan put the papers down on the desk in front of him, folded his long fingers across his waistcoat and looked me in the eye.

"No," I said without releasing his gaze, "we're buying it."

"Why?" he asked a challenging tone to his voice.

"It's personal," I replied still not breaking eye contact.

"You don't let your personal life get in the way of your business decisions. You never have done."

"There's always a first time," I said still not breaking eye contact.

Jonathan looked away and picked up the small pile of papers in front of him. He rearranged a few pages and then looked back at me again.

"What's going on, Robert? I've been working with you and your family for years," he said leaning forward as if labouring his point, "personal business never comes into any acquisition arrangements. What the hell's happening?"

I thought carefully about my answer. Before I had a chance to say anything, Jonathan indicated toward Hannah sitting outside my office. "It's got something to do with that girl out there, hasn't it?"

I considered lying.

Then I thought about the life growing inside of Hannah and I thought about her brother and the farm and decided to be cautious.

"It doesn't matter what it has to do with," I said leaning back in my chair. I paid Jonathan an exorbitant hourly rate, he could damn well do as he was told and stop asking me questions.

I didn't have to explain myself to anyone. Then I looked at Hannah. Well, except maybe Hannah.

"We're doing this my way," I said. "I know it's not the way we've always done things, but sometimes things change."

"There's something you're not telling me, Robert," Jonathan said before biting down on the end of one of his precious silver pens.

I ignored the comment and remained looking at Jonathan.

He leaned forward taking his time to place the pen down on my desk and then said, "I have to remind you that you're proceeding against my advice." Jonathan took off his glasses and placed them with extreme care next to his pen.

"That's fine," I said. "Draw up the contracts. Send me the disclaimers, tell me what you need to tell me." I leaned forward, placing my elbows on my desk, "but I'm doing what I need to do to make this deal come together the way it has to come together."

"There is nothing about the way you've been running the business lately, Robert that makes any sense to me," Jonathan said a note of exasperation in his voice.

Well, I wasn't about to tell him that a lot of things weren't making much sense to me anymore. That I was reassessing my moral compass.

"It doesn't have to make any sense to you," I said, "it's about it making sense to me and me making sure that my family are looked after."

I watched as Jonathan returned his gaze to Hannah. She sat reading email and I noticed that she had her hand sitting protectively across her stomach. Maybe I was being paranoid, but I wondered if anyone else noticed.

"Well, Robert," Jonathan said as he began to pack papers into his briefcase, "I've known you long enough to know when you've made up your mind, nothing's going to move it. I will make the changes to the contract and I'll have a new set of documents delivered this afternoon. Also accompanying them will be a note from me advising you that what you're proposing is contrary to my advice."

I watched as Jonathan carefully stowed his pen and glasses and snapped the gold buckles on his briefcase. I held out my hand and as Jonathan took it, I said, "Anything less of you and I wouldn't think you were doing your job."

Jonathan acknowledged the compliment with a nod of his head. "Is there any chance you're ever going to tell me what went on down south?" I started to walk Jonathan to the door and he stopped and said, "You know everything that you say to me remains confidential."

I paused for a moment, my hand on the handle of the door and said, "There's been some underhand business practises going on in one of those factories. The accounts we've received don't reflect the true position and there's a lot of dairy farmers down there who are reliant upon untruths. Things need to be straightened out."

Jonathan thought about what I'd said, digesting the words in his usual unhurried way. "And you've decided you're the man to sort it out." A flicker of a smile graced his mouth. "I get it. You're going to be the Robin Hood of the dairy industry. And no doubt, you've found a way to squeeze a few more dollars out of the deal."

"Something like that," I said as I opened the door. It wasn't quite the position, but I wasn't going to belabour the point with Jonathan. I knew that once I got involved with the factories, I could salvage the position not only for the factory workers, but for the farmers as well. Once I had control, I could weed out all the dishonest management and I could make sure that one way or another the factory became profitable and, most importantly, that Hannah's brother didn't lose his farm, even if I had to put a consortium in place at a loss for a little while.

As far as the long term investment was involved—I didn't normally go for long term investments—hence Jonathan's questioning my approach; but for Hannah and her family I was prepared to hang in there, instead of doing my usual cut and run.

"You'll have those papers by this afternoon," Jonathan promised as he walked out of my office.

I closed the door behind him and then watched with interest as he stopped by Hannah's desk to chat. I saw Hannah put on a brave face. I knew how unwell the pregnancy was making her feel. Her feet had barely hit the floor this morning before she vomited. I told her she could stay at home, but she insisted on coming in to work. She didn't want anyone to know what was going on and only I knew how bad she really felt. To look at her out there, smiling and chatting away, no-one would ever have known the discomfort she was labouring under.

Except me.

*H*annah

I found it hard to believe that another four weeks had passed since I was down south with my family.

Despite my occasional reservations about the hoopla involved with marrying a Redfern, life had somehow settled into a comfortable routine.

As I sat across a table at the Museum Cafe with Stacy from Olive's Boutique and a wedding planner that she recommended, I wondered again how I'd gotten here.

Danielle Van Hoven arranged weddings for the high society of Auckland and Stacy insisted that she was the only woman in the country who could do justice to a Redfern marriage.

Robert had been insistent that we marry at the Wintergardens. Danielle had been making the required arrangements. I sat there, with a glass of sparkling water and a small bowl of rice for lunch, trying to pretend that I was feeling okay, despite the occasional pain that kept running up my back.

"I'm pleased to see that you're checking your food intake," Danielle said eyeing my meagre bowl of rice. I thought about the life growing inside of me and wondered how much larger my waist would be before the big day.

Food obviously wasn't one of Danielle's issues. She took great delight in tucking into a rather large toasted sandwich. I thought there would be little chance of shoehorning her ample curves into one of the designer wedding dresses that Stacy had been parading in front of us both at the boutique earlier this afternoon.

Danielle stopped chewing long enough to tuck a stray lock of her red hair behind her ear. The movement brought into stark contrast the black base hiding underneath. Then she eyed me again, putting her sandwich down on the pristine white plate in front of her.

"Come walk with me," she said immediately losing interest in the food. I followed her through the marble foyer of the museum. It echoed with the sound of the hurried footsteps of schoolchildren and bus loads of tourists. The sound bounced off the polished marble floors and up toward the cavernous ceiling of the open three story foyer. How we would ever hold an intimate reception in here, I didn't know, but Danielle seemed determined that everything would be okay.

I continued to try to explain to Danielle that I wanted a small, intimate reception. My instructions were falling on ears that refused to hear and it had nothing to do with the surrounding decibels. The wedding was rapidly becoming a major production, with half of the who's who of Auckland finding their way onto the invitation list. My small reception —with the assistance of Robert's grandmother—had grown into a gargantuan production.

I had another pain run down my leg and my bladder screamed for relief. I must have consumed far too much fizzy water. "Can you excuse me a moment," I said to Danielle and Stacy over the reverberating sounds in the foyer, "I need the ladies." I pointed towards the restroom sign and they both nodded.

"No problem," Stacy said.

"We'll meet you in the atrium," Danielle said pointing towards the large glass dome that connected the old war memorial museum to the new and modern circular extension. "I still haven't decided whether or not that space would be more suited to the kind of celebration needed for a Redfern wedding."

I resisted the temptation to roll my eyes and made my way to the ladies room.

My nausea had abated over the last couple of weeks, but I was still wracked with a tiredness that I'd never experienced before. I sat quietly relieving myself and wondering how much longer it would be until I felt like myself again. When I stood and turned to flush the toilet I realised, with a clutching sense of horror, that the toilet bowl was filled with blood.

I tried not to panic, but my breath came in short, sharp pants. I could feel the edges of my world tilting to one side. I put out my hand and steadied myself against the cool wall of the tiny cubicle.

I was bleeding!

My baby was dying.

I couldn't think straight.

I closed the lid on the toilet and sat down.

Robert.

Robert would know what to do.

I fished in my bag for my phone and another sense of terror rolled through me. I couldn't find my phone. What the hell had I done with it? I took a deep breath, trying to calm my racing pulse and head. I closed my eyes and concentrated on breathing.

In. Out. In. Out.

I opened my eyes and took another look inside my bag. There it was, hiding in the bottom under old supermarket receipts and my wallet.

With shaking hands, I scrolled through my numbers and pressed the button for Robert's mobile.

It rang.

What was I going to tell him?

"Yes?" Came the sound of Robert's familiar voice.

"Robert, I'm bleeding."

"What?" He sounded confused. "Have you hurt yourself?"

"No. It's the baby." A sob escaped from between my lips before I had a chance to stop it. I couldn't cry. If I cried I'd fall apart. Danielle and Stacy were waiting for me in the atrium.

"Oh, God. Where are you?" I could hear the concern in his voice.

"At the toilets in the museum." I stifled another sob. "Stacy and Danielle are waiting for me in the atrium."

"Don't move."

"I have to go and meet Stacy and Danielle, they'll wonder where I am."

"Wait for me in the atrium. I'll be right there."

"You've got meetings this afternoon."

"I'll cancel them. Go and do as I say. Wait for me in the atrium. Don't say a word. Find somewhere to sit down and I'll be right with you."

I did as I was told without arguing. I found Stacy and Danielle sitting on a low, orange couch below the curving staircase that led to the second level of the atrium.

"It's stunning, don't you think?" Danielle gushed. "It holds 500 easily so it will be the perfect venue for your reception.

The idea of five hundred people at my wedding reception should have sent me into a tailspin. Instead, I sat down beside the two women and I merely nodded. I allowed Danielle and Stacy to continue planning a reception that I was beginning to think would never happen.

I barely heard the rest of the conversation, but I think I grunted in the right places. I had no idea how long we sat there, but Robert, true to his word arrived out of nowhere.

"Ah, there you are," he said breezing into the middle of the discussion as if he walked in on wedding plans every day of the week. "Sorry to interrupt," he said with a smile. I'd never been so glad to see anyone in my entire life. I could have openly wept. "I overlooked the fact that I needed Hannah for an urgent presentation, so Danielle if you can just take this from here with Stacy. I'm sure the two of you can continue to organise the big day on behalf of the two of us."

Danielle stood up, a beaming smile on her face. "Of course, Mr Redfern, not a problem."

Robert put his hand out towards me, and I was never so glad to take an arm as I was to take his as he walked me out of the museum.

"How are you feeling?" I could hear the concern in Robert's tone now that we were out of earshot of the wedding planners.

"I don't know. I think I'm in shock."

"I have the best obstetrician in Auckland on his way to the apartment and we're going straight there now," Robert said. He guided me to the car which sat on a broken yellow line at the front of the museum. As much as I hated Robert breaking the rules and behaving as if they didn't apply to him, this time I wasn't angry or upset as he opened the door of the car.

"Miss Scott," Graham acknowledged me as Robert closed the door and made his way around to the other side. He got in the back seat beside me and buckled the seat belt around me with excruciating care. Before I really knew where we were, I found myself at the apartment.

Robert took a call and I heard him saying, "Yes. Okay. Will do."

"That was the doctor," he said as he opened the door to my bedroom. "He said that you're to go straight to bed and he'll be here as soon as he can. He wants you off your feet and resting."

"Robert," I sniffed as I kicked off my shoes and climbed onto my bed, "I think I'm losing the baby."

"No, no," Robert said sitting down beside me and taking my hand in his. He looked me in the eyes, his huge hazel eyes filled with compassion and love. "The doctor says that this happens often," Robert began to rub my hand, "You need to rest. You've probably been overdoing things and that's my fault. I've put too much pressure on you. The doctor says that bed rest is the right thing, but he's coming to check you out, anyway. He's the best in Auckland," he reassured me. "I've been on to an agency and we'll have a nurse here before the end of the day if that's what's needed. I've cleared my appointments for the afternoon and I'm staying right here with you."

"Robert, you don't have to do that."

"It's done. Now stop fussing and stressing yourself. You're the most important thing in my life."

The look on his face and the tone of his voice was the last thing I could deal with. My resolve crumbled. Fear raged through me and a terror that I'd never known before rendered me helpless.

I burst into tears and began to shake.

"There, there," Robert's strong arms were around me in a moment. I could feel his kisses raining down on my head. I hung onto him. Robert. My rock. What was I going to do if I lost this baby?

I couldn't stop the tears flowing. I hadn't wanted this baby. I hadn't wanted to be married and now all I could think about was everything falling apart.

If I lost the baby, I couldn't go through with the wedding. Maybe I couldn't go through with the wedding anyway and this was the universe's way of punishing me for taking Robert's money.

Exhaustion washed over me and the sobbing began to subside. Robert lay down beside me and I must have fallen into a fitful sleep.

The next thing I knew, Dr Merton and his nurse were both stood in the darkened room with Robert.

I felt like some sort of strange women from the eighteenth century being cloistered because of the impending illness of childbirth.

The doctor examined me while the nurse held my hand and wiped away my tears.

"I think everything is going to be okay," he said. He had kind eyes and a gentle bedside manner. I could see my own reflection in his glasses and somehow that seemed reassuring.

"Complete bed rest for you, madam, for the next week," the doctor said. "This happens often. You're early in the pregnancy and sometimes you can have a bleed through. Resting up is the best chance you have of this baby staying firmly where it should be." The nurse nodded in agreement. "If this pregnancy's going to terminate itself, then it's going to do it in the next few days. You need to stay in bed and take things easy."

I nodded through a fresh set of tears. Relief or terror I couldn't be sure? I just knew that the doctor's words were reassuring. My life had seemed so out of control since I'd moved to Auckland and now, for the first time, I had a chance to try to control something. Even if that something was simply choosing to remain in bed for the good of my growing baby.

I could remain here and allow Robert to take control of everything—it was what he excelled at.

After the doctor and the nurse left, Robert spent the

afternoon fussing. He brought me chamomile tea and a tablet so I could watch an endless stream of mindless television.

I lay in bed thinking about how much life had changed for me in the last three months since I'd been in Auckland.

I thought about the first night I went to the charity benefit with Robert. How I'd agreed to become engaged to him in exchange for a huge sum of money. I checked my bank balance and saw all of that money still sitting there.

I needed to return it to Robert—it was the only sensible thing to do.

A voice in my head said, *you need to return the money and go home.* I thought about the hoopla of the wedding. The stress it was putting me under. The idea of going home to the peace and tranquility of the south didn't seem such a stupid idea.

CHAPTER 32

*R*obert

I was used to fixing things.

That was what I did.

Throw some money at the problem and the problem disappeared. It was the way it had worked for me all of my life.

Hannah lay in her room and, for the first time in my life, I couldn't fix the problem by throwing money at it. Granted, I'd made sure that she had the best medical help that was available. The doctor's advice? Stay in bed and wait it out.

My gut roiled at the thought of the advice.

Surely there was something else that could be done?

Apparently not.

I stood up and walked towards the large picture window in my office. It was arguably the best view in Auckland. From here I could see from one side of the harbour to the other. Yet, the only building that caught my eye, was the penthouse apartment across the water where I knew Hannah lay, trying to hang onto our growing baby.

I couldn't concentrate.

I looked around the large expanse of my plush office. Out the window beyond, past Hannah's vacant desk and out to the staff who worked for me. They all sat in neat little rows at their desks, fingers tapping over electronic keyboards, their rapt attention drawn to the white glow of the computer screen in front of each of them.

Then I looked back to the view of the city and the ocean and islands beyond.

I thought about the massive expanse of green fields that I'd looked out across at Hannah's brother's farm. The freedom he had each day to enjoy the sunshine and the scent of the grass beneath his feet.

What the hell was I doing holed up in a concrete and glass prison? Sometimes I lost track of whether it was day or night. I needed to come to my senses.

How many hours a day did I spend here? How many years had I been sitting in this very room and only now I noticed the marbled blue of the ocean out the window. Why had I never seen the boats crossing the harbour before? What about all those people below me, enjoying the waterfront?

I ran that waterfront every morning to stay in shape. But did I appreciate it? Did I hell. I was too busy worrying about how to screw the next dollar out of anyone who came into my immediate line of vision.

"Fuck this!" I said to no-one in particular. I was going home to see how Hannah was doing. This shit could wait.

I loosened my tie, dropped the lid on my laptop and then hesitated. In all the years that I'd been running the company, I'd never left early, let alone walked out of my office without my laptop.

Things were going to change.

The company would survive if it took me a day to return a few emails.

I picked up my jacket, threw it over my shoulder and

walked out of my office.

It was 11.15am.

"I'm taking the rest of the day off," I said to the shocked woman on the front desk, whose name I was embarrassed to admit to myself that I could never remember.

She looked at me dumbfounded.

"Of course, Mr Redfern."

"Take messages for me," I fumbled for her name and she smiled at me.

"It's Cynthia."

"Yes," I said. "How long have you been with us?"

"Five years, Mr Redfern."

"Call me, Robert."

Things were going to change around here and me spending more time with Hannah was a start.

Fuck it. Things were *really* going to change. As soon as I got back tomorrow—or the day after, or whenever it was that I got back to the office—I was going to send an memo giving every single member of staff the day off for their birthday.

The idea made me smile.

The thought of going home to Hannah at this time of the morning filled me with an unexpected sense of delight and anticipation.

I stood in the lift and thought about the last time I'd been happy coming back to the apartment. It had been when I knew that Silo would be there to greet me.

I missed that damn cat. How had I allowed myself to be so removed from loving something?

It hurt so much when I found him that morning on the side of the road. His body still warm. I kept torturing myself. If only I'd been more careful to make sure he didn't get out of the apartment.

I tried to tell myself that I didn't really care—but who was

I kidding?

Silo's death had come so soon after the loss of my parents I think I just cut myself off from everyone. No-one had been able to get through to me again—until Hannah came along.

"Mr Redfern, I wasn't expecting you?" The nurse who had come from the agency jumped to her feet, her white shoes squeaking against the wood of the kitchen floor.

"How is she?"

"The same as this morning. She keeps complaining that she's bored and she wants to get out of bed."

I nodded.

"Go take a break," I said. "I'm home for the rest of the day, so you can take the rest of the day off if you like." She looked at me, a prim and proper woman from the agency, with mousy blonde hair. "With full pay," I added.

"Of course, Mr Redfern," she said, "I'll get my things."

After I'd shown the nurse to the lift, I returned to Hannah's room and opened the door. "How are you feeling?"

She looked up, let the tablet she was holding fall flat on her legs and greeted me with a huge smile. "What are you doing here, it's not even midday?"

That same warm feeling washed over me that I felt when Silo had rubbed around my legs and purred. There was no way that this woman was ever going to leave me.

No matter what happened with this baby.

*H*annah
I'd spent far too much time in bed wallowing in my own thoughts and my own self-doubt, but if I wanted to make sure that I kept this baby, then there was nothing else I could do.

A bird in a gilded cage had nothing on the way I was feeling at the moment.

Robert, as usual, had spared no expense and my every whim and wish had been taken care of. My only wish was that our baby stay safely tucked up inside of me and that was the one thing that no amount of money Robert could throw at it could fix.

I buried the doubting voices in my head. It became clear to me that I didn't want to lose Robert or my baby, so I was determined to do whatever the doctor asked me to do—even if it meant not moving for a week.

Complete bed rest didn't seem like such a hard thing to do, but now, by day three and no end in sight to the time I would spend in this room, my mind had gone round and round Robert and come back to the same conclusion—I had fallen deeply in love with the man.

Then cabin fever started to kick in and I began to have my doubts about Robert. Maybe he was marrying me only because of this child. I might be in love with him, but how did I know that he really loved me?

Maybe I would be better off simply to go home.

The door opened and Robert walked in.

"What are you doing here, it's not even midday?"

"How are you feeling?" he asked, concern painted across his features. I thought I would never tire of looking at the perfect arch of his eyebrows, and the square set of his jaw. His lips called out to me to kiss them.

I couldn't describe how grateful I was to see his beautiful face.

My fears and concerns around his love for me vanished as he sat on the side of the bed and took my hand.

"I'm scared," I said. I couldn't bring myself to lie to him.

"There's nothing to be scared about," he replied as he lifted my hand to his lips.

Despite my relief at seeing him, the thoughts in my head simply fell out of my mouth. "Robert, I've had some time to think about things while I've been lying here. I think we need to put at stop to this marriage. The whole thing's out of control. I'll return the money that you put in my bank account and I'll go home to Mum and Daniel and we'll forget that any of this ever happened."

I was so sure that this baby wasn't going to stay with me, no matter how long I lay here in this stupid bed.

Robert squeezed my hand so hard I thought that the blood vessels in my fingers were going to explode. "No!" he said, "that's not happening." Robert pulled his tie from around his neck and dropped it on the bed beside me. I noticed the dark curl of his chest hair peeking out from above the buttons of his shirt and a thread of lust took me by surprise. "It's not just because of the company that I want to marry you."

"What do you mean, it's not just because of the company?" I watched the colour drain from his face.

"Forget that I said that."

"Robert, I can't forget that you said that. What do you mean because of the company?"

Robert shifted uncomfortably on the bed and sighed. "Well, the reason." He stopped, looked out the window to the ocean view beyond and then turned his gaze back to me. "Did you not think it strange that I made the offer that I did the very first night that we were out together?"

"Of course I thought it was fucking strange." I couldn't contain my anger, "That's why I want to give the money back now."

"Settle," he said in a tone of voice that had the desired effect. "I don't want you getting upset. The baby."

Maybe he cared about the baby but he didn't give a shit about me.

"Now listen to me," he said holding up a finger, "not a word until I'm finished. Do you understand?"

I nodded my understanding and then struggled to decipher the rollercoaster of emotions running through my body.

Robert said, "There is a clause in the constitution of the company that says if I'm not married by a certain time that I will lose control of the company and it will go to my brother."

I couldn't quite believe what I was hearing, but strangely it made sense.

Robert continued, "I didn't watch my father sacrifice everything while Ed and I were growing up to see it thrown away." I went to open my mouth, but Robert wagged his finger at me. "My brother doesn't particularly care about the family business or the family name, but I do."

I tried to process the information that Robert was giving me. "So what you're telling me is that you asked me to marry me because if you didn't you were going to lose your job?"

He looked uncomfortable and undid another two buttons of his shirt.

Robert wasn't playing fair.

It occurred to me that Robert probably never played fair.

Robert always got what Robert wanted.

"Something like that," he said.

"Well, it either was, or it wasn't?" I could hear the near hysteria in my voice. Why should this matter so much to me?

"Yes, that's the case."

"And were you ever going to tell me about this?"

"I'm telling you now." He said in a matter-of-fact tone.

"I'm pregnant. We're a few weeks out from the wedding of the year, according to the wedding planner and you're telling me this now."

"Will you calm down?"

I closed my eyes and took a deep breath. I wanted to hit him.

"You weren't ever going to tell me, were you?"

"Hannah, that doesn't matter. What matters is that we're going to have a baby and we're going to get married. Who cares how we got here."

He tried to pull me into his arms, but I braced myself against his chest with my forearms.

"I care." Why, I wasn't sure, but I did. "So you're doing this out of obligation." I couldn't help putting in the knife, "I suppose there's a clause in there that says you have to have a child by a certain date?"

He blanched.

"There fucking was!"

"Hannah, calm down."

I lay back against the pillows and closed my eyes. All the fight knocked out of me.

"No, there's no clause like that, but it's expected that there would be heirs."

"Fuck you, Robert!" I felt like one of the cows in my brother's herd. "So now I'm part of a nice little tidy package that fixes everything for you. You get to keep your company. Everything looks the way that it should. You get your grandmother off your back. No wonder she's been so pleased that we're getting married. So all of this is just a complete fucking sham, Robert?"

He made another attempt to calm me down, but I wouldn't be calmed. "You knew it was a sham when you got involved with me. I put two hundred thousand dollars in your bank account and you signed a contract."

"I don't need you to be logical right now." I couldn't keep the sarcastic tone out of my voice and he smiled.

That smile melted the glacial anger that I kept trying to hold onto.

Robert reached for my hand and this time I let him take it. "The point is, Hannah that we've both moved on. This is not just about the contract for me anymore. Hell, if you want me to show you how much I love you I'll tear the fucking contract up and pay you the money, anyway. What do I have to do to show you that this marriage is no longer about the contract or the company? It's about the fact that you have become the most important person in my life. We can abandon all this and go and live anywhere in the country. Hell, anywhere in the world."

"You could never do that." I couldn't imagine him living anywhere else. His life was here. "Your life is your business."

"No!" He shook his head and moved a little closer to me. "My life is here, with you. You are about to become the mother of my child. You will both be the centre of my universe. I have never cared about anybody the way that I care about you. I used to look at my brother and wonder what it was he saw in my sister-in-law because I'd never experienced that kind a connection. I experience that with you."

I didn't know what to say.

"Let me show you, Hannah how much I love you, how much I need you in my life. I want to look after you and our child. Please give me the opportunity to do that."

I needed to process what he'd said to me. "I need to think about it," I said feeling like a bitch and turning away from him.

"I want my Mum."

"She's on the next flight up here," he said.

"Really?"

"Ring her now and tell her to pack. If there isn't a flight, I'll send the jet."

"You'd do that for me?"

An exasperated look crossed Robert's face. "Hannah, I'd do anything for you. Ring her now, get her up here, she might even talk some sense into you."

Robert looked at his watch. "If you hurry and ring her, she'll be up here before the afternoon's out. I will arrange for the jet to pick her up."

"I need you to go," I said feeling like even more of a bitch. I still needed to process the information that Robert had given to me. The idea that he needed a wife and an heir to continue on with his business seemed so cold and devoid of emotion.

My mind whirled and all I could think about was the revelations he'd just made.

I didn't know what to think any more.

He leaned down and I allowed him to kiss me on the crown of my head. "Ring your mother," he said as he got up off the bed and headed for the door.

I pulled my phone off the nightstand and pressed Mum's number.

I must have fallen into a fitful sleep.

A knock at the door woke me. Robert didn't knock.

I didn't want to see anyone. But the knocking persisted.

"Come in," I said scrubbing my hands against my eyes.

Mum stood in the open doorway.

I burst into tears.

"Oh, love," she said as she crossed the room.

"Mum, I don't know what to do."

"You need to do as Robert tells you, love," Mum said as she wiped the tears from my face. "He's a wonderful man. He cares so much about you and he's so worried."

I couldn't help feeling like a total fraud. True to his word, Robert had flown mum up so I wouldn't feel alone. These were not the actions of a man who didn't care about me.

"You don't know the half of it, Mum," I muttered between sniffles.

"Do you want to tell me?" Mum rubbed my back and then said, "Maybe you shouldn't tell me, Hannah. Sometimes things need to be kept between a husband and a wife. But I can tell you something. That man, he loves you. He's terrified that you're going to lose this baby and he's also told me that you're having second thoughts about the wedding."

"I don't know what I think anymore."

She soothed me by making the clucking sounds she'd made when I was a child. In a second I was transported back to falling off the railings by the milking shed, my knee spilling blood into the dirt and hobbling back to the house sobbing. Mum sat me up on the sink in the kitchen and made everything better.

Could she make everything better now?

"It's okay," she said as she handed me a box of tissues. "I felt exactly the same way you're feeling just before your Dad and I got married."

I blew my nose and wiped my eyes again and mum tucked a stray piece of hair behind my ear before she carried on with her story. "I know the reason you ran from home is that you didn't want to end up married and pregnant." She gave me a weak smile and I couldn't help but return the gesture. "But sometimes we can't escape our destiny, Hannah."

"Destiny," I sniffed.

"Sometimes there's a plan that we can't see. I thought about that when I was walking down the aisle to marry your father. Sure enough, we've had our good times and we've had our tough times, but we did the best we could for you and your brother. And look how things are now." Mum pulled my hand into her lap and looked into my swollen eyes. "I know you always wanted to go to university and get an education, but we just weren't able to make that happen for you."

"It's okay," I whispered, "I don't think I've done too bad." She took a moment and really looked around the room, taking in the generous windows with their view of the city below. The designer furniture that was probably worth more than the entire contents of the farm house and she laughed.

"You're like a cat, you always manage to fall on your feet. That's why your dad and I weren't worried about you. And there's still time for you to get an education, Hannah, there's always time."

"You think?"

"I know. You're an intelligent girl. I'm sure Robert wouldn't have any issues at all if you said you wanted to educate yourself. Heck, the way he feels about you, he'd fly the tutors in from anywhere in the world."

Now she made me smile. I had to agree. "He probably would."

Mum leaned forward. "How are things going with this baby that you're carrying?"

"The doctor says that I just have to wait. I have to be on bed rest and things may or may not be okay."

"But they're looking better, yes?" Mum asked.

I nodded. "I think so, yes."

"Well then, you need to stay calm and not upset yourself and I know that's hard with the hormones and all racing around your body."

I laughed again. "I keep forgetting that you've done this."

"Oh, yes. You're never alone. Always remember that."

I leaned into mum. She collected me in her comforting arms and all of a sudden I was that girl again sitting on the kitchen bench with a banged up knee.

I looked into her eyes. She'd seen so much. Generations of our family and now I was carrying the next generation.

"It will all work itself out, Hannah," she said. "You've just got to trust. You've got to trust Robert and you've got to trust yourself and you've got to take a chance. Sometimes you have to take a chance."

"Even if I'm scared that it won't work out?"

"Especially because you're scared that it won't work out."

"I only told Robert that I wanted you here less than three hours ago."

"There you go, then. He's a man of action and a man of his word. Believe me, he'll move heaven and earth for you my girl. And there's not many men who will do that. He knows what you need and he cares about you. He cares about you with a ferocious passion."

I knew about Robert's ferocious passions, everything he did he did with passion.

"I think that's what scares me so much," I said.

"Well don't let it," she replied. "It's one of the greatest assets in the world to have a passionate man want to take care of you."

"But I wanted to make my own way in the world."

"You can still make your own way in the world, my love. We all do that one way or another. But you can do it with a good man by your side, supporting you and cheering you on."

I thought about all the things my mum had achieved. All the committees that she'd been on at home. All the charities that she'd helped. She'd always been there for us. Every school trip, every school camp. I hadn't seen those things as important, but they were incredibly important because they gave me a sense of self and a sense of security. I'd always felt loved and now I had a chance to offer the same thing to another human being. Maybe I needed to rethink my desire to run and maybe it was time for me to stay and settle and become Mrs Robert Redfern.

CHAPTER 33

*H*annah
I walked up the pale steps towards the Wintergardens and to a man that I now knew I loved with all of my heart.

"Are you ready?" Daniel asked, a twinkle in his eye.

"As ready as I'll ever be," I said as I took another large gulp of the cool autumn air. "You know this was only supposed to be a tiny family affair?"

Daniel laughed. "You're marrying the most eligible bachelor in Auckland and you thought you'd get away with a couple of people at the wedding."

We stopped in front of the large bank of press who had been corralled outside the gardens so they could take photographs. Grandmother Mary had relented, allowing the press access to us prior to the ceremony. It wasn't unusual for her to insist that an entire area be blanketed out to prevent photographs being taken. We would still have a private photographic session after the formalities of the ceremony, together with an exclusive interview. The proceeds of sale from that interview would go to the children's hospital.

Grandmother Mary had allowed me to choose the charity in this case and when I received her nod of approval and I saw the smile in her eyes, I knew it wouldn't be long before she put two and two together and worked out we were due an addition to the family fairly soon.

Robert had insisted that we keep my pregnancy a secret and that he would announce the news to the world and to his family well after the wedding.

"I don't know how you cope with this kind of attention," Daniel moaned as he pasted another smile on his face for the grateful reporters and photographers.

"This is a long way from the milking shed, isn't it Daniel?" one of the reporters said as he stuck a microphone under Dan's face.

Daniel looked at his surroundings and eyeballed the reporter, "It's not too different from home," he said in good humour, "all we're missing is a couple of hundred from the herd, right sis?"

I nodded in agreement.

"Come on," Daniel said as he squeezed my arm, "I know you're supposed to be fashionably late, but I think you're milking your moment of fame here."

I knew I could always rely on Daniel to bring me back to earth.

Trudi came and stood beside me, resplendent in her burgundy crushed silk dress while Stacy fussed with my train. "You look stunning," Stacy said when she was happy with the arrangement of my multiple layers of ivory silk and lace. "I've been waiting to dress someone for Robert Redfern's wedding for years and you're perfect."

I could feel the heat of the blush that crept up my cheeks.

Taking great care to ensure that she didn't disturb the

Redfern Tiara that sat on top of my head, Stacy pulled my thin veil down over my face and the entire world went a little fuzzy.

"Perfect," she nodded her approval and turned her attention to Trudi, my Maid of Honour.

Once Stacy was happy with Trudi's appearance, Danielle, who had this carnival planned to the millisecond, confirmed her approval and we were on our way into the gardens themselves.

"Let's get you married, sis," Daniel said as he walked me down the long corridor of white roses and ivy that had been installed alongside the central pond.

As we turned the corner into the gardens proper, my eyes found Robert. He stood beside his best man and brother, Edward. I held my breath at the sight of my handsome husband-to-be.

The Redfern men stood, shoulder-to-shoulder in front of the celebrant and a who's who of Auckland. But I only had eyes for Robert and he for me. It was as if the entire assembly of people who stood around us vanished.

All I saw was the man that I loved. The father of my child. The man that I knew I would spend the rest of my life with.

Robert wore a morning suit, with a gold cravat. The single white rose pinned to his black jacket matched the ornate bouquet of two dozen roses I held in my hand.

I took my place beside him and he leaned over and whispered, "You look incredible."

"Thank you," I whispered back, "you're looking pretty hot yourself."

I was rewarded with a wide smile. "You think we can escape this lot and run away together?"

"It could be a bit late for that," I said trying not to giggle. But his words had done what was needed. He'd settled my nerves and allowed me a minute to take a breath.

The celebrant welcomed everyone and somehow I missed a lot of what she said, until I heard the words, "And who gives this woman to this man?" It was Dan's cue. He gave my hand a squeeze and then passed it to Robert.

A look passed between the two of them and I remembered Robert telling me that Dan would kill him with his bare hands if he hurt me.

My brother kissed me on the cheek, through the light veil and then, taking the hand of his wife, they both went and took a seat beside my mother. She sat in the front row, resplendent beside Grandmother Mary.

I watched as Dan gave mum a hug and she dabbed some tears from her eyes. I knew she was thinking about Dad as well. I had a feeling that he could see us all. He'd be looking down with a beer in his hand, nodding his approval. His family had come a long way and I knew he'd be proud of where we all were now.

Edward went and sat with Nicki who held their newborn baby, Emily in her arms.

Robert and I now stood facing each other in front of the celebrant. She handed Robert a small card, I knew it was the vows that he'd written. Robert pocketed the card and his intense hazel eyes looked straight into mine.

"I, Robert James Selwyn Redfern, take you, Hannah Rachel Scott to be my wife. I promise to love you and to honour you and to keep you, in sickness and in health. I promise to share all my worldly goods with you. To laugh with you and to cherish you and to make sure that you never want for anything again in your entire life."

The celebrant handed me a small card. I cast my eyes across the words that we'd carefully crafted together and then gave her the card back. "I, Hannah Rachel Scott, take you, Robert James Selwyn Redfern to be my husband. I promise to love you and to honour you and to comfort you in sickness and in health. I promise to support you in all of your outlandish endeavours and walk beside you on the road of life."

Robert's smile at the last line—one that we'd debated for some time—gave me great comfort. I didn't want to be a burden or be supported by Robert, I'd made pains to tell him that I wanted to be a part of his life. We decided that the words were more appropriate coming from me and to hell with what anyone else might think.

I wore Robert's mother's engagement ring on my right hand and now the celebrant handed Robert a wedding ring. As he slipped the cool band of gold over my knuckle and I did the same to him, I thought about the thousands of men and women before us who had carried out this very ritual in front of the people who loved them and the people that they loved.

I wanted this family to work.

I wanted to remain married to Robert and I was determined that I would do whatever I needed to do to make our little family work.

"Robert, you may now kiss your bride."

I turned my face up to my new husband. Robert lifted the veil from my face and the world came into crisp focus.

Robert's lips touched my own and there was only him and me. Everyone else disappeared.

I closed my eyes.

My hands slipped around the neck of my new husband and I lost myself in the security and overwhelming sensual pleasure of being his wife.

"Get a room," I eventually heard my brother calling.

"It's a bit late for that," Robert said as he pulled his lips away from mine and we turned to face the standing and cheering assortment of friends, acquaintances and family.

"Ladies and gentlemen," the celebrant said, "may I present Mr & Mrs Robert Redfern."

There was another cheer and applause. I could hear the cameras clicking around us, but I only had eyes for my handsome new husband.

ℰpilogue - 1 year later
Robert

We sat in the poky little cabin that Hannah had brought me to the first time we came down south. Baby James babbled to himself while he lay on a small rug surrounded by brightly coloured plastic toys.

Hannah had taken a moment to sit on one of the small winged chairs in the window, a tablet in her hand. I had a surprise that I'd been waiting for today to give to her.

"Happy Anniversary," I said as I passed her a scroll of paper.

"I thought you said we weren't going to do anything." She said a reproachful look in her eye.

"I like to keep you on your toes," I replied. "Go on, open it."

Hannah untied the thick purple ribbon and then unrolled the piece of paper. She screwed up her face as she read the words in front of her. It was something I'd never tire of watching, the adorable way her face scrunched up around her nose when she couldn't work something out.

"What?" she asked and then took another look at the paper.

"Read the letter that's underneath it from Jonathan." I'd promised my faithful solicitor that I'd never send him another piece of work ever again if Hannah found out what I was doing over the past couple of months. He'd managed to keep this from her until today.

I watched as Hannah scanned the words.

"You've set up a Trust?"

"Yes, and the beneficiaries are you and any children you may have," I explained. "The trust has purchased a number of land holdings in the area, to generate some income." I'd had Daniel point me in the direction of the local farms that needed assistance and I'd put a package in place that would see not only Baby James' trust prosper, but also the businesses of the local farmers. It was a long term investment, a win-win for everyone involved. The farmers would have the chance to purchase their land incrementally from the trust and in the meantime, the trust would use the cash-flow to diversify its portfolio.

Hannah still had a puzzled look on her face.

"If you look at the list of assets," I said pointing to the bottom of the second sheet of paper.

"Oh, Robert," she said, her eyes filling with tears. "But I thought you hated this little shack."

"It was the first place that you brought me when you brought me home," I said, "and since we're going to be spending so much time in the area, I thought it fitting that you should be able to stay here and do with it what you want. I have an architect flying in tomorrow. She has a great reputation for extending buildings and staying within their character. I think we can make a lovely home away from home here for all of us."

Hannah crossed the room and threw herself into my arms. "Thank you," she said as she peppered my face with kisses. It was something that I'd never tire of.

"I have a gift for you as well," she said.

"We agreed."

"You've just bought me half the district, I don't think you have any say in the matter any more."

Hannah walked into the bathroom and then came back

with a small animal carry box in her hand."

She put it on my knee and sat down next to me. Our son continued to gurgle and smile from the mat on the floor in front of us.

"Open it."

I had a strange feeling as I opened the box.

Two round yellow eyes stared back up at me from a tiny, black furry body.

"Hannah…"

"Meet Silo the Second," she said. "If we're going to spend half our time down here, then we need a good ratter. No home is complete without a cat."

I scratched the kitten under the chin and it immediately began to purr, a little traction engine of noise. I picked the kitten out of the small box and it snuggled into my chest.

"He loves you all ready," Hannah said, "I knew he would. You're such a cat person. I knew it the minute I saw old Thomas rubbing around your legs that very first day we visited the farm. He's very particular about who he'll say hello to."

"And what about when we have to stay in the apartment in Auckland?" I asked. The thought of losing another cat to the road made my stomach churn.

"He'll be an inside apartment cat. He'll adapt."

My crazy, intelligent, farm girl had an answer for everything.

"Have I told you today how much I love you?" I asked.

"No," she replied.

"Well I do," I said as I pulled Hannah to me.

As I kissed my wife, I could hear my son's happy gurgles and the purring of a little kitten.

Life, it seemed was now complete.

I was so glad that I'd taken a chance on a spirited farm girl all those months ago.

ABOUT THE AUTHOR

Hello from Auckland, New Zealand.

Thank you so much for taking the time out of your busy life to read my story. I do hope that you enjoyed Hannah and Robert's road to happiness.

People oftentimes ask me why I write about billionaires. Aren't they 'yesterday's romance'? they ask. I don't think so. I think that billionaires will be around (in one form or another) for a very long time. At least I hope so, because I do so love writing about men who have everything—except the love of a good, sensible woman!

I'm not sure why babies have been arriving in my stories so much lately...too much sex!? And I can never resist putting a cat or dog (or even a fish) in my story somewhere.

I love meeting new readers so do make sure that you drop me an email and say hello. I always reply to my readers.

For anyone who doesn't know where New Zealand is, we're sitting below Australia at the bottom of the world. It's a fantastic place to live and I'm so blessed to call this peaceful piece of paradise home.

Hope to catch up with you soon.

Until then, take care.
Love Toni x

For more information about Toni Kenyon:

www.tonikenyon.com
toni@tonikenyon.com

ALSO BY TONI KENYON

Thank you for reading Robert & Hannah's story. Don't forget to sign up for my book club **here** so you'll be the first to know when my next billionaire is available.

If you'd like to leave a review - and it only has to be a short sentence and a star rating - I'd be so very grateful. Your review (good or bad) helps other readers find my books. :-)

Romance from Toni Kenyon - a fresh look at the world

THE PACIFIC BILLIONAIRE'S PROPOSAL

Adam

I had been called away from my evening engagement and found myself at the corporation's current development site located on the upper slopes of Auckland's sprawling city centre. The largest city in New Zealand had seen exponential growth over the last decade and Banks Corporation had been perfectly placed to take advantage of the construction needed in the central city area.

The city I loved lay spread in front of me, its twinkling lights making promises in the twilight that I knew it wouldn't deliver on tonight.

I knew I looked somewhat out of place on a construction site in a tuxedo, but I willingly donned the regulation fluorescent high visibility vest, hard hat and steel capped boots—I was a stickler for safety. I never complained when my site managers insisted that I, along with everyone else who visited the site wear the required safety gear.

Pulling at the restrictive collar of my shirt, I was tempted to remove the black tie that threatened to escalate my body temperature to boiling. I hated attending fundraisers but I knew I had to get back to the gallery if only to make sure that I didn't let my mother down. I hated leaving Rachel on her first official outing after the death of my father, but she knew, as did I, that I'd be letting the family down if I didn't respond to the emergency call.

"Where are they?" I shielded my dark brown eyes from the glare of the lights that illuminated the area of the five tower redevelopment we were currently working on.

Following the sudden death of my father, the division of the family empire that I now found myself at the helm of had, over a matter of years and through careful negotiation with land owners and the city council, managed to acquire a substantial network of buildings on the fringe of the spreading central business district. This grungy part of the city had been one of my pet projects for the last three years now.

In my dogged and determined way I'd worked hard to drag the area into the 21st century. I'd seen off environment lobby groups, the transport authority, the city council itself and a rag-tag bunch of neighbours from the art deco district who didn't want to see this particular neighbourhood refurbished. I'd made enemies along the way and I suspected one of them might be at the root of this problem.

Blair Shrieve, my site manager for this and every project we'd worked on, pointed to the top floor of the adjacent abandoned building.

The towers had been used in the past few years as low cost accommodation for inner city dwellers. I'd taken a lot of flack for gentrifying the area and reducing living options for many people who'd lived in this part of the city for most of their lives.

A spate of protesting, vandalism and squatting around the inner city sites had been somewhat of a running sore and a problem for our competitors as well. There had been a recent suicide on the other side of town—one of our competitors doing another refurbishment with a lesser quality site—and their project had gone into receivership as a result.

I had put in place a twenty-four hour watch on our own projects. I didn't want any copy cat actions, or anyone drawing any more unwanted attention to this development.

"You did the right thing calling me, Blair," I said, "I don't want anyone else getting wind of this, okay?"

"Agreed," Blair said nodding his head, "I've no idea how the hell they got in here."

"They?" I needed to be sure how many people I might be dealing with here.

"CCTV camera only saw one person going up there," Blair said.

"Right." Now I knew I was only dealing with a loner. My only worry was that it might be some drug addled street person who might give me a difficult time.

I looked up and I could see the silhouette of a figure on the top floor of the partly stripped building. "I want you to double security," I said to Blair, "I'm going up there to deal with this."

Blair knew better than to try and dissuade me and simply handed me a small crowbar. "Just in case."

I was fit enough to take on almost anyone. Regular workouts with a personal trainer and a background in martial arts meant that short of this person being so fuelled on illicit drugs that a tranquilliser gun might be needed, I should be okay.

I gripped the cool steel of the heavy crowbar in my hand and made my way across the old carpark. Picking my footing with care. The last thing I needed was to turn my ankle on the uneven ground. Heavy machinery had taken its toll on the brittle surface and in the interim, small tufts of grass and yellow buttercup-type weeds had infiltrated the black tar creating a crazy-paving look around the edge of the expansive space.

The fourteen story building had been stripped of its old cladding from the bottom up, the central orange spine of the crane kept me company as I climbed. As I ascended the first seven floors of the skeletal building, I concentrated on the lights of greater Auckland spreading out before me.

I loved my home city. I'd been born here and I'd sat on my father's knee watching the city itself grow with me. Peter Banks had been a self-made man. The company still retained holdings in the overseas manufacturing plants that had enabled the family to migrate to New Zealand and which also supplied a number of our building operations in and around Auckland and the entire country.

All eyes would now be on me, Adam Banks. Waiting for me to falter and make a wrong move.

I wasn't about to let the simple matter of a protester, or a homeless person bring down the empire my family had built.

When I got to the eighth floor, the stairwell closed in on me. I cursed my suit and tie and wondered what chance I actually had of making it back to my mother's gallery opening.

The heat of the night, the exertion from the climb and the musty smell from the abandoned building began to take their toll. I pulled the bow tie from my throat and stuffed it in my suit jacket. I undid the top two buttons of my shirt and cursed myself for not taking my jacket off before I donned the high visibility vest.

The chances of me making it back tonight were getting slimmer by the minute. Once I'd gotten a hold of this homeless person, I was going to have to think about how I'd deal with them. The irony of the matter was that my mother's charity was fundraising for the local mission. Raising funds to enable the sort of person who was trespassing on our property to have somewhere to stay and a hot meal in their stomach.

I pulled the door open on the 14th floor and set about regaining my bearings. Surely they would have heard me coming? Or maybe they were so off their face on drugs or alcohol they were slumped in a corner somewhere.

Most of the space had been gutted in preparation for the refurbishment. The odd mattress that looked as if it had seen better days or might walk itself to what was left of the windows to be thrown out, jostled with discarded fast food packets.

I made my way around the perimeter of the building and found my intruder, camera in hand, taking shots of the city from the 14th floor.

"You're trespassing and you shouldn't be here," I said relieved that I wouldn't have to use the crowbar I'd been clutching for the last seven or so minutes.

A young, blonde woman who from the rear looked as if she had curves in all of the right places turned around to look at me.

I recognised her immediately.

Zoe

My day had darkened. It matched the sky outside. If I wanted to get a good shot of the rising moon tonight, I needed to be up on the 14th floor of the Banks building in the next half hour or so.

Construction work next door over the last sixteen months had caused irreparable damage to the rare and second-hand book business that my family had run from this shop for generations.

I took another look at the large crack that had appeared in the wall of the shop, behind the counter. It seemed to be zig-zagging its way higher and higher towards the ceiling. No doubt it had something to do with the earthworks that were being completed next door.

It broke my heart to watch the beautiful old and historical buildings of my city being consumed by the heartless steel and glass of the type being constructed next door.

Banks Corporation and the construction conglomerate that they headed had a lot to answer for. They were responsible for the destruction of what had been my childhood playground.

I turned the latch on the old front door and the tinkling of the familiar bell that rang when anyone entered the shop sounded like a death knell.

That sound had brought me so much joy when I was a child hiding out the back of the shop, surrounded by books and comics. It heralded the entry of someone new into the store and every new person through the door I knew would be a book lover like me.

I had grown up in this very store and I'd watched the coming and going of many tenants in the buildings next door. Huge foot traffic that had been essential to keep the life blood and income running through the shop.

Everyone in the area knew Moody's Book Shop and there was rarely a soul who passed through the door who didn't become a regular customer.

Unfortunately, our customer base had grown old with my parents and, as my parents had both passed on, so had a large proportion of our secure customer base.

With the buildings next door in flux and now being renovated. The front of the once warm and inviting store had become a construction site. Barely a day went by when there wasn't a row of orange cones sat on the crumbling footpath. With construction came large double trailer trucks and concrete mixers with their suffocating diesel fumes. They cut out the natural light that used to bloom into the window and turned the inside of the shop into a toxic cave. What had once been a welcoming sanctuary filled with light and colour and people, had become a suffocating, bleak and lonely space.

Running my hand over my favourite chaise lounge, the one I'd paid to have recovered and restored, not for the first time, I wished that I'd been more vocal in my opposition to the plans of the council for the area.

But I was only one person. How could one person of little means fight an entire city and the likes of the Banks Corporation? Their wealth and power was legendary.

I looked at the unpaid rates and utility bills that sat on the shelf below the cash register and wondered where the money was going to come from to cover these escalating costs.

I'd borrowed as much as I could against the building. I knew there were repairs that needed doing and I couldn't afford to meet them. The way things were going, I'd have to sell up and move away from the city—like everyone else in the area. Banks Corporation would be responsible for moving me on. What they were really angling for was to purchase my building at rock-bottom prices and force what was once an Auckland institution out of business and into extinction.

As if I wasn't having enough trouble dealing with the online reading community.

I sighed.

The reason I'd started my book blog was to try and bring people back to the shop. I turned the lights off in the shop and plunged the familiar space into near darkness.

I knew that I needed to get to the top of the building next door if I had any chance of getting a decent shot of the city tonight. The conditions were perfect to get a great picture. These were the things that I needed now. A good picture to catch a reader's eye. Then I could maybe convert them into a regular viewer of my blog and even if I couldn't entice them into the store itself, I hoped I could entice them to purchase some of the stock that I carried on-line.

My strategy was working. It was time and labour intensive, but I could see it coming together, if I could just keep paying my expenses in the meantime. Short of transplanting my family business to another location—which remained cost prohibitive with the escalating rental market, I couldn't see another way to ensure that my business carried on.

I'd already sold my house to keep the business and cleared out the storage area above the shop. A bedroom and small kitchen and bathroom were all I really needed. The shop front and the back storeroom where I'd spent my childhood were my home.

Rising costs and lack of turnover had meant that only this morning I'd had to give notice to Mrs Pearson, or Mrs P as everyone affectionately called her. Mrs P had been with the shop for all of my life and it had been like losing my mother all over again.

I wiped away a tear and climbed the stairs up to my small bedroom. My clothes were rolled and sat in an arrangement of small, square bookshelves. I knew I had fourteen floors to climb, so I found a pair of shorts and struggled into them. I'd been comfort eating and most of my clothes were getting a little tight. I'd always had curves and envied my friends who seemed to be built like wire clothes hangers. I only had to look at something sweet and I could feel my curves expanding.

Pulling my long, blonde hair into a pony tail at the back of my head, I grabbed a bright pink v-neck t-shirt from the shelf and wriggled into it. It barely covered my midriff and I vowed to purchase some more clothes for myself from the Red Cross shop down the street. The change of seasons was almost upon them and I thought the ladies would have a new supply of clothes in by now.

Picking up my camera, I scanned the small, untidy space for anything else that I might need. Satisfied that I had everything I wanted, I quickly headed down the stairs and out the back door.

Having walked these streets for so many years and been on site for much longer than the builders next door, I knew exactly where I could squeeze through the security fence to get to the tower block that was being refurbished.

I ignored the DO NOT ENTER and TRESPASSERS WILL BE PROSECUTED signs and scurried like a thief across the compound to the safety of the shadow of the building.

I didn't own a car and had never learned to drive. There was no need. I'd lived within walking distance of the shop before I had to let my small home go and, even though the public transport system in Auckland left a lot to be desired, I still managed to get around. Besides, I spent most of my life in the shop now, so a car would have been a totally unnecessary expense.

I made it to the top of the building just in time to capture the sky's vignette as it morphed from blue to pink over the silhouette of the city's skyline.

I had planned to take a number of shots while I was up here. Catching the mood of the city at it's most magical as it transitioned from dusk to dark.

I knew there was a full moon rising tonight. It was the second in the cycle which meant that the huge orange glow of the orb made it appear larger on the horizon. I'd capture enough images being up here to keep my blog going for months.

I had just begun to click the camera's shutter to get the first shots when a voice gave me a hell of a fright.

Shit. I wasn't alone.

Download your copy The Pacific Billionaire's Proposal

Rockstar Romance from Toni Kenyon

PRIVATE LOVE IN A PUBLIC PLACE

Mags O'Brien lives on the alcohol-soaked, drug-enhanced concert circuit, managing out-of-control rocker Julian MacAvoy. She helps him spread his musical gospel to his adoring followers, despite the fast-spinning turnstile on his bedroom door, and the broken hearts he leaves in his wake.

Mags believes she's immune to Julian's magnetic personality but when controversy hits the tour, she finds herself in danger of falling at his feet, slave to his appetites and her own desire and need.

Julian refuses to be tamed, but the pressure of the ravenous crowds clamps tighter and tighter around him. His chaotic world starts to crumble when he realizes his motivation to continue touring comes from an unobtainable woman. Can he force her to make the agonizing choice between himself and her estranged husband?

An erotic and candid look at life on the road.

Download your copy Private Love in a Public Place

Praise for PRIVATE LOVE IN A PUBLIC PLACE

I'm a huge fan of Rock&Roll love stories. This one rates right up there with Olivia Cunning's "Sinners" & "Sole Regret" and "FitzWilliam Darcy". I can't wait for the 2nd book to come out in April! This story has it all...

Heartbreak, Steamy but Very Real love and really tough choices. At one point, I cried like a baby and in the next, I was yelling at my KindleFire. LoL...

Bottom line- Totally worth adding this book to your collection!

Sexy and gritty, raw and engaging, "Private Love in a Public Place" takes you on a personal behind-the-scenes tour of a rock star's life on the road from the perspective of his manager, a woman who loves the artist as much as she loves the man himself. ... This is a fresh, steamy and surprising love story guaranteed to entertain!

Mags is open and real, a woman I could relate too in a job many of us would see as glamorous (manager to a rock star or babysitter perhaps) but which she made very real, faults and all. Jules is that mix of arrogant tosser and little boy lost, who you can't help but fall in love with. A rock star who shows us he's human.

Other work from Toni Kenyon

CATCH

Tamsen Parsons is happy with her wacky world. So she leases fish to big business, her bedroom resembles a gypsy fortune-teller's caravan and she's got the flat-mate from hell. Still, the sun's shining and she can smile.

That is until uptight lawyer Matthew Solomon breaks into her serene world. He's over the corporate climb, unsure what he wants in life anymore and the sexy and aloof Tamsen looks like just the sort of short-term tonic he needs.

What Matt doesn't count on is his interfering mother, Tamsen's out-of-control best friend and falling in love.

Can a gypsy-fish-minder really bring this bad-boy to heel?

Download your copy Catch

Praise for CATCH:

Wonderfully written and will read over and over again. Definitely one to tell others to read as well. A Keeper.

Kenyon writes a sexy, fast paced, contemporary romance that'll have your heart racing. Tamsen is a terrific heroine with a unique job (nice change from the usual romance heroine) and Matt is definitely a hot hero worthy of her. The sensuality is scorching hot, so be warned you'll need a long cold drink in hand when reading Catch. Kudos to Toni Kenyon for a marvelous story - definitely an author to watch!

This book keeps you wanting to read more. Once you think you have it figured out, you get thrown for a loop.

RETURN TO ALA MOANA BEACH

Ty Carter's an expert bomb disposal technician who doesn't take anything lying down. But a bullet to the back cuts short his tour in Iraq, returning him to a wife who he believes deserves more than half-a-man as a husband.

Lulu Carter wants nothing more than the man she married to come home. Instead, an injured and disturbed stranger turns life upside down for her and their children.

Only Ty and Lulu can decide if the love they shared is worth fighting for and whether they should stay married after such a traumatic event.

Download your copy Return to Ala Moana Beach

Praise for RETURN TO ALA MOANA BEACH:

Amazing book, couldn't put it down. their separation was heartbreaking...but it's a lovely story and shows the reality that many soldiers went through...

A beautiful and moving story about what happens after a soldier comes home. The characters and the gorgeous setting illustrate a realistic and lovely world. Hawaii is a character by itself. Not only does the author portray the returning soldier well, but she does an excellent job describing the feelings and thoughts of his family. The story revolves around the veteran's trauma, but also everyone who cares about him. I love it.